A SHAMELESS LITTLE LIE
(SHAMELESS #2)

MELI RAINE

A SHAMELESS LITTLE LIE
(SHAMELESS #2)

BY MELI RAINE

I did it. I admit it.

I fell in love with Silas. My bodyguard. My protector.

My new informant.

We're playing a cat-and-mouse game. I'm not sure whether I'm the cat or the mouse, but I can definitely tell I'm in a trap.

A trap with no way out.

I'm not who everyone thought I was. The truth is out there, finally turning the lie about me inside out. I *am* the shameless little lie. It's finally been revealed, and now even more people want to kill me.

As a presidential campaign hangs in the balance, a delicate web of international relations and economic stability at risk, power becomes more important than anything else.

Even my life.

Especially my life. I'm a nothing. A no one. Just a tool, remember?

But tools can be used to open locks. Cracking open the truth and exposing it could change the balance of power. Tip the scales. Make a presidential campaign turn on a dime.

Too bad Silas doesn't believe me when I tell the truth.

And that may make him the biggest tool of all.

CHAPTER 1

*M*onica Bosworth has eyes that could cut gemstones.

I've known this since I was a little girl. When no one else is looking, she gives me glares and once-overs, the skin around her orbs tight and contemplative. She evaluates me like I'm a specimen she's trying to understand.

Or eradicate.

And right now?

Definitely eradicate.

Lindsay makes a gasping choke, the kind of sound you hear when someone expires. It's the sound of everything she knows about herself dying. She's alive, though. More than alive. I can tell from the different expressions that migrate across her face in real time that she's processing all of it second by second, realization by realization.

I am just there, frozen and silent, unable to find a single, solitary way to connect with anyone in the room.

Even Silas.

Monica turns to Marshall, her voice so flat and even. It's like a steamroller is ironing out her words. "We have a situation now, Marshall. We need to control the information. Who else knows this?"

Silas won't stop looking at me.

Drew wraps his arm around Lindsay's shoulders and stares straight ahead. His neutral demeanor is one that comes from exquisite control. Underneath the surface, it's very clear that he would rather have his hands around his mother-in-law's throat right now, squeezing every spare drop of oxygen from her lifeless body.

"I don't know, Monica," Marshall says, drawing out his words deliberately. "You tell me. Who else knows this?"

Flinching but recovering quickly, she looks at Lindsay. "I would prefer to answer questions privately."

"What you prefer doesn't matter, *Mother*," Lindsay slings back. "What you *prefer* has been the dictate of my entire life. I'm done. I've been done for a very, very long time, but this? *This* takes the cake. You slept with someone else? Daddy isn't my father? You lied to me all these years?"

I stand, my chair falling over behind me, one of the rolling wheels scraping hard along my calf at a diagonal. It stings, so I know I'll bleed. The pain is nice. I could sit with the pain. Make friends with it.

Pain can be a source of comfort when chaos is your only alternative.

Senator Harwell Bosworth, the man expected to be the next president of the United States, is my *father*. Hidden in plain sight. My entire life, I've been led to believe that my father killed himself when my mother was pregnant.

And now?

It turns out I've spent my entire life around him and *didn't know*.

"The rumors," I hiss, drawing out the last consonant like a snake's kiss. "The rumors about you and my mom. They're true. Oh, Mom. Oh, God, Mom," I moan, starting to lose my breath, dropping the tether line that keeps me connected to the world. Silas's hand is warm on mine, but it's not enough.

Nothing I know about myself is true.

The one person in the world I could trust unconditionally is dead.

Yet she's now the person in my life who has betrayed me the most.

Monica opens her mouth, steely eyes staring at me through narrow slits. She opens her mouth as if she's about to say something, then shuts it tight. Good. Because if Monica Bosworth says one direct word to me, I'll be arrested.

For assault.

The press wants to milk me for scandals? Oh, I'll give them one.

It hits me.

I'm not the scandal here.

Monica is.

"WHO?" Lindsay screams. Monica jerks like she's being executed by a firing squad and Lindsay's one-word demand is a bullet that wounds but misses the lethal mark. "WHO IS MY FATHER? WHO DID YOU SCREW, MOTHER?"

All of the air in Monica drains out of her, like a tire deflating, a hot-air balloon being decommissioned, a soul entering certain hell. Drew watches her, protective arm around Lindsay, but he drops it as Lindsay jumps to her feet, crosses the room, and slaps Monica with a crack so hard, it almost breaks the woman's shell.

Almost.

Eyes unfocused, mouth drawn, face like marble chiseled in prison, Monica just takes the hit.

I've never seen anything like it.

Fear spikes through my body, sudden and unexpected. The prickly sensation in my veins, on my skin, in my pores, is so all-consuming. It robs me of speech. All I can do is stare.

All I can do is *freeze*.

"ANSWER ME!" Lindsay screams again, this time curling her hand into a fist, elbow pulling back, the expected punch caught by the quick reflexes of her own husband.

"Don't," Drew says, his voice filled with heavy anguish. "Please. She's the wife of a presidential candidate. I can't let you assault her, no matter how much you want to." His voice drops so, so low, and yet I can hear him when he adds, "Or how much *I* want to."

"She deserves it." Lindsay's voice sounds like a demon.

"And so do I."

We all turn toward the new voice to find the senator in the doorway, looking at Monica with so much compassion. It's almost unseemly, like we've been invited to watch them have sex. Her tear-filled eyes meet his and it hits me.

He knew.

He knew all along.

How many more secrets do they share?

"You knew," I gasp, my breath hot against my tongue, sour and sweet at the same time, lightly flavored with salt from tears I only now realize are running down my face.

Lindsay catches my eye, her look so raw and vulnerable. We're connected. We're not sisters–different mothers, and different fathers–but our sisterhood is here nonetheless, our bond forged by lies.

Monica, Harry, Anya–they all lied to us.

And who is the fourth? Who is Lindsay's biological father?

Monica ignores me. Harry looks at me with a steely expression, his jaw set, body tight and formal, but his eyes–oh, those eyes. I didn't know a person could plead for mercy with just the skin around the eyes.

Somehow, he does.

"No," I say, shaking my head, breaking his gaze. "No."

"No, what?" Silas asks under his breath. "What's wrong?" He clears his throat and squeezes my hand. "Aside from the obvious."

"I can't." I drop his hand and pivot on one very shaky, rubbery leg. I'm half turned toward the door. Marshall is standing, frozen, taking in the sight of Harry, who now looks at his wife with very different eyes than the ones I got.

"If anyone deserves to be slapped, it's me," Harry says.

"That can be arranged, *Daddy*," Lindsay spits out.

"Lindsay, I–"

"You *knew*," she says, interrupting, mirroring what I'm thinking. "Who is he? Mom won't tell me. You know everything, right? Of course you do. You always know more than you let on. That's your job, isn't it? That's how politics works. Keep secrets and tell lies and leverage what you know to make sure you have more power than anyone else."

Harry looks at her with tenderness.

It's the look you give a child you've raised and nurtured since birth.

I have to leave. I will my body to move, but it won't. Trapped by my own frozen impulse, my breath going in and out of my lungs without any effort on my part, I am paralyzed by too many thoughts. So many. It's as if they're coming out of my lungs, over my lips, microscopic pieces crawling along the fine ridges of muscle and bone that make up my body.

"We can discuss that in private," he says to Lindsay. "Later. First, I want to speak with Jane. Alone."

"*Already?* Already I'm pushed aside because I'm not your real daughter?" Lindsay barks, eyes widening with grief, her belly curling in as if Harry had gut-punched her.

"You are my daughter in every real way, Lindsay. Just not blood," he says, his voice filled with pain.

"That is a major, major, big way, *Daddy*," she says, her voice dropping to a growl.

"Yes. It is," he agrees. "And we're going to need a long time and many conversations to get through this, but I know we can."

"I don't need a bunch of long conversations. I just need one piece of information: who is he?" Lindsay is tenacious. Uncompromising.

And *right*.

Monica catches Harry's eyes. She doesn't even have to shake her head. The two have some sort of unspoken agreement.

"Later," he says firmly. "I promise we'll tell you everything you need to know."

"Not good enough," I say, the prison of my mind releasing me. "That's not good enough." Our eyes meet and I look at my father. My actual father. I have one who is alive and here, staring at me with compassion and complexity. I feel like I'm naked and flayed, my blood running out of my body as if sacrificed to the truth.

"You don't get to dictate what's 'good enough,'" Monica interjects, finally coming out of whatever spell she's under.

"You don't have a say right now, *Stepmother*," I shoot back, rage flooding me, replacing my blood.

Lindsay lets out a weird sound, a whoop that cuts off suddenly with a sob. Monica ignores me, but the jab hit a nerve. A thin line of sweat forms on her upper lip and her eyes go shifty. She won't look at me now. Good.

But Harry does.

"Jane," he says, voice dropping. "Don't."

"You can't tell me what to do."

"*Please* don't," he amends.

"Then get her out of here. Now," I order, looking right at Monica, whose chin rises in defiance as she continues to ignore me but looks at Harry with a very clear expression. It's a challenge.

Pick one of us.

He does.

"Monica," Harry says, "I need you to leave."

CHAPTER 2

*L*indsay gives Monica the most twisted, evil smile I've ever seen in my life. It's cruel and gloating, celebratory and mocking. A work of art in expression, it's a smile you don't want to see too often.

You certainly don't want to be on the receiving end of that kind of grin.

Especially as a mother.

"Get out," Lindsay says with that grin, her words barely necessary. "You heard Daddy–er, whatever I'm supposed to call him now."

Harry ignores her jab. Monica's face goes slack. Not only is all emotion gone, it's like she's turned into the opposite of emotion. When matter and antimatter meet, they neutralize each other. Monica is single-handedly neutralizing everyone else's emotions.

Except for Lindsay's.

And mine.

"Harry." Monica says one word. It's like a thousand screaming sentences in one syllable.

"Go," he says. "I'll deal with you later." Capturing his wife's full attention, the senator–correction, my *father*–makes it clear there is no arguing. That's an order.

Drew inhales sharply, then covers it with a cough, moving away from Lindsay to stand next to Duff. They whisper in voices so low. It's as if they're lip reading each other.

Given the fact that Monica isn't moving, the tension in the room rises like mercury on a hot day. Lindsay marches to the door, Drew behind her, tall and imposing. Her hair hangs in damp waves against her face, eyes wild.

"If Mom won't leave, I sure will. It's getting a little too crowded in here." She looks right at me, shaking her head, giving me a pleading look that says *Can you believe this?*

"Lindsay," I croak, voice gone. "Can we talk later?"

"Damn straight." Her words remind me of Drew. They say couples pick up each other's quirks. "When you're done, text me. There aren't enough bars in the world to handle the level of drinking and talking we need to do, Jane."

"But–" Monica pipes up. "Lindsay, she may have had Tara killed. She betrayed you, and–"

Lindsay turns and waves Monica away. "I will never, ever believe another word out of your mouth, Mother. As of now, I trust Jane more than you. Hell, I wish Anya were alive. I'd trust *her* more than you."

And with that, Lindsay leaves.

The door slams shut like some lesser god dropped a giant marble slab on it.

"Awkward," I mutter, my body vibrating with the sheer force of so much emotion. It won't settle down for a very long time. All the molecules that make up my physical body collide with my emotional shards.

Marshall approaches Harry. "We can have her removed." His eyes barely cut to Monica, but it's obvious who he's talking about. The red splotch on her cheek from Lindsay's slap is fading. I want to refresh it.

Lindsay can get away with assaulting a presidential candidate's wife because she's Monica's daughter.

What are *my* boundaries now? How much has changed? How much has stayed the same?

I have a sudden impulse to follow Lindsay, to go down the

long hallway to the big kitchen, to sit at the counter and eat snacks and drink coffee like we did in high school. The sheer normalcy of it is so alien. I lived like that? My life was predictable and comfortable once? It seems impossible now. All those sleepovers here at The Grove. Nights when the senator would pop his head in while we were watching movies and check on us. The repeated invitations to go on vacations and trips with the family so Lindsay would have a friend to hang with.

Was I really invited because I was Lindsay's friend? Or because I was Harry's secret daughter?

A flash flood of memories hits me, hard, *rat-a-tat-tat*, like a machine gun scattering random ammunition from my life. Changing schools when I was eight. Asking Mom how we could afford the expensive prep school I started in seventh grade. Assurances that it was covered by a scholarship. How the private security guys assigned to Lindsay kept watching me, too. How Mom waved it off as overeager agents trying to do a good job.

How the only pictures of my "father" burned in a small kitchen fire when I was eleven. How I was told my "father" was an only child and his parents were dead. How I was taught without being told not to bring him up.

How every bit of that was a lie.

How every time I wondered, I felt shame.

"Everyone get out," I say loudly. "You heard the senator. Get. Out." My words sound like they're coming from a completely different person who coincidentally lives in my body. I'm confident and angry, determined and clear.

Everyone but Monica starts to move toward the door.

"Harry," Monica says, stepping toward him, her jaw so tightly clenched that her neck muscles stand out, long twin bands running from collarbone to just below the earlobe. "Don't be hasty." She looks at me like I'm an annoyance. "Don't say anything to her you'll later regret."

My turn to lunge.

Silas's heat is pressed against my back in an instant, my arms twisted back against his tight abs, my elbows thrashing and shoulders pulled with a painful tear. I fight him with every ounce of vengeful strength I possess.

It's not enough.

Rage directed at the closest thing to evil in my life right now pales in comparison to Silas's ability to stop me.

"Don't! You'll be arrested," he hisses.

"I am Senator Harwell Bosworth's daughter! You can't arrest me!" I scream, kicking my feet up, tipping another chair over. My hips try to gain leverage against the enormous conference table and flip it through sheer fury. "This is just a *family* spat." My eyes lock on my father's in that second and I see all of his pain. There's so much. It's like his soul is turned inside out and reflects on his corneas, gleaming and raw.

"I told you. She belongs on the Island," Monica says coldly to no one in particular. "Mentally ill, like her mother."

"And you belong in hell, you cold, worthless, lying bitch!" I counter, wrenching my arms as I try to get to her, claw her, shred her.

Erase her.

But Silas won't let me.

"She's a liability," Monica says, gaining power from my emotions. Who does that? Who is revitalized by another person's *pain*?

"You're the liability!" I scream. "Wait until the press gets ahold of what you've done!" If my mouth weren't so dry, I'd spit on her.

"Harry," she says calmly, her long-suffering inhale so practiced, it's like she's acting in a soap opera, "the press says she slit Tara's wrists when they met at a bar. She was covered in blood in the news." Monica's blonde, perfectly coiffed hair moves with her as she calmly, coolly shakes her head as if we're discussing some environmental disaster or a surprise earthquake. "Are you really going to listen to someone like that? I know she's your daughter, but–"

"Everyone except Silas and Jane get OUT!" Harry loses his composure, his face going a deep shade of red that looks dangerous. He's intimidating and imposing and he knows it.

Under any other circumstances, I'd freeze. It's what I do under stress.

I'm overriding my own circuits, my emotional programming completely unprepared for this.

And it is *so* liberating.

"GET OUT!" I echo, struggling against Silas, who has a locked grip on me, both arms around my shoulders, hooked at my elbows, his right leg across my front, arms like steel bands. His biceps are huge against mine, pressing my breasts flat against my chest wall. Sweat coats the spaces where our skin connects.

I'm more dangerous than Monica.

I've underestimated how good that feels.

"We're not done here," Monica says to me, needing the last word.

"NO, WE'RE NOT!" I shout back, depriving her of it.

Marshall reaches for her elbow–which is not pinned against her ribs, like mine are–and she snatches it back, moving primly through the small space between her and where he stands at the closed door. As they exit, she doesn't look back.

Silas's hold on me remains steady. My muscles twitch, eager to be flexed, needing to physically harm someone. The feeling is beyond instinct, more than impulse, a craven desire to be violent and draw blood and to revel in it.

I *want* to cause someone else pain.

Monica is my number one target, but in a pinch, my *father* will have to do.

Silas and I are breathing hard, his breath its own kind of threat as it heats my neck, my hair, my shoulder. My shirt is crooked, pulled hard to the right. I'm pretty sure I've lost a button or two. I'm nothing but struggle, every piece of me in motion.

Harry is the opposite. A stone statue, only his eyes moving.

"I know it's hard to understand, Jane. I did what I thought was best at the time."

My father doesn't tell Silas to stand down. He's looking at me with contemplative eyes, as if I'm a problem to unwind, a situation to manage. Lindsay told me her parents treat her like this. A pang of empathy turns into a loud chime in me, growing in intensity, the sound taking over.

I'm his daughter now.

I've been his daughter all along.

How is he about to treat me now?

"You did what you thought was best at the time?" My elbow slips and I get Silas hard in the diaphragm. His grunt is the only indication I've hit a target. He doesn't loosen his grip.

"Of course I did," Harry replies, giving Silas a look. Immediately, he releases me, taking three steps back. He moves closer to the senator.

"At which time? When my mother told you she was pregnant with me? When she gave birth? When she raised me without a father? When she lied to me about who my father was? All those times I had a 'Daddy-Daughter' dance at school and you came with Lindsay? When, Senator Bosworth–excuse me. When, DADDY? When did you think it was 'best'?"

The word "daddy" feels like I'm spitting a live slug out of my mouth. It is gross and foreign, unexpected and gag-inducing.

It's also Lindsay's word. Not mine.

Even if he is my father.

"I deserve that," Harry concedes.

"You deserve nothing but that. Nothing but condemnation and anger and–you completely amoral, soulless beast!"

He flinches but doesn't yield, taking my hits like a stoic boxer hardening himself for the ring.

"Jane, your mother and I–"

I start to rush him, the mention of Mom too much, too blinding. Silas inserts himself between us. For a microsecond I think about hurting him. A proxy, though, isn't enough.

I want my father to feel pain.

"Don't you dare talk about my mother. You don't have the right to speak of her. You used her. You used her up. You let her become a patsy in some twisted game and she became the fall guy and she died because of you!"

Sweat sprouts along his hairline, face going chalky.

12

"That's not what happened," he insists.

"Then tell me what happened, Harry. All I know is that my mother is dead because you *let* it happen. Tell me that isn't true. Tell me I didn't live with a mother who lied to me my entire life about my biological father. Tell me you didn't make her hide the truth. And tell me you did everything–*everything!*–possible to prevent her death."

His silence hurts me more than I want it to.

I run to the door, jumping on feet that aren't mine, racing to get out of here. My calf stings and I look down at it as my hand grabs the doorknob and I open it.

"Jane!"

"Go to hell, Daddy!"

And for the second time in less than ten minutes, the man most likely to become the next president of the United States has the door slammed on him.

Silas is behind me in seconds, as if he walked through the wall. He follows me until I reach the outer door that leads to where the black SUVs are all parked. He elbows past me and opens it.

"Where to?" he asks.

"I'm not going anywhere with you."

"I'm sorry about that. It's my job. I held you back as much to protect you as I did to defend the Bosworths."

"Leave me alone."

"I'm afraid I can't do that, Jane. I have to take you somewhere." Compassion pours out of those icy, sea-blue eyes.

"Somewhere? Where would that be?"

"You tell me."

"I finally get to choose? Really? Is that because I'm the senator's daughter?" My heart doesn't know how to beat anymore. It's screaming and crying like a terrified little child.

Which it is.

"It's because you're due for some freedom. Jane, where do you want to go?"

"I want to be alone."

"Not possible."

"So much for freedom!" I shout.

"I have to protect you. You tell me where you want to go."

I look at him. *Really* look at him. He's sweaty, face slightly flushed, and he is *pumped*. The guy held me to protect me from myself. Just doing his job, right?

What else can I get him to do in the course of duty?

"Take me home, Silas."

"Home? You don't have a home, Jane."

"I meant take me to *your* home." I'm overwhelmed, struggling to find words around the red swath of pain that fills every space around me.

"My place? My apartment?"

"Yes." My impatience is making it impossible to say anything at all.

"Why?"

I stop and stare at him, my heart beating in my chest like it's hammering its way out, as if it's about to crack my breastbone in half and slip away over the sand and into the ocean. The sky is crystal clear and textured, the different layers of blue competing with one another for the crown of Most Striking. The air smells like freshly cut grass and salt. For the rest of my life, that scent will bring me back here as I stare into the beautiful eyes of a man who is paid to keep me alive.

And then I say the only words that matter. The only words that make sense.

The only words in the world.

"Silas, take me home and screw me until I can't remember a single moment of what just happened back there in that meeting."

CHAPTER 3

I expect a *no*. But today is not a day for my expectations to be met. Not one tiny bit.

"That would take a very long time," he says, deadpan.

"Hey–I've got all the time in the world." I look him over like he's a piece of meat, as if the question of whether we'll have sex is a formality and I'm already picking out which condom to use. "You look like you've got the stamina."

His muscular shoulders push against the cloth of his perfectly tailored jacket. I wonder what he looks like naked. Warmth pours through me, a mix of anger and angst and outrage, all ready to be vanquished by breaking every rule inside myself so I can just be broken and not have to deal with anything.

"Jane."

"If you won't do it, I'll go find someone who will."

"I don't doubt that you could, and in a heartbeat," he says, crossing his arms over his chest, looking at me with a mixture of lust and restraint that makes me want him even more.

"Oh, please. If I were that hot, you'd have slept with me by now."

"It's not for lack of interest."

"It's... not?"

"You know damn well I'm interested. Last night should have made it perfectly clear."

Last night. That was *last night*. Last night I was in his arms, his mouth on mine, hands exploring, my body offered to him for comfort, for connection, for passion.

Last night I knew who I was.

Last night, I wasn't Senator Harwell Bosworth's daughter.

Last night feels like a century ago.

"Nothing in my life is clear, Silas. Not a damn thing." Brazen, emboldened by the casual disintegration of every part of my identity, I step into his space and stand on tiptoes, kissing him.

He kisses me back.

And then it's like he swallows me whole, bringing me into his body and world, eliminating the rush of evil that seems to have enveloped me over the last few hours, days, weeks, months. I feel free again, centered and real as his tongue slips into my mouth, an act of stealth and openness that is a paradox. Silas kisses me with his entire being, breathing for me as I relinquish myself to the blinding possibility of being fine again.

It could happen. Some day.

For right now, I'll take having the broken pieces of me held together by his hands, his body, his mouth. A sweet kiss can heal, but a hot kiss can transcend. I press hard against him, our tongues warm and wet, moving faster, his claiming of me going deeper, so far down inside me, I feel full. Complete.

Grounded.

"I will not take you home and screw you, Jane," he says as our kiss ends, his mouth still against mine. "Not now."

"Why not?"

"Because I don't believe in taking advantage of people when they're weak."

"You think I'm weak?"

"Did I say *you* were who I'm talking about?"

"You're the weak one? *You?*" My fingertips drag against the cloth of his suit jacket and I swoon, imagining my hands slipping his clothes off him. Power resides in his muscles, attached to bones and tendons and veins that make up the body that moves against mine right now. He's hot and sweaty and primed for *me*.

"You're breaking through every defense I've got."

"Why do you need defenses with me?"

"That is a great question we can discuss over lunch."

"Lunch?" Images of our naked, sweaty bedroom antics suddenly get swept away by... *lunch?*

"Yes. It's a meal you eat around noontime when you're hungry."

I punch his shoulder. "I know what lunch is!"

"Good. Then it's a date."

"A date? Aren't you on the clock?"

"We're going to ignore that."

"Who said you get to pick and choose which rules we break?"

"I do." His voice is a low, slow caress.

I take a breath to argue, but let it out slowly instead. He's right.

"A real date?"

"Yes. One where I pick the restaurant, we drink wine, and no one bombs your car or turns out to be your father."

"Is that a guarantee?"

"It's a plan."

"You're not going to let me throw myself at you, are you?" I ask, my hands up in the air in defeat and incredulity. Tornadoes of emotion overpower me. I'll do anything to make them stop.

"I also don't believe in being used for revenge sex." He dips his head slightly in a self-effacing gesture that makes him even more irresistible.

"Revenge sex?"

"Revenge sex, angry sex, call it what you want. When I make love with you, it'll be for all the *right* reasons. Screwing you so you can forget you're Senator Bosworth's daughter isn't a good enough reason."

His words—*when I make love with you*—cut through all my fierce pain. Silas didn't say *if*.

He said *when*.

"Your reasons count, but mine don't?" I ask, the lingering need to be livid hard to shake.

"When your reasons don't involve genuinely wanting me, then no."

"I wouldn't ask you if I didn't want you, Silas." My voice is pleading. Desperate. Angry.

Lustful.

"And I wouldn't say no if I didn't want you, too, Jane."

What am I supposed to do with *that*?

"This is just plain old awkward." My words are true. We've traded a lot of lies in our short time together, but I just laid it out.

"It doesn't have to be."

We're so close to each other, faces inches away, the casual conversation masking both our racing hearts. I get the impression he's as overwhelmed as I am, yet Silas is in complete command of himself. Any guy who can turn down a woman who throws herself at him and pivot it into a proper date has a sophisticated inner life.

One I want to know.

"You're kissing me right here at the senator's estate." Somehow, he pulled us into a tight corner where a small solarium pokes out of the house. We're surrounded by thick bushes, some flowering. I'm sure someone, somewhere, sees us. We're just public enough to be seen, but private enough not to be obvious.

"I don't care."

"You don't care about kissing me, or you don't care about getting caught?" This conversation is Byzantine, with twists and turns that don't make sense, and yet it holds a strange beauty, an intangible quality that isn't diminished by the many layers.

"You tell me. Do you think I don't care about kissing you?"

"No. I think you do care."

"Good. I don't like mixed signals. I'm direct, Jane, unless my job prohibits it."

"I *am* your job."

"And I'm very, very good at doing my job. The best. Always."

My answer is muted by his kiss. As he buries one hand in my

hair, playing with the layered strands like he's touching fine silk, he gives me a strong, possessive kiss that assures me. I'm riveted in place, knees weak, his mouth confusing me even as it makes promises.

This time, I break first. "I just found out that I am the biological daughter of a presidential candidate. And Lindsay!" My hand flies to my mouth, fingertips brushing my pleasantly raw lips. "Poor Lindsay."

"She'll be fine, eventually. She has Drew."

"Who could her father be?"

At my question, his face goes slack, eyes suddenly all business.

"You know I can't tell you that."

"You *know*?" I let my heart beat a few times as it spreads its wings. The cage it's been locked inside dissolves as we speak.

"We have suspicions. And rumors. A few tips."

"Drew's hidden this from her all along?"

Silas opens his mouth to respond, then shuts it, lips going tight, his head shaking slightly. "I said too much. Let's pretend I didn't."

"I'm done pretending when it comes to paternity questions."

"I can understand that," he says gently. "But this isn't about your father. It's about Lindsay's."

I start to cry, silent and soulful. "I feel so bad for her."

"It must be hard."

"At least I don't have Monica for a *mother*."

"Lindsay's had a rough life," he agrees.

"What about your life? Your mom? Kelly? How are they? What's happening with your sister's death and–" My stomach roars with a grumbling, growling sound, like a tiger lives inside me.

"Perfect timing," he says with a sad smile. "Let's talk about it over lunch." As he guides me out of the little corner we're in, his body language changes. He's back to all business, stiff and formal, on guard.

I immediately assume I've done something wrong.

"Where?"

"In town. By the water, where the old port shopping is. Except we'll stick to indoor locations with obvious back exits," he clarifies.

"You're really selling the romance here, Silas."

I expect him to laugh. Remember? Today is not my day for having expectations met.

Peering intently at me, he gives me a soft, concerned look. "This is too much."

I jerk in his arms. "The date?"

"No. All of it. Tara's death. Your–" His entire body tightens. "Your exam back there. The test results. Monica."

I interrupt him. "And your sister. Kelly. Your mom."

He starts to pull me closer, but pivots instead. I'm led away from the kiss, the hug, the comfort. Reality means getting out of here as fast as possible. Reality means never taking the time to feel anything as it actually happens. This is my new reality.

This is all I know now.

Duff is sitting in the driver's seat of the black SUV Silas guides me to. I wonder how he knows which car to bring me into, how he communicates with his team, what it takes to make everything move so smoothly. I plan to ask when we're settled into the SUV, but as I try to climb up into the backseat, I pause.

And begin to shake.

My blood turns cold, like someone is flushing pipes, as I look at objects around me–the back door handle, the button on Silas's cuff, the distance between my eyes and the black asphalt. It all starts to spin, pulling in and out, toward and away, and I am nothing more than a human version of a wax doll.

"Jane?" Silas's voice comes to me from the end of a long tunnel that separates us. "Jane!" His voice is urgent and softer.

And then it's gone. *I'm* gone.

What a relief.

CHAPTER 4

*M*y ear is stroking something so soft and smooth. It's comforting and inviting, so I rub against the softness, reveling in sensation, sighing.

And then the something *moves*.

"Hey," Silas says, his voice coming from above. "She's awake."

I open my eyes, then shut them quickly to make the spinning stop. The world is full of random objects that move in and out, forward and back, my depth perception put in a blender and puréed.

"What?" I whisper, his hand on my shoulder. I want him to stroke my hair, to bring me ginger ale, to keep me safe and let me relax.

"You fainted," he says, voice somehow both taut with worry and gentle with concern. "Right into my arms."

"You have good arms."

"I like them."

"So do I."

I roll in his lap and look up into those bright eyes full of mirth and worry. "Can you sit up?" he asks.

"No."

"That bad?"

"It feels so nice here. I could sleep here forever."

Someone clears their throat in the distance. It's a masculine sound.

"She okay?" the throat-clearer asks from another continent away. Or maybe the front seat. It's hard to tell.

"I think so," Silas responds, easing me up slowly.

"I did not consent to sitting up," I murmur, snuggling in.

"And I didn't consent to being your pillow."

"But you're a good pillow. The best pillow *ever*."

"Jane?" Silas asks slowly. "Are you on something?"

"On something? I'm on you." My muscles go slack, body in need of this all-too-short moment to enjoy being at rest in a place of sanctuary.

Rumbling makes my head move lightly as he–is he *laughing*? "No. I mean, did you take a drug, or a pill? You're acting very weird."

"Have we met? Come on. You try going through what I've been through these last few days, then faint, and come out of it perfectly sane," I grouse.

As I come to a full upright position with my back against the upholstered seat, I realize it's not just me, Silas, and–*oh*. The throat-clearer is Duff.

Drew is behind him, their heads huddled together as they speak through the window.

"I'm fine," I lie. "Just tired and a little weary from having my entire life blitzed to smithereens."

"That would exhaust anyone," Silas assures me.

"I need my own place," I say, the plaintive tone so obvious to me. In any other situation, I'd be mortified. But right now, I just want home. Any home.

My home.

"You do," Drew says, breaking away from his conversation with Duff and looking into the backseat. "And we'll get there. Right now, we're trying to figure out how best to handle this new complication."

I bristle. "I am not a complication."

"I don't mean you," he clarifies. "I'm talking about Monica."

"Oh." Asking him to elaborate will get me nowhere. Silas slides out of the seat next to me, opens the door, and stands with Duff and Drew, talking in low voices. In the door, I find an unopened bottle of water, grateful for a moment to meet my body's needs. As I drink, I realize how little I've been able to focus on this bag of flesh and bones that carries my personality, my soul and mind, around. A flash of memory in Alice's studio, posing, makes me feel more connected.

The body will not be ignored. Deferred? Sure. Ignored?

No.

Secretly, I watch Silas, my face tipped down but eyes cutting to the right. His hands are on his hips, pulling back the sides of his suit jacket, showing his belt with a small pistol on it. His white business shirt is wrinkled and a little lopsided. One part of it is untucked. That was my fault, I'm sure. The way he held me back from injuring Monica was no small feat.

The water hits my stomach and soothes my parched throat. I smooth my hair and straighten myself. Posture, clothing, thoughts. Being in order is never more important than when you've been in nothing but disarray.

And I'm the very definition of chaos right now.

My skin feels like electric impulses multiplying by the second. I'm hot. I'm cold. I'm tired. I'm wired. I'm a bundle of conflicting emotions and sensations that don't add up to anything substantive, but that suck all the energy out of me.

But I am *here.*

I got angry.

I defended myself.

And I left on my terms.

A cracking sound, like a slab of marble snapping in half, fills the air. The glass window to my left explodes. I flinch, a rush of annoyance flooding my veins, making me turn and look. Instantly, my irritation turns into pain as little shards of glass rain down on me. The open car door slams and all the men outside drop out of my sight like they've fallen through trap doors in synchronicity.

Crack!

Crack!

Crack!

Silas shouts, "Get down, Jane!" and I want to tell him I can't, I need him back in here, it hurts, I am tired, so tired, please make it stop.

"JANE!" he bellows.

I open my mouth to answer and a chunky piece of glass falls in, my tongue stinging as it gets trapped between the tip and my lower teeth. Copper wetness floods my mouth and I spit the piece out, red blood all over the back of the front seat.

Ringing is all I hear. It's maddening. The world has gone slow.

So slow.

The door with the shattered window opens slowly and Silas crawls in, ignoring the glass everywhere. I want to warn him, to make sure he doesn't bleed like me, but the ringing is so loud, I can't speak. He wouldn't hear me if I said a word because everything is a tinny cloud of sound. The whole world is glass and high-pitched ringing and movement and fuzzy. Blurred edges dominate everything. I see nothing *and* eternity with every movement of my eyes.

I can't feel my heart. Is it still there?

He pulls me down to the floor of the vehicle, his hard yank unyielding. My shoulder feels like it's been ripped out of its socket. The reactive scent fills the SUV's cab, an unpleasant odor that sets every nerve firing, mingling with the blood until I can't think, can't move, can't process.

Can't save myself.

Silas is inches from me, eyes combing over my face, my body. His hand goes to my jaw, thumb brushing against my bloody lip.

"You're not shot." His words carry no question. Just an affirmation. I barely hear him, but I know what he's saying.

Crack!

Another gunshot outside.

I start to shake, my vision pinpointing, but a wave of nausea cuts through it all and shoves a big bolus of adrenaline through my body. We're on the floor, my calf painfully pinned beneath me, my skin being cut by glass. The sting feels deliberate and cruel, as if the glass is trying to hurt me on purpose.

Just like whoever is shooting.

"Why?" I ask Silas, coming out of it, the ringing like a mournful chorus. "Why?"

"Why what?"

"Why are they shooting? Why are they *here*? They aren't supposed to be here."

Ignoring my words, he holds his gun in one hand, the flinty metal odor of fresh gunfire mingling with the taste of my own blood, making my stomach curl.

And then a series of gunshots, a rapid mixture of sounds that make it clear multiple people with different firearms are going at it, followed by screams.

Oh, no.

Sounds like Lindsay.

Drew is calling out orders. Her screams mute suddenly, like a radio turned off with a quick flick of a wrist. Abrupt and fractured, the sound of that scream ending is like hearing the devil smother an angel. Was she shot?

Please don't let Lindsay be shot.

All of the men pop up outside the window into standing positions. Silas cocks his ear, listening. He doesn't drop his weapon but he sits up, peeking through the intact back window.

"Gentian!" Drew barks.

Silas crawls backwards out the slightly open car door and stands.

I hear the rustle of leaves, strangely, even beyond the bright ringing in my ears. It's a loud, furious sound. Noise that a big animal in the bushes makes. Not what I expected to hear.

I sit up, brushing glass off the seat, pieces scraping against the butt of my hand. As I turn to the right, my attention caught by movement, I realize the big animal is a human.

A very dead, very bloody human.

Duff opens the SUV's door and looks at me like Silas did, only without emotion. He's cataloging my injuries, triaging me, his expression changing as he sees blood. "You're bleeding, Jane. Any serious injuries?"

"No. Just copper," I say, pointing to my mouth.

He frowns. "Copper?"

I wave him away. "I'm fine. Just scratches. It hurts, but no more."

Duff appears to be older than me, older than Silas and Drew, with a long scar at the corner of one eye that drags his skin back tight. It gives his eyes a lopsided look, like it changes the color of the injured one, that orb more the shade of the sea mixed with sand. He's tan and tight, skin stretched over muscle and anger like it's a sentry. I've never seen him smile, his resting face severe. He smells like sweat and lemon and old wood.

Then copper overpowers everything again, in my mouth, my nose, my memory. It *sears*.

His hand reaches for mine, offering to help me out of the SUV, but I don't move.

Duff waits two beats. He looks to his right as a black SUV rolls up, intact. The driver rolls his window down.

It's Silas.

"Get in," he orders. His command makes me move, taking Duff's outstretched hand, gliding like I'm a robot being programmed. Duff boosts me up to get in the passenger's seat, snaps the door shut, and before I can reach for my seatbelt, Silas peels out.

"What was that?" I squeal as I struggle to find the buckle and secure myself.

"Someone got past the perimeter and started shooting."

"I can tell *that*. Who was it? Someone after me? Someone trying to kill Harry?"

"We don't know."

Silas's phone rings. He pulls it out of his jacket and tosses it on a flat spot on the console, pressing the Talk button and putting it on speakerphone.

"What the hell was that, Drew?" he asks, shaking with adrenaline and rage.

"You sound like the senator. He's pissed. But we have a complication. The guy got in by using the slip."

What's 'the slip'?

"What?" Silas sounds incredulous. "There are only two passwords for that special entrance, and–"

"He used Spider's password."

Silas's eyes bulge out of his head. I assume "Spider" is Harry's code name.

"You're shitting me." I know from Lindsay, way back in high school, that her dad's — er, *my* dad's — security team changed his code name every week. From the shock registering on Silas' face, I take it this is still the case, which makes it even worse.

"I am not."

"Why would he give it to someone?"

"Claims he didn't."

Silas lets out a low whistle. "This just went from bad to worse."

"No, Silas. This just went from worse to apocalyptic." Drew's voice has a resonance to it I've never heard before. He's livid but level headed, calculating quickly to determine sequences of events and projecting out to the future. Constantly in vigilant mode, Drew's life revolves around outsmarting the enemy and protecting the client.

A breach like this is huge.

"The intruder was trying to shoot Jane, though. Not entering the house to get the senator or his wife."

"We don't know who the intended target was. The guy's dead. We'll never know."

"But he used Bosworth's private code? You're sure."

"Positive."

Silas sighs. "I need to get her to a safehouse. Not Alice Mogrett's. Too much movement already. She needs a place to land."

"I can hear everything you're saying," I blurt out. "Quit talking about me as if I'm not here. This is getting really old."

"We're working on getting you an apartment, Jane," Drew

says, his voice professional. The difference between the way he talks to Silas and me is stark. "It's taking longer than expected."

"Why?" I ask.

"Because no one is willing to rent to you."

"But *you're* renting *for* me!"

"It's... complicated."

"I told you my solution," Silas says to Drew with more authority than I've ever heard.

"Gentian." Interesting how he changes to Silas's last name. "I told you it's too risky. You're crossing a professional line."

"Happened a long time ago." The look he gives me makes it clear *I'm* on the other side of that line now.

"Fine, but I won't enable it. I have a company to run, and you know how politics works. Word gets out and..." A barely concealed growl lurks in Drew's words.

"What are you two talking about?" I demand.

"Silas offered to have you stay at his place," he tells me in a sick, nasty voice.

Shock makes me touch his arm, my voice going breathy. "You... did?"

"Yes. Only as a temporary solution."

"What about your mom and Kelly?"

"They're on their way to my sister's place. Mom thought it would be more stable for Kelly to live at the home she knows best during the initial–you know."

"Adjustment period?"

He looks relieved. "Yes."

"I don't want to live in your apartment, Silas," I say evenly, with confidence.

Drew clears his throat, the sound the equivalent of *Ooo, burn*.

"I respect that," Silas replies, but I can see he's troubled. He's nodding to himself, then suddenly his expression changes.

"Give me a minute." He holds up one finger and hits mute on the phone, brows turned down and tight, his face a mask of concentration. He pulls over, the car skidding slightly. Suddenly, a second car barrels up behind us, pulling a three-point turn until Drew is facing the house, his window down, looking up at

Silas in the driver's seat. There are three guys in the car with him, all wearing suits and sunglasses, like a really bad imitation of *The Matrix*.

Great. I'm back to being an entity. An item they move around. A logistics problem. So much for being treated like a person.

With great disgust, Silas kills the phone call and looks at Drew. He opens his mouth to say something, but I cut him off.

"Drew!" I call out, surprising myself.

"What?" he shouts back, not bothering to look toward me. Why should he? I'm just a client.

"You can't do this."

All of his guys freeze. More eyebrows go up.

"Excuse me?"

"I was just shot at. I am covered with glass shards and cuts. I need more than that," I announce.

"Oh, right. Medical attention. Duff can take you to the emergency room and–"

"I need more *information*. I need more freedom."

He gives a dismissive sound. "Medical care we can manage. Information? No. And freedom?" His eyebrows shoot up. "Are you crazy? After what just happened?"

"I just found out that I am a presidential candidate's daughter. I don't care what people think I've done or not done, but show some compassion for the fact that I've just been thrust into a spotlight that has the potential to be worse than everything I've been through for the past seven months, and trust me–it's been hell."

"How do you think my *wife* feels, finding out he's *not* her father?" he hisses back at me. I'm the target of his anger now. I'm sure it feels good to unleash on me, but here's the problem.

I'm pissed, too.

I need a target.

"I've gone along with being turned into an object you moved around at will because I felt like I had no choice. Now I do. And now I'm leaving." I start to climb out of the car and sprint toward the main passageway from The Grove's backyard to the

29

front of the house. A big red bloodstain covers the edge of the sidewalk, the dead body covered with a sheet. Bullet casings litter the ground. As I move, the air chills the thousands of small cuts all over my skin. My mouth stings with pain, and my vision starts to fade in and out.

I grind my teeth and make myself keep moving.

Silas comes up behind me. "Jane."

"No."

"Jane," he says, voice firmer and insistent.

"No!"

"Jane." His hand touches my shoulder. I shake it off and, on unsteady legs, look straight ahead. Eyes on the prize. I want to walk through a cluster of flowering bushes and get to the front of the house. From there, I have no idea where to go, but it's better than here.

"If you leave, you'll be dead in twenty-four hours," he declares, matching my steps.

"You're just saying that to control me."

"Have I ever lied to you before?"

"I don't know." I pause. "Have you?"

"No."

"But I have no way of verifying that."

"True. But I think you want to trust me." His voice is softly urgent.

"I want to trust someone. Alice is the only person I really trust."

"I want you to trust *me*." The insistent tone gets me right in the diaphragm, making my breastbone ache up to my throat. A part of me wants to trust him, too. A big part of me.

It's where my heart lives.

"You have a funny way of showing it."

"I–I was trying. I really wanted to take you out, talk like regular people, do the getting-to-know-you bit..."

"Well, Silas, I have to say, you sure do know how to make an impression on a first date."

His smile is broad, the explosive laughter a bonus. As he

moves, chunks of broken car-window glass fall to the ground off his lapel, making little tinkling sounds.

"It takes a lot of work to make that kind of impression." We both look over at the intruder's dead body and stop laughing.

"Look. Trust me for now. You don't have to trust me forever. Just *now*. Let's go to my place, get cleaned up, and have that date at my place."

"I told you, I don't want to live at your place!"

"Not live. Just... breathe. Pause. Rest."

"I have one condition."

"Name it."

"Do you like to play Candyland?"

His grin is so genuine. "No, but I know someone who calls herself the world's master..."

CHAPTER 5

"*I* have another condition," I inform him. As charmed as I am by the offer to spend time with his niece, I need more. Every part of the world feels like a sharp dagger pointed at me. Each molecule is a threat. As I breathe in and out, I'm inhaling threats and exhaling denial.

It's exhausting.

"Of course you do."

"You have to open up and give me more information about threats. You *have* to. Drew's being an asshole."

"Drew is doing his job."

I've ruffled Silas, who clearly doesn't like my criticism of his boss and friend.

"And I am protecting my sanity. I can't have some crazed man sneak into my... father's estate using his personal code and start shooting at me and be kept in the dark."

"That is really all there is to know." He shrugs. Blinking hard, he's trying to be neutral and cool.

You can't fold emotions and put them back in a Do Not Show box when you've kissed someone as passionately as Silas has kissed me. Once you cross that line, that's it.

Show anger? Passionate hate? Incredulous disgust? Sure.

But lying to someone whose hands have held you bound to

them while your lips and tongue whisper secrets through strokes and aches, fevered bites and longing licks?

No.

"Silas. If you want me to trust you, you either need to tell me the truth or become a much, much better liar. That is bullshit and you know it."

"Let's talk on the car ride to my place."

Grudgingly, I move with him toward the SUV, because really– what choice do I have?

"I'll have clean clothes for you there. Someone was supposed to deliver them by now," he adds.

I halt. "You set this up before I said yes?"

"I was reasonably confident you'd agree."

"You were cocky."

"Same thing."

"*Not* the same thing." I stop walking. I turn to him. The sun makes it impossible to see his eyes, but I know he's laughing at me.

"You're argumentative."

"I am defending my boundaries."

"That's another way to put it. Come on. Let's get you into a shower."

I make a sound that suggests he's being inappropriate.

"Look at your skin, Jane. You're covered in glass shards and blood. You need to clean and dress all of that. In fact, maybe an ER is a better option than my place."

The thought of going to a hospital, of the endless forms and discussions and explanations, feels worse than dealing with pain. "No. Fine. Your place. But I am not living there."

"I understand."

"And if you have ice cream in your freezer, I will eat it all."

"Are you done listing conditions?"

"One more. If you really are taking me out on a date, I'm getting lobster, buddy. Lobster tails and filet mignon. I am going to be high maintenance."

He smothers a smile with his hand.

"And that is different from–what?"

I glare at him.

But I love his laugh. "Go for it. Add a bottle of Dom Perignon, Jane. Live it up."

"Yes!"

"I'm sure you're worth it."

"But don't think because you're buying me dinner that I'm a sure thing."

"I don't assume anything when it comes to you," he says, his voice full of warmth.

"You used to."

"My mistake." He looks pretty happy for a guy who was so wrong.

"You *admit* you were wrong?"

"Of course."

"Most guys don't."

"I'm not most guys."

Thank God.

I lean back and close my eyes, letting Silas command the clean SUV along the surface roads before we hit the I-5. Thick traffic seems to bother him. He drives just enough on the shoulder to take the next exit.

"Why are you going this way?" I ask.

"Gridlock makes us a sitting target."

"You think someone might shoot at us on the I-5?" After what we just went through, I know he's right. Suddenly, traffic isn't just an annoying given in Southern California.

It's directly connected to my ability to stay alive.

"They infiltrated The Grove. That speaks to an inside job. I don't rule any danger out." Scanning the horizon, he looks at every lane, every car, eyes moving as if he's been programmed.

Because he has.

"Inside job? If I had to lay bets, I'd pick Monica Bosworth." I'm totally joking, but realize he's not laughing. I look at him. Grim lines bookend his mouth, his jaw tight.

"Silas? You guys think *Monica* was behind the shooter?"

"No," he says slowly. "But we can't rule any suspects out."

"She's close to being the first lady of the United States! You think she would give an intruder her husband's private code so the guy could come to their estate and kill me?"

"It sounds crazy," he confirms.

"It *is* crazy."

"We rule nothing out."

"Sounds like you're ruling Monica *in* as a suspect." Secretly, the thought gives me a hopeful thrill. If evil has a face, it's hers. At the same time, years of knowing her as Lindsay's aloof, power-hungry mother fill me with an unearned soft spot for her. All those years of vacations weren't that bad. She could be witty and funny.

As long as you weren't the target of her sharp tongue.

"Think about it, Jane. Your paternity was just revealed, Monica's cheating and Lindsay's paternity were part of that meeting– and within minutes someone tries to shoot you on Senator Harwell Bosworth's personal grounds? The guy got past all our security. You don't do that without an insider feeding you information." He gives me a sideways glance that makes me groan.

"Drew thinks I'm responsible, doesn't he?"

Silas goes quiet, making a left turn, the sound of the blinker filling the space between us.

I keep my eyes closed and try not to move. Every time I move, my skin stings.

"You're smarter than anyone ever warned me," he finally says, voice rueful and admiring.

"If that is supposed to be a compliment, you're really, really terrible at them."

"It's meant to be a compliment."

"If my intelligence comes as a surprise, you haven't been paying attention."

"Is that an insult?"

"Yes."

"You're very good at them."

"I'm also good at compliments."

"And Candyland," he adds drolly.

I'm caught off guard by the reminder of Kelly. "I am," I reply, softening my tone. "How is she?"

"About what you'd expect. Mom and I broke the news to her gently. It was... hard." His voice chokes with emotion as he swings the car to the left again, veering around a delivery truck before turning.

"I'm so sorry." The enormity of what Silas is living with makes it hard to breathe.

He nods.

My eyes fill with tears. I reach up to wipe one away and accidentally drag a small sliver of glass across my cheek, scratching myself. The teardrop drips into the open wound, stinging more.

"If I can help in any way," I start to say, but emotion overcomes me.

"Jane," he says gently. "You have more than enough on your plate. Kelly will be fine. She's a sweet little kid who misses her mommy. My mother and I are handling it. She has two adults who love her very much. That's more than most people have. If anyone needs help, it's you."

"My needs are simple. I just need people to stop trying to kill me." *Crack! Crack!* The sound of the bullets flying past us a few minutes ago echoes through me. From car bombs to someone killing Tara to a mad gunman–my "simple" life isn't ever happening.

The tears just keep rolling.

"That simple, huh?" he asks rhetorically.

"Right. Seriously. If they would just stop, I could pick up all the destroyed parts of my life and try to build a new one." *Sniff.*

"You know that's not how this works."

"*Shhhhh.*"

"Why are you hushing me?"

"Because all I really have left is the ability to live in a state of denial when needed, and you're stripping it away." I wipe my tears with the heel of my hand, watching for glass. A right turn, then a left, and suddenly we pull into an underground parking garage.

"This isn't your apartment building," I note.

"No. We're changing cars."

"Oh."

A quiet peace settles between us as I obediently follow him. He punches a key code into the door handle of a boring navy sedan and motions for me to climb in. The car smells like pineapple air freshener that has baked into the cloth interior. It reminds me of my mother's car for no reason whatsoever.

I drop my head and let myself cry.

Silas says nothing, his silence one of companionship. He isn't awkward or tense. He's just there, a presence. I can lower all my defenses and feel what I'm actually feeling in real time. No need to store this away to be dealt with later.

I have more than enough of a historical archive to mine in future days when life has calmed down.

If it ever calms down.

The thought of living like this for the rest of my life horrifies me.

And makes me cry harder.

My chest starts to to constrict, throat tightening, my lungs working harder and harder to get enough air. Every time I start to feel calmer, all the small abrasions on my skin scream. Too many parts of my inner and outer self need attention at the same time.

What do organisms do when they cannot handle an overwhelming amount of stimuli?

They self-destruct.

There is a point where living with your own mind becomes its own torture. You can't turn off the racing neurons. You can't stop processing trauma. You can't quell the endless screaming inside. People turn to drugs or alcohol or food or sex or gambling to transform internal pain into an external release, but it just manages symptoms.

It never cures what causes all that crazymaking.

Ultimately, you're trapped by... *you.*

I know it's a temporary state. If I just get a hot shower, some food, and some rest, then tomorrow will be better. Call me the Scarlett O'Hara of the twenty-first century. Tomorrow is another day.

But damned if getting through *today* doesn't feel like an endless saga to endure. My own private war.

"Need a tissue?" Silas asks, bending toward me to open a compartment. A small tissue box is in there, next to a few blister packs of pain-relief medicine and some peppermints.

"No. If I wipe my tears again, I'll just scratch myself with glass. I'll shower and cry in there."

"I'm sorry."

"It's not your fault."

"I'm sorry you have to feel all of this."

"Me, too. I'm sorry you can't even be with your mother and niece right now. All because of me."

"I... I'm not here because I have to be, Jane."

"But you're working."

"Yes, I am. But this job shifted from work to personal long ago. You know that."

His words make me cry harder. This time, there is texture to my sobs. I'm a mixture of pleasure and pain, of sorrow and joy, of hope and despair.

And that is all Silas's fault.

We pull into his apartment complex in more silence. This time it's even deeper, this need to cry. I'm too raw, inside and out, to make sense of anything. The kinder he is to me, the more bewildered I am. It was so much easier to co-exist with him when I thought he hated me. There was clarity.

This? It's so much better and at the same time, so much more fraught with danger.

Because it's not my safety I'm worried about with Silas.

It's my heart.

CHAPTER 6

The hot shower turns out to be a bad, bad idea.

I'm not thinking, so I turn into a muscle-memory machine, walking into Silas's bathroom and doing my pre-shower routine. Find a towel. Turn on the water spray. Pull the curtain. Start to undress. As I yank my shirt off, I inhale sharply through clenched teeth. I'm essentially dragging shards of glass along my skin.

I move very, very slowly, using my injured hands to pull the dirty, torn cloth of my shirt off my skin and over my head. A small sprinkling of glass strikes the tile floor, making little *ping ping ping* sounds.

Soon enough, I'm naked.

As I turn, I see that the bathroom door has a full-length mirror attached to the back of it.

I view myself in harsh light for the first time in a while.

It's not pretty.

Bruises dot my thighs, calves, and arms. A particularly dark one is on my upper hip, close to my ass but lower, on the side. It looks like a piece of dark blue tie-dye, a 1960s freedom festival gone wrong. Small scratches, some healing, some fresh, make me look like someone threw me into a burlap bag with a sack of angry cats.

My bangs are too short, making my wavy hair coil up. My dirty, uncombed hair is–funny enough–a lot like Kelly's was the night I met her. Before her bath.

At the thought of little Kelly, I look at my own face, eyes wide with emotion. I give myself permission to feel. Like I told Silas, I can cry in the shower.

Turns out, I can also cry before.

I count back the days.

Six days ago, I was sitting at my table at the coffee shop in Santa Barbara, completely unaware of the car bomb planted in my vehicle.

Five days ago, I was at Alice's ranch for the first time, posing.

Four days ago, I was called back to The Grove and forced to submit to a medical exam that made Silas intervene.

Yesterday, I met Kelly.

And today, I learned the identity of my real father.

Then someone broke into his private estate with a code only Harry, Monica, Lindsay, and his security team knew–and tried to kill me.

There aren't enough hot showers, bubble baths, or pitchers of sangria to deal with my week.

I pull the shower curtain back and gingerly step in, bracing for the spray.

I scream.

Bang bang bang.

"Jane?" Silas yells, instantly on the other side of the door. He pushes his way in.

The pain of too-hot water cleaning the remaining glass off my skin renders me mute. I open my mouth to reply, knowing I need to. Each gasp makes it harder to tighten my throat and make my vocal cords work. The searing burn takes over all my skin and I step back, trying to escape it.

"JANE!" The only thing between us is the shower curtain.

"WHAT?" is all I can manage to say back.

"You screamed." He sounds unsure of himself suddenly, his body in shadow, magnified by the bathroom light and my own despair.

"The water. It hurts," I say back, choking out whatever answer I need to give to make him leave me alone so I can cry.

"We really should have gotten you medical attention," he adds through the curtain. "Once you're done, we'll go to an ER."

I reach for the shower faucet and turn the water to a cooler temperature. Then I begin to lightly skim my arms, feeling for glass. Nothing.

"It's okay," I tell him. "Do you have antibiotic cream?"

"Yes. In a first-aid kit."

"Then I'm fine." I say it with a finality, a heaviness that I hope signals to him that he should leave.

I can hear him touch the door. Then footsteps, walking away.

Good. He gets it. He gets *me*.

I'm glad someone does.

Once the first round of water escorts the broken glass off my skin like it's going on a perp walk, I sink into the warm water and let myself fall apart.

We hold up these versions of ourselves to the world. I harbor no illusions anymore. Any belief I have about myself is up for question. Nothing is permanent, nothing is real, except the very painful and stark acknowledgement that people want me dead.

Dead like Tara.

Dead like John and Stellan and Blaine, like my mom, like my dad–

No.

Not my biological dad. He is alive and well and working damn hard to be the next president of the United States.

My nose clogs and I laugh as the water absurdly continues, oblivious and stalwart, doing what it knows best. The laws of physics don't change because I learned a crucial part of my identity today. I haven't changed, either. Not my body. Not my core. I'm the same Jane who woke up this morning and had a cup of coffee.

For a few brief, wet seconds, the shower water just pours down on me. Same Jane. Same breasts. Same body.

Same ruined life.

The unfairness of it all grabs my gut and twists it. The cold, cruel shower tile presses hard against my cheekbone as I fold in half. Emotion turns me into a wretched, naked thing with an open mouth turned upward, seeking absolution. Seeking relief.

How can I get a break when the pain is inside me? My very existence feeds the shame industry, all of the news headlines beating their big drums until my head explodes. Silas protects me from social media and the newspapers. My phone is filtered. I'm rarely in public.

And yet, I know.

I know the crazy gunman at The Grove will be blamed, somehow, on *me*.

Tara's death is my fault.

My own car bombing is my fault.

That's all I'm good for, I realize as I gasp, clawing at my own wet throat, seeking air. Silas heard me scream when the hot water hit my skin's wounds, but this silent scream will go unanswered.

I can't turn what I feel inside into sound.

And so instead it will vibrate through me, multiple frequencies turning my organs and veins, neurons and impulses, into a ragged mess of noise and danger, all trapped inside my scarred and torn skin, the bones my only anchor.

A person can only handle so much pain.

I know this isn't the end, either.

There is more coming.

Steam curls around me until the shower fixtures float in and out of my vision, lazy and hazy. For a few moments they seem surreal, my mind unable to stay in place for long enough to register my surroundings, hands fumbling for soap on the small ceramic tub shelf. I drop it, the loud thud as it hits the bathtub floor like a head striking concrete, a gavel banging in a judge's hand, the sound echoing until it softens, like the crash of lovers' bodies on a bed.

Against a wall.

On the floor.

I bend to find the soap, fingers slippery, the object that makes me clean eluding my grasp over and over. My nailbeds are slightly tinted, blood pooled in them and dried. A flash of Tara, dead, like a doll in a horror film, makes my stomach roil. I know that's my blood. Not Tara's.

But is there a difference anymore?

Finally, I just can't take it, and I slip and slide down to the bottom of the tub, head down, forehead pressed so hard into my knees, it's like I'm trying to fuse the bones. I cry under the hot spray until ice-cold needles pierce me.

Until I shiver my way into a single internal frequency. From many, one.

One very tired self.

I finally stand on legs that don't deserve to work. The shower turns easily to the off position. Dripping wet, I step onto the bath mat and pick up the large, folded towel Silas left on the counter. If only life were like this. If only someone took care of me, anticipating my needs, trying to offer what I want.

Such a change from anticipating people who want to hurt me. So different from thwarting people who want to kill me. We focus on predicting and preventing their actions based on *their* needs. *Their* wants.

Not mine.

Never, ever mine.

Crying into the big bath sheet isn't a choice. I can't help myself. I couldn't stop if someone held a gun to my head. Here, in Silas's bathroom, staring at a red, swollen version of my face, the dark, wet hair like a sad crown on my head, I can finally be. I can feel. All the emotion I shoved aside so I could act and react is finally coming home.

While it may not live here, it's a familiar visitor, and it has some sights it really wants to see before moving on.

"Silas?" I call out, wrapped in the big towel, my hair hanging around my ears, wet and feeling nicely clean.

"Yes?"

"You said there were clothes for me?"

Silence.

"Hang on." His voice fades as I hear footsteps, then

muttering as he comes back. "Looks like they didn't bring any clothes."

"What am I supposed to wear?" I look at the pile of filthy, torn, bloodstained clothes on the floor. "I–I–" Panic blooms in me.

"Give me a sec." His voice fades again. One minute later, he's back.

Tap tap tap.

"Who is it?" I say, voice filled with sarcasm.

"It's Silas." He laughs at himself. "Can I open the door?"

"Sure."

He does, extending a small stack of neatly folded cotton clothes my way.

"This is the best I could do." As I take it with one hand, I realize it's a set of sweats. UC Irvine is on the front of the sweatshirt.

"What is this?"

"The smallest stuff I could find in my drawers."

"You want me to wear *your* sweats?"

"*Want* isn't the word. It's all we've got until I get someone to do their job and deliver what they promised." His voice is terse.

I look at the clothes. My bra has glass in it. My underwear should be declared a biohazard. I can't wear my old stuff.

I have no choice.

"Okay. Thanks," I say, pressing the door closed. He's blocking it but moves with an elegance that makes me smile.

I'll take any reason to smile.

As expected, the sweats are enormous. It's like swimming in cotton. But the pants have a drawstring and I can walk around without being a nude model.

Minus the artist.

I find Silas in the kitchen, pulling two pints of ice cream out of the freezer. He does a double take, dips his head as if he's embarrassed, then laughs.

"You look like a mad scientist got his hands on you and shrank you ten percent."

"I would trade what happened today for that."

He opens a cabinet door and grabs a bottle of red wine, holding it up to me in a gesture of offertory. "Want some?"

"Wine and ice cream?"

"One of my men's health magazines says it's the best way to establish rapport with women."

"How sexist."

"Doesn't mean they're wrong."

I snatch one of the pints from him. Bourbon vanilla. "How about making a wine float?"

He's taken aback. "A *what*?"

"You know. Like a root beer float? A wine float."

He has a corkscrew in his hand and takes the bottle, gripping it between his thighs, peeling off the foil from around the cork. His movements are hypnotic, watching him open the wine a form of pleasure in and of itself. The soft cotton of his well-worn college sweatshirt rubs against my stiffening nipples and I force myself to turn away, struggling to control the wildfire of desire that makes me wonder what it's like to be between those thighs.

I'm jealous of a wine bottle.

"You seriously want to pour red wine over ice cream and eat it?" he asks, deeply amused.

"It's worth a try. Anything is worth a try."

Pop! The cork comes loose. Silas gives me a funny look.

"Anything of *value* is worth a try," he declares, pouring into a wine glass, careful with the stem. He frowns at me. "Did you put the antibiotic cream on those cuts?"

"No. Not yet."

"But you will." He's firm about it.

"Yes, I will. Priorities."

"Wine and ice cream come before basic first aid?"

"They *are* first aid."

Laughter fills the tiny space between us, Silas lifting his wine glass to his mouth, white teeth showing before he takes a sip. "Hell of a day," he says, shaking his head slowly. Letting out a breath, he drops his shoulders, body moving from action to rest.

"I've had better." I grab the wine bottle before he can offer and pour myself a glass, drinking half in one long gulp.

He does the same.

"So, how does this work?" I ask, so tired, I'm punchy.

"How does what work?"

"While we wait for some clothes for me, I'm stuck here."

"Stuck." He makes a very male sound in the back of his throat, like I've offended him.

"Don't take it personally."

"I'm not." But he is.

"I need my own space. I have not been afforded that in ages. I need," I say, gasping slightly, fighting an unexpected wellspring of emotion, "I need to be alone so I can start to reassemble the pieces of me."

"You don't seem broken to me."

"Then you're not looking at me very hard."

"Oh, trust me, Jane. I am."

CHAPTER 7

*M*y blood pumps through me like it's trying to find a way out. All the tiny cuts that dot my skin pulse along with it, one hand on my wine glass, cupping it for balance under the bottom, stem poking between my ring and middle finger. The other hand rests on the counter, outstretched slightly toward him, as if searching.

Questioning.

He steps forward, halving the distance between us. Covered in dirt and glass, Silas is a mess. He's breathing a little faster than a moment ago, and I see dried blood on his wrist.

"You need a shower," I tell him.

The skin between his eyebrows folds in and he looks down, as if surprised by his disheveled state. "Huh. You're right."

"I'll babysit the ice cream and wine while you're gone."

His impish smile makes my blood pump harder. Swigging the rest of his wine, he pours another glass.

"Drinking?" I tease. "On duty?"

"Occupational hazard."

"The shattered glass and bruises aren't enough?"

He smiles but turns toward the bathroom, refreshed wine glass in hand. I hear the shower turn on, then muffled sounds.

Finally, he's under the water. Unlike me, he doesn't scream.

A whoosh of air as I exhale deeply feels so good. No matter how safe I feel with him, Silas holds me back. He might be thawing toward me, but he's still my biggest obstacle. I can't get comfortable.

And definitely not naked.

At least, not unless I'm posing.

As I laugh at my own crazy mind, I drink more wine, needing my muscles to relax, craving the release. The body tenses when it's under attack. Silas isn't coming after me. I can let my guard down.

Except I can't.

He's in the room next to me, separated by one wall, naked in the shower where I just was.

Naked.

I turn away from the tiny kitchen doorway and walk to a small window at the opposite side. Dark clouds, menacing and clearly filled with rain, change the light outside, giving the parking lot and grounds an eerie look, like the old sci-fi movies from the 1980s or 1990s my mom used to ask me to watch with her. I sip my wine, then pull the neck of Silas's oversized sweat-shirt up over my nose, inhaling deeply. It smells like his after-shave and laundry soap. I close my eyes and give myself permission to take him in, to revel in his scent, safely ensconced in cotton and politeness.

And for the next few minutes, I just breathe.

"Jane?" Silas asks, making me jump and spin around.

His features change, going to a puzzled look. "Is your nose okay?"

I look down at the front of me and quickly pull the neckline back where it belongs. "What? Yes. I'm fine." Red heat turns my cheeks into apples as I blush.

"What were you doing?"

"Nothing."

"You were looking down your own shirt. Is there something on your chest? Does it need attention?"

His words are out just fast enough for us both to react to the double meaning, but too quick for Silas to alter them. I bite my lips and pull them in to stop laughing.

He doesn't bother to restrain himself.

"I obviously didn't mean it that way."

Too bad.

Taking a deep breath, he motions toward the kitchen doorway. "Let's sit on the couch and talk."

"Sure," I say, the wine loosening me up. As I walk behind him, I see he's wearing a tight t-shirt and flannel drawstring pajama pants that are not nearly as loose as mine. Barefoot, with damp hair that curls at the ends when it's wet, Silas looks like most of the guys I knew in college.

Only bigger, older, smarter, and *way* hotter.

Just a small difference, right?

I sit down first, curling up against one end of the couch, pulling my knees up and legs under me. He doesn't take a spot at the other end, as I expect, but instead sits right next to me, in the middle. His thigh touches my knee. We're that close.

Okay, then.

Warmth pours over me, the feeling so pleasant it's jarring. I like feeling something other than pain. My skin prickles from all the small scratches, but it lights up with a heat that comes from anticipation. I don't know where Silas is going right now, but I sure do like the direction.

"This isn't how I thought our day would end," he says, a little sheepish, testing me.

"It's not even three o'clock, Silas." I hold up my glass of wine. "But it's cocktail hour somewhere."

"We can order takeout for dinner. And in my line of work, after a day like today, if you aren't drinking, it's because you're dead." He says it with a wry look.

I laugh, but the sound is brittle, a social nicety. His proximity makes me want to lose all impulse control and crawl into his lap. Kiss him. Touch him.

Ride him.

The temperature inside me rises as I make myself drink my wine, needing to occupy my hands, my body, my mouth before I make a fool of myself. I've never felt like this before–ever.

Turning to sex as a way of escaping my life never occurred to me. As I sit here, my body encased in flaming cotton and getting wetter by the second, I wonder if I've been missing out.

Except–the only person I want to use sex as an escape *with* is Silas.

"What about you? You must have dated a lot in college," he says suddenly, clearly a little uncomfortable with my strange silence.

"That's an abrupt topic change," I point out, but I'm not displeased.

He stares at my mouth. "You invited me to have sex with you until you forgot your own name, Jane. We were about to go out to lunch on our version of a date instead. I'm just circling back to first-date conversation."

Funny how he's not circling back to the having sex part.

"Asking me about who I dated in college is first-date conversation? I'm sure you have a dossier on me that's a foot thick. You know everything about me."

"But not from you. I want to hear it from your mouth." His eyes drift down again to stare at my lips. "Tell me."

"My first year, I dated, sure." I play with the stem of my wine glass between my fingers, feeling like this is the most awkward date ever. How do you date someone who has seen you naked, saved your life repeatedly, blocked someone from sexually assaulting you, kissed you after you played Candyland with his newly orphaned niece, and held you back from clawing your newly revealed stepmother's eyes out?

We are *long* past the basic-small-talk phase of getting-to-know-you. We leapfrogged over it while playing different roles.

Client and bodyguard, though.

Not potential romantic partners.

"Why'd you stop then? Find a serious boyfriend?" There's an edge to his question.

"No."

"Then why?" His head tilts just so, eyes kind. He really wants to know.

He really *doesn't* know.

"I wanted to focus on my studies," I lie, the untruth slipping out of my mouth so quickly, like letting go of a bad taste.

Silas drinks his wine as if he's taken lessons in drinking and was top of his class. "That is a cover story."

"I graduated summa cum laude!" My protest is fake. My admiration for his ability to read me is very, very real.

"I'm sure you did, but you don't go from dating a lot the first year to–what? Nothing?"

I reluctantly nod. "Nothing."

"Nothing, or–" One eyebrow goes up. "*Nothing* nothing."

"Nada."

"Jane. Why?" A look of dawning recognition fills his face. "Damn. That was when the party happened."

"Right." I didn't realize I was holding my breath. The shaky sound of relief pours out.

"You came back to college, and then..."

"Every time a guy came on to me, all I could see was Lindsay's body, bound and abused, bleeding and naked. Then I imagined it happened to me. Every time someone touched me, I–it was too much."

Any other guy and I wouldn't say that, fearing it would scare him away. But this is Silas.

Who else can you talk about trauma with if not a combat veteran?

"Then that makes you a–"

"Virgin," I confirm.

His eyebrows go high and he clears his throat. "I was about to say 'compassionate friend.'"

"Oh." So much for not oversharing.

Very awkward silence hangs between us. Long gone is the casual presence we provided for each other. Tension fills the air, sex and passion and questions and nerves all mixing together, the unspoken wondering making each move risky and full of questions.

I reach out first. It's not intentional. My hand moves as if some higher force is at work, one I don't know about but that has taken over. Perhaps it's impulse. Maybe it's desire. Whatever you call it, the power of that short journey across the space between us comes from unconscious movement, propelling me to reach for his chest and press my hand to it.

"Silas, I..." A long, slow exhale leaves my ribs aching, the right words on the tip of my tongue. They rest, poised and waiting to line up in a neat, orderly queue. Before I can speak, though, the mood shifts.

Radically.

He takes the lead, moving closer, each inch between us telescoping as he closes the gap. I am suspended in time, his body heat warming me, the moment his chest brushes against my arm sending shivers through me. I want this. I want him.

I want *us*.

Impossibly soft lips and a commanding tongue break down my wall, the one I don't want, the one I hate having between us. Silas dismantles it with a slant of his mouth, brick by brick, pulling me closer to him, his hands cupping my jaw. The rough stubble of his beard sends electricity across my skin. His heat potentiates mine. My body is drawn to him, seeking a kind of warmth that simple temperature doesn't convey.

The brush of his thick thigh against my forearm, the slide of my palm under his loose t-shirt, the fresh, clean scent of his wet hair, the way his fingers balance along my neck as he teases me, all turn Silas into nothing but touch. The scrabbling pain of existence starts to yield as he continues, never breaking contact, always seeking more from me. He's giving and giving and I am taking and taking, eager and alive and needing every drop and more.

Rising up on my knees, I move over him, straddling his lap, the long, hard ridge of his erection riding along my wet heat. Our pajamas separate us, my hips curling to find him. As I bend down to rub against him, the first brush makes him groan into my mouth, his tongue moving with hot need.

The kiss is bruising, his hands pulling me up against him as the friction makes me moan, too, our voices and tongues playing a dangerous game that the rest of our bodies mimic. My hips cannot stop, the long lines of round, corded muscle in his ribs a sculpture made just for my hands. The white-hot desire turns me into a primal, feral being who wants nothing more than to make him come with my body, and for him to make me shatter.

However he wants.

"This feels so good," he murmurs, his mouth on my neck, the kisses on my earlobe making me shiver violently, then rub harder against him. If I could crawl inside him, I would. Every part of him touching me reassures me I'm alive. Every kiss is a reminder that he *wants* to kiss me, *wants* to stroke the inside of my lower lip with his tongue, *wants* to plunge his hand into my hair, wants *me*.

And every inch of my body lights up as his body moves in rhythm against mine, seeking pleasure through friction and promise, seeking more of me. The real me. The me that isn't in pain when his tongue does that, when he rasps against my ear like that. When his hand slides up under his oversized sweat-shirt and cups my full breast like *that*.

"Like that," I gasp against him. The way his thumb grazes my nipple tells me he knows. He hears. He needs, just like me.

He *craves*.

I feel my own hot breath against his chin as he looks down at his hand on my breast. "You're perfect. This is perfect."

"This is either one big mistake or the greatest leap of my life," I whisper.

"Maybe it's both," he says before silencing me with a kiss that makes my body curl in delight, all the way down to my toes. Our foreheads touch as he pulls back slightly, hand resting in the space above my navel, palm flat against my bare skin. "But I know it's not a mistake for me."

In the mad rush of my impulsive reaction I kiss him hard, the need to have him in me an awakening. I breathe to be with him. I stroke the soft skin at the nape of his neck to connect with him. I move my hips against him to have his body give mine pleasure. I am made for him. I have a purpose.

And he does, too.

"You," he whispers, pulling my head back, fingers tangled in my damp hair. "I don't know what this is, Jane, but before we go further, I have something to say."

My stomach drops.

"Mmm?"

"I'm sorry."

"Oh!" I wasn't expecting that.

"I am. Truly. I believed the evidence, but now I'm questioning everything. My world is filled with ambiguity, but it's a series of blurry edges backed up by stealth information. All the briefings on you pointed in the same direction: guilty. And yet all of the investigations came to the conclusion that you'd done nothing wrong."

"I know."

"In my line of work, if people think you did it and congressional investigations or law enforcement research shows you didn't, that's not proof. It just means you outsmarted the best of the best."

"And... do you think I'm that smart?"

He smiles and looks at me with an intensely amused look he's trying to hide. "I do."

I sit up, breaking the intimate contact. I can't have this conversation *and* have me rubbing against his erection. That's some kind of a deal breaker.

"Which means you think—"

"I already said I was wrong, Jane. I meant it." His chest rises and falls in a slow rhythm, then picks up with a long, deep breath. "I truly mean it. And the fact that I'm wrong indicates this is more complex than I ever imagined."

"How so?"

"It means *Drew* is wrong. It means various informants are wrong. It means I hurt you." Soulful eyes meet mine, his expression pained. "And that is the worst of it all. I've always prided myself on being a man of honor. Of dignity. One who treats people with the respect they deserve. You didn't deserve how I treated you. You don't deserve anything you've experienced." He reaches for me.

I let him touch me, the instant calm in my blood a sign that being with him is better than fleeing. I don't know what I'm supposed to do right now. All of my instincts are wrong. In the past, when someone challenged me like this, I did what I knew.

I ran.

Withdrawal is a defense mechanism. I'm a master at it. You can't get hurt if you never let people in.

What Silas is teaching me right now, second by second, as his hands cup my jaw lovingly, eyes searching mine, is that withdrawing from someone who cares for you is a form of pain, too.

"Can you forgive me?" he asks, somber and serious.

"There's nothing to forgive," I assure him, rushing to quell the agitation inside.

"Yes. There is. I didn't believe you. I do now. You don't have to forgive me. I'm asking for it, though, to show you I acknowledge what I did to you."

"Thank you." I take my finger and trace his eyebrows. Dark like his hair, they arc along the bones of his eye sockets, the trail down to his cheekbone surprisingly soft. His stubble is light, so he shaved this morning, but it peeks out, a reminder of how different my own body is from his. Sunlight plays on his face as I make my way down to his lips.

Unmoving, he lets me explore.

I climb into his lap again, this time moving slowly. If I was burning before, now I'm smoldering, his confession and request for absolution making me dizzy. The implications of such a heartfelt admission are infinite.

A man who is so open and so remorseful is one you can give your dearest possessions to, who will protect and honor them.

A man like Silas is one you love for all eternity.

We've moved out of the realm of attraction and into a state quite different. Bodies demand connection, but so do souls.

"I forgive you, Silas," I rasp, the words coming out like a whimper. "But you're giving me a more precious gift."

He tilts his head, eyes curious. "What's that?"

"You're making it very hard for me not to forgive myself."

"Forgive yourself for what?"

"For letting the world beat me down."

"First of all, why in hell would you ever do that? And second, forgiving yourself should come before forgiving me. I withdraw my request for forgiveness. You have to forgive yourself first, Jane."

I let out a small laugh and stroke the edge of his cheekbone, down to his jaw. "I've never done this before," I confess, breath shaking, body relaxing into his.

"Forgiven yourself?"

"Fallen."

"Fallen?"

"Like this." He makes it so easy, my bones trusting him, my body knowing what my mind hasn't quite accepted. As his palms anchor me to him, wrapped along the contours of my curves, I find a peace in our kiss, a rising warmth that turns what was just sexual into an intimacy that fills me with a deep calm.

His mouth tells me how much he wants me, but those words–oh, how they soothe the damaged pieces inside, the parts that broke a long time ago and were left to remain fractured, unhealed. Silas moves against me with unfettered want, his openness turning our rawness into a spiral that climbs heavenward. I'm not wearing a bra. When he cups my breast again and whispers, "Every part of you is beautiful," I trust even more.

His mouth, eager and pliant, takes charge as his kiss grows more demanding. I moan against him, our bodies tensing as coiled ecstasy waits to be unleashed.

The drawstring of my pants is easy to open, and soon Silas's calloused hand is on my ass, squeezing with a possession that thrills me to the core. My pulse throbs hard and heavy between my legs. This isn't enough.

I want him naked and over me, thrusting into me. I want him to trust me enough to show me his stripped self, the one we have in private, alone, but never show the world. I want to see it all, every shred, and when he's done showing me and has to put on his mask to go out into the world and pretend he's never that wild, that raw, that vulnerable, I want him to come back to me and do it all over again.

I want to be his confessor, his lover, his confidante, his–

Tap tap tap.

"Jesus!" Silas hisses as I startle so badly, I fall backwards, his agile hands saving me from a terrible head bump on the coffee table. The knock at the door is unexpected and most unwelcome.

Silas's phone buzzes.

He stands up, reaching down into his pajama pants to not-so-discreetly adjust himself. Winking at me, he squares his shoulders, turns away, and faces the door. Grabbing his phone, he reads it as he walks to the door, opening it quickly.

It's Duff.

Holding a duffle bag.

"Jane's clothes," he says, walking in and giving me a polite nod as I try to look like I wasn't just humping Silas. It's harder than you'd think.

"Took you long enough," Silas mutters.

"Wasn't me. Pranin back at the main office said there was a mix-up."

"Don't let it happen again." Silas looks back at me, the glance so short, it's microscopic.

Silas starts to gesture for Duff to leave, but the man stays put.

"Drew wants me to brief you on some cases." His eyes cut to me, then back to Silas. "Including this one."

"I'm right here," I call out. "You can say it in front of me."

"No, Jane. I can't." Duff's reply is like a stab through the heart.

"Fine," I huff, leaving the room and heading into...

Silas's bedroom.

I spin on my bare foot and return, angry and aroused and a boiling mixture of too many feelings combined with all these tiny cuts from the glass scratches earlier. I can't stop the flickering memories of a few hours ago, the blood, the guns, the crack of ammo. I touch my bruised cheek.

"Where am I supposed to go?" I ask Silas through clenched teeth. If I bite any harder, I'll chip a tooth.

"You can hang out in my bedroom and wait."

Even Duff reacts to that, and not in a kindly way, eyebrows

high, the scar by his eye twisting his smirk into a menacing grimace.

Silas turns a deep shade of red and refuses to look at anyone. "Hallway," he snaps at Duff.

When the front door closes, I scurry back into his bedroom. The clothes Duff gave me include pajamas, pink flannel, and soft white cotton for the top, a t-shirt that is a little too tight but it's comfortable. I change quickly, my skin on fire from all the cuts and from Silas's touch.

Peeling back the tightly made bed, the cover soft and smooth, I slide between the sheets and fume.

As blood pounds through me, slowing down with time, my limbs try to let go of the day. We cling to ideas and expectations, minds unable to release, but the body is last to learn anything. It's the final station in the long cargo train that delivers all our parts to the locations where they belong. Emotions and thoughts, ideas and beliefs, all get transported to way stations and final destinations, settling into fiber and flesh.

Some go dormant.

Others never rest.

But eventually I do, the weight of the world letting go in my dreams, leaving me on my side in a bed that smells like Silas's cologne and soap, the sheets sending messages my brain will have to interpret as I stand down and give in.

I can trust sleep.

Then again, I don't have a choice.

CHAPTER 8

The first conscious moment I'm aware he's in bed with me comes as I slide my palm against his flat stomach, the layered grooves of his abs bringing me out of slumber. He's so warm, the skin unlike mine, a line of hair in the middle of my hand thickening as I move my hand down. It's warm, hotter as I hit a line of fabric, then brush against something hard and unyielding.

He makes a low sound in his throat. My nose grazes his shoulder. I sigh, the long sound of coming to, the luxurious, slow exhale of post-sleep awakening. My arm is around Silas's waist. He's on his side, turned away from me, and here I am, feeling his bare skin in my sleep.

"Oh!" I say and begin to retreat.

His hand clamps over my wrist. "No. Don't stop."

"But I–"

"Jane," he says roughly, "*please* don't stop."

His voice holds a richness, his breath coming quickly. A ragged sigh emerges as I make a wordless sound to tell him *yes*, I'll continue. *Yes*, I want to touch him. *Yes*, I want to see the center of his heat.

And *yes*, I want that heat in me.

"I didn't mean to touch you in your sleep."

"I wasn't asleep."

"I was."

"I know. And the fact that you reach out to me even when you aren't aware of it is enchanting," he whispers as he turns over, my arm now around his back. Silas kisses me until I am very, very much alert.

My hand runs down the long, hard lines of his back to his ass, the coiled power in his legs so strong. He moves toward me, pressing with a mix of urgency and patience. Nothing holds us back now but ourselves. No interruptions, no killers, no meetings, no constant vigilance. For now, we're a man and a woman who want to be stripped bare and to enter into each other's bodies to create a new space.

A refuge.

A haven.

My pajama shirt rides up as Silas blankets my body with his, the tickle of his chest and torso a warm rush of pleasure. He's kissing me with abandon, taking his time, the attention feeding some part of me that needs to be treated like this. We sink into the bed, my back arching, breasts pressed against the thick heat of him.

"If this is too much," he says as he ends the kiss, breathing hard against my cheek, "say the word."

"It's not that it's too much," I gasp. "It's not enough."

"I know exactly how you feel," he replies, his mouth heavy against my lightness. Silas grounds me before I can float away, his tongue so delicious, the delightful play between our lips a choreographed layer of emotion running in tandem with our hands.

You would think that passion would take me out of my anxious mind. You would be wrong. As Silas explores me, all of my looping increases, the frantic thoughts barraging me like gunfire on an open range. I want to stop thinking about my life. I want to get rid of the horrific images of the last few days. I want to stop the voices that tell me I'm unworthy.

I want to give in to what he offers me.

I want to just *give*.

We do not choose to remain distracted by our crazy minds even in the face of extraordinary pleasure. Silas's hands and mouth tell me where I need to let myself wander. Oh, how I want to. Oh, how I wish it were so simple.

Our minds choose what they choose, free range and autonomous, the subconscious nothing more than abstract art at work, smearing emotions like paint. We see what is shaped by experience. No two people can share the same thought, the same reaction, the same process.

All we can share is bodies. Space. Touch. Time.

My skin reacts, gooseflesh rippling like a roaring river, my nipples turning to whitewater peaks, body swelling with the overflow of melting abundance that comes with a thaw. This feels so good.

He makes me feel *so* good.

But the world wants me to feel bad about myself. It's the only way I'm allowed to function. And when thousands–millions–of voices are telling you one thing, it's impossible to let his hands say another.

"What's wrong, Jane?" He stops abruptly, so fast, it makes me jerk, like he's slammed on the brakes of a car.

"Nothing," I whisper, suddenly self-conscious, hating that he's noticed something.

"You seem scared. I don't want you to be afraid. We can stop anytime."

"No," I say, only it comes out more like a moan than a word. "I'm not scared."

"You're shaking."

"That's not from fear. I'm shaking from *excitement*." Every time he touches me, I'm renewed. Silas is here because he wants to be. He wants to reach down and strip off his shirt. He wants to grind his hips against mine as his thigh parts my legs. He wants to move against me like he's trying to find his way in through every inch of my skin.

He wants me to stroke him over his pajama pants until he makes a hushed, choking sound that turns to a rush, a grunt, a growl filled with sex and lust.

He wants *me*.

And I want him right back.

Before he can hesitate, I reach between us and slip his pajama pants down until the hot cotton of his boxers cools with my breach. He's hard, the long thickness of him centered against his lower abs. Moving on his side against the back of the bed, he does something I never expected.

He opens himself up to me.

While I am technically still a virgin, I've messed around enough to know how the preliminaries work, and Silas is using a different playbook from any other guy I've been with. Men don't stretch out, casual and open, like this. Foreplay and sex play is frantic, fevered, done in darkness while half drunk.

Not out in the open, lights on, eyes locked.

His gaze pins me in place. He wants to own me. We're about to take all the time we need to get to know each other's bodies.

Confidence and a determined attitude that how this all rolls out is natural. Special.

Ours.

It's ours, only ours, and just like that, with an intense look and a smile of genuine pleasure welcoming me into his world, Silas clears me. The rest of the never-ending chatter in my mind floats off like dust on the wind. I move against him and kiss him with an earnestness that makes our lips so sweet, the stroke of his hands against my bare back so perfect. None of the rest of the voices in society are here. This is not their place. They do not deserve access to me 24/7.

Only Silas does.

I watch my own movements with a heated rush as I wrap my fingers around his waistband and slowly, exquisitely, pull off his boxers. His erection pulls with the fabric, then springs back with a thick power that makes me want to pull him into my mouth, give him pleasure.

Make him want me as much as I want him.

Kicking his pants off the bed, Silas props himself up on one hand and grins at me.

"Your turn."

I look down, my shirt half off, pants still on. The lights are on. We can see each other completely. There is nothing being hidden.

There is no reason.

Impulse makes me rise up on my knees, untamed breasts bobbing slightly as I pull the shirt completely off, stretching to point myself closer to him, giving Silas a show. Those deep-blue eyes never leave me, tracking my breasts, my hips, my face.

I sit on the edge of the bed and hook my thumbs into my panty waistband. Arching up off the bed, I slide them down, then sit on the cool cotton comforter while I finish removing them.

Before I can do it, I'm dragged back, Silas's hot mouth on mine, our bodies askew. He's kissing me like he's drowning, like I am how he breathes, and I'm matching him.

The way the light shines off the muscles in his back as I give myself the luxury of opening my eyes while we kiss makes me think of Greek gods. Of men in the woods, strong and sculpted by hard work and necessity, by honor and truth. We move our naked bodies against each other, his skin coarse with hair, mine smooth and shivering.

After a while, I lose the sense that we're two separate bodies, until he moves me back and sits up over me. Silas takes his hands and places them gently, reverently, on my hips, gliding up over my ribs, my breasts, and along my underarms.

I lift my hands up until my wrists cross above my head, skirting through my shorter hair until they rest on the pillow.

"Beautiful," he murmurs, bending down to plant an open-mouthed kiss on each nipple. As he finishes the first, his tongue lingers, making me tighten and pulse. I forget to breathe as he blows gently on the wet skin, which curls inward, closing like a rosebud, waiting for another time to reveal itself.

I'm all gasp and throb by the time he kisses his way between my legs. My heart quickens, breath picking up, but he pauses.

"These scrapes," he says, one gentle finger tracing a couple of cuts. "I hate seeing them on you. They're marks of my failure."

"No," I whisper.

"Yes. I'm so sorry you're hurting. I'm going to do everything I can to make sure you don't hurt anymore."

"Everything?" My answer is loaded with innuendo. He picks it up.

"I've wanted you," he murmurs to my belly, "since we first met."

"You hated me," I whisper, my fingers loose in his hair.

"No. I mean before. When you met with Lindsay after she came home. I thought you were the most captivating woman I'd ever met."

"When we were at The Toast? You–you *did*? You thought *that*?"

"I did. It was hard to hide it."

"I just thought you were a super-innocent, nice guy."

"You're half right."

"Which half?"

His lips move against the tender skin right below my navel. "Let me show you."

My abs tighten every second his lips graze me. The light stubble of his late-day beard feels like an electric skin, like someone has added a layer to me, all wire and heat and wetness. I'm tingling everywhere, his hands moving my thighs apart, until I arch up and gasp at the warm pleasure he gives me with his tongue.

I didn't know.

I didn't know that a man could touch me like this, so masterful and bold, yet make me feel delicate and worthy at the same time. I didn't know that a man could play my body like an instrument, bringing blood to a *crescendo*, breathing *con slancio* that soaks into my pores as he licks me, his passion raw and atavistic, laid out as if it were a given.

I didn't know.

I do now.

Too much emotion turns my blood to lava, the light strokes of his hands on me a quick accumulation of aching unanswered prayers. My body moves toward him, drawn by need, his gravitational pull too much. If I thought I was overcome by my crazy, dangerous life, I am learning as he runs his hands up over my hipbones straight to my breasts, touching me like a man who is determined to study me until he's an expert, that *crazy* and *dangerous* apply to this, too.

What do I do with my hands? I want to touch him, explore him, my palms curling around his shoulders and touching the thick muscle I find. My mind races as he turns me into nothing but quivers. Exposed like this in the night, I open my eyes, shadows mingling with the whispers of the flesh.

And then it all fades, a soft infusion that makes me feel light, so light, I'll float away. His fingers perform magic across my ribcage, calloused hands pulling me to him through the simple act of pressure. His body gives and I take, my hips arching toward him until he stops, pausing only to give me something even better.

His mouth.

The kiss is firelight and peace, sanctuary and trust, my hands finally free to feel all of him, finding a long torso, the well-worn terrain of hard work. This man protects people with his body. It must be a fortress. As I touch him, his hand dips between my legs, the fevered rush of his kiss giving me a taste of myself, the hedonism so intoxicating.

Come with me, his fingers say, turning me up until I'm about to explode. *Let me take you to a place where there is no shame.*

So I do.

Pleasure crowds out all of my doubts, emptying my mind with a suddenness that defies the neat orderliness I assumed it required. I kiss him back, hard, and grind into his hand, then move until I'm straddling him, his erection pressed between my legs, the wet friction making me gasp as he looks at me with dark eyes that promise more.

I'm not sure how much more I can take.

My pulse is in every pore of my body, synched perfectly to give me an exquisite sense of Silas, as if his naked journey matches mine. He reaches up and moves a strand of hair off my face, eyes boring into me, trying to see my soul. I move against him and he groans, closing his eyes, giving in to me. Having him release the protective wall that makes me feel safe is an illicit, welcome pleasure.

It means he trusts me.

It means he wants me.

It means I am *in*.

In his head. In his heart. In his life.

And now it's my turn to let *him* in.

A simple roll of my hip and one wet thigh's slick shift and he's poised at the entrance, so close to slipping in me, his body a study in restraint.

"Are you sure?" he asks.

"Yes."

"We need something," he says, turning toward his bedside table drawer. A condom is in his hand as he rolls back over, and within seconds, he puts it on.

He looks at me, breathing hard. Intensity deepens between us. I can't look away.

He won't.

"Not like this," he whispers, moving me out of range, making me almost cry out in frustration. "Let me make sure it won't hurt." Kissing me deeply, he pulls me to him, then rotates our joined bodies until I'm on my back. Strong arms bulge as he holds himself above me, my knees falling to each side, my heart slamming between my legs like it's relocated.

"I want you to tell me to stop if you want to stop, Jane."

"I don't."

"Do you understand, though? I mean it." He kisses me, a sweet kiss that is too chaste for the moment. I want raunchy and naughty, dirty and wild, and right now, he's so earnest.

I grab his ass with both hands and pull him in.

Turns out he's stronger than me, even in that region.

The next thing I know, my mouth and body are plundered, the pain of being entered completely outweighed by the intensity of this kiss. My mouth is now taking more than I knew possible, emotion transforming me from the inside out. He licks, he sucks, he bites, he tells me all his secrets but I can't understand any of them, my fingers finding every scar on his back and arms, over his abs and chest, back to his perfect ass, until he moves inside me, pulling back with a hiss.

And then he moves inside me again, slow and steady, the air changing between us. I smell musk and sweat, sex and juices, but I also sense a scent that is new. Wholly original.

As I breathe, his head dips down, kissing my shoulder as he thrusts. Coiled power radiates from him, my hands on his ass loosening their grip, riding up the small, curved surface of his lower back into the corded rope of his spine.

"Widen your legs," he commands, my body intuitively submitting, waiting for him to give me guidance. "Relax."

"I am relaxed with you," I whisper into the hard curve of his ear, taking in every second and scent, every thrust and stroke, marveling in real time that we're together like this, accepting it, welcoming it.

Loving it.

Lush kisses and deep strokes turn us into a twisting, entangled, sublime knot, his body so big above me, my own so deeply *here*. Grounded and present as a tactile sense inside me builds, I kiss him back, so connected to him that I lose my own edges.

I blur into him.

There is pain, yes. It's a tender, yanking ache that isn't fading. But it's a reminder. A talisman, of sorts, but one you can't hold in a pocket or your hand.

My breath breaks away and fills the curved space between us, his hair against my shoulder, his wide chest and big body making me feel wanted. A flicker, a sunburst, a change, turn me into a bonfire, and suddenly he tells me, "I can't hold back. Are you ready?"

The push and release are so hard, so good, so–oh, oh, I'm flying, the heat lifting me up until all that is left is Silas. I am enough, gasping and moaning, letting go of voices and thoughts and fears and pain until all I am is whatever he gives me. We're moving against each other to give and give and give until we're empty.

Emptiness is underrated.

Our breath is so fast, so ragged, like smoke scraping against a diamond. In the soft, dusky light I catalog my senses. Electricity races across each pore. My legs shake, newly awakened. Silas's breath thunders in my ear, his chest against mine, my soft breasts moving to fit against his thickness.

Hearts can break so easily.

But hearts can also be the greatest cure of all.

"Jane," he says to me in the quiet. I turn just so, trying to control my shaking as he slides out of me. I look at him, unabashedly watching his body as he moves, enjoying every second of this unfettered view.

"Mmm?"

"You okay?"

"Better than okay."

"Did I hurt you?"

"No."

"Come on," he urges, propping himself up on one elbow, facing me. He strokes a long, gentle line from my chin to one breast. "Tell me. It hurt?"

"Only a little. And it wasn't your fault." I smile.

"Oh, but it *was* all my fault." He smiles back.

"It was worth it. You're worth it," I say. The words feel inadequate.

"Thank you," he says.

I jolt, absolutely not expecting *that*. "For what? Sex?"

"For trusting me."

"How do you know I trust you? Maybe I'm some devious double agent who sleeps her way to information."

"I don't think so." A yawn overpowers him, so intense, he shakes a little. It's endearing. I melt a little more.

"You don't?" I arch one eyebrow. "Then my evil plan is working."

"If your evil plan involves letting me have lots of sex with you, then let's make that evil plan work."

"You liked it?" I ask, shy again.

"I like you."

"That's not an answer." I reach between us and find him, hard again.

His turn to arch an eyebrow. "Again?"

"You said you wanted to work my evil plan."

He pulls me into his arms. "I like the way you think, even if you might be a spy."

I kiss him quickly, then begin to stroke him. "Oh, I see something I'd like to spy..."

"That involves going deep undercover, Jane," he says, then moans as I do just that.

Turns out he's right.

My evil plan does require a lot of practice.

So we do.

CHAPTER 9

I wake up to an empty bed, a sun-bathed room, and the seductive scent of coffee in the air.

As I sit up, the sheet slides down my body. I'm naked.

And in walks Silas, carrying two mugs of hot coffee, wearing nothing but a smile.

"I'm still asleep," I mutter. "This is all a dream."

"If you say so," he laughs, setting the coffee down on the end table closest to me, ripping the top sheet off me completely. "Coffee first, sex second."

"I will need coffee to be awake enough to have sex."

"Not if this is still a dream."

"If you deny me my coffee, it becomes a nightmare. Trust me."

He kisses me, tasting like coffee and male pride. "Drink up, then. You'll need the energy for what I'm about to do to you."

"Don't you mean *with* me?"

"Just wait."

We drink our coffee around grins on our faces. The world changed in one single moment last night, forever different. Giving myself to Silas feels natural. Real. Authentic and true. When we made love last night, all the fear washed away. That wasn't a revenge screw, or an angry screw, or one iota negative.

I feel rejuvenated. Recharged. Revitalized.

And now, I want more.

I'm halfway through my coffee when Silas places his mug on my end table, leaning across me intentionally, dragging his forearm across my nipples, the tiny hairs covering his muscled arm tickling my skin to pearly pebbles.

"Oh. Excuse me," he says, not at all sincere. "I just needed to make a little room."

I admire the long, tight curl of muscle from his thigh to his ass, how ridged and rolling his body is. Shadows and light make looking at him a joyful process. For a few seconds, I view him as a painter looking at a subject, but the moment fades quickly. My heart races and I lick my lips. He's too gorgeous, too close, and smells so good. Tan and peppered with darker hair, his arms and legs are powerful machines, finely honed and trained to protect.

And kill.

But mostly protect.

Those big, speckled eyes are fringed by long lashes, thick eyebrows arching up a strong brow. His hair is messy and he has stubble. Relaxed and playful, this is a side of Silas he's revealing to me slowly.

As his lips kiss a trail where his arm just dragged, I gulp my coffee, spilling a few drops down my collarbone, two rolling right into the valley between my breasts.

"Let me clean that up for you," he says in a low voice thick with desire, his tongue curling to a tip at my navel, then flattening as he rides all the way up my torso, between my breasts, ending at the hollow of my neck. I lean back and let my body take over, my sigh turning to a moan, as he faithfully does as promised.

He keeps his promises. *Always*. I know that about him, and I'm learning it's true in bed, too.

Every time our skin connects, I marvel at how good this feels. Two parts of me are at war inside: the Jane who wants to let go and enjoy, and the Jane who is so new to being this intimate with a man that she freezes, worried she's doing the wrong thing. I am both of those Janes.

But there is only one Silas.

"I need my coffee," I protest, but giggling at the same time.

He lets out a mock sigh. "Coffee isn't better than sex."

"No. It's not. But it's close," I tease as I turn just enough to reach my cup. I don't have the courage to tell him I'm sore from last night. That I'm nervous.

That I need a little bit of time to sort everything inside me and let it all settle.

He grabs his own mug and takes a sip, sitting next to me.

I open my mouth and to my surprise, blurt out: "I didn't know sex could be so, so, so..."

"Incredible?"

"I was going to say 'athletic.' But 'incredible' works, too."

Unrestrained laughter from Silas shakes the bed. "You," he gasps, "are killing me."

"That's a nice change. Because normally, I'm the one someone's trying to kill."

His laughter stops abruptly.

And then my phone buzzes. Seconds later, his does, too.

We both groan in unison.

"I am not going back to The Grove," I declare before either of us locates our phones. "No."

"I won't make you," he says, resolute. "But I have to see what's going on."

My phone is on a chair on the other side of the room. Silas walked in here naked and completely unselfconscious. Just a few hours ago, we had messy, naughty, awesome sex, and he's seen my body in darkness and in daylight.

And yet... standing up and walking across the room without a stitch of clothing on feels so provocative. Exhibitionist.

Crazy, right? I pose naked for Alice's paintings but can't bring myself to go get my phone?

Taking a deep breath, I toss off the sheet and just do it. When I turn around, I see it doesn't matter. Silas is staring intently at his screen.

I look at mine.

It's Lindsay.

75

We need to talk. Now. Meet at The Toast in an hour?

"Anywhere but The Grove," I mutter. Besides, The Toast has great coffee. Much better than the stuff Silas made for me.

On the other hand, the service here at his place is top notch. We can work on the coffee.

Another text makes the phone leap to life in my hands. I back out of Lindsay's text to find one from Harry Bosworth.

Er... my father.

Come to The Grove in an hour, Jane. We need to talk.

My father wants to see me.

My not-sister wants to see me.

I have to choose.

No, I reply back to Senator Harwell Bosworth, the man who is one election away from being the leader of the free world. I don't choose him.

I choose Lindsay.

"Lindsay wants to see you," Silas says, holding up his phone. "Text from Drew. She wants to meet in an hour, but Drew convinced her to move it to one p.m. I have legal stuff scheduled with Kelly and my mom this morning. I can't go with you. Duff's on his way to take over."

I fight disappointment inside, pretending to be joking. "Duff's taking over?" My eyes roam up and down his nude body. "In what capacity?"

A fierce jealousy fills Silas's face. "Don't even joke like that."

My pulse seems to stop. "I'm sorry. I was just–"

He breathes out, a long line of resigned air. "No, *I'm* sorry. That was an overreaction."

I look at him, hard. "It really was a joke. I don't–Duff's not–I was just making a stupid–" I reach for his hand and stop myself from babbling. "You're the only person I want."

"Good. Because the feeling is mutual."

"You asked me last night about dating in college. What about you?"

"I didn't date much." The lack of elaboration sets off alarm bells in my head.

"But you've dated. Had relationships?"

"Yes."

"And the last one?"

"She died."

I go numb. "How?"

"In combat."

"Oh, my God."

"Right." He's closed off, but I can tell he's ready to say more if I ask.

"Was she someone you were really close to?"

"She was my fiancée."

"Oh, Silas." A strange blend of empathy and jealousy plumes through me. "I really am sorry." I want to ask him why he didn't tell me before. Part of me is hurt that he hasn't trusted me with this information until now. Then again, we're unfolding ourselves to each other slowly, painstakingly.

I'm sure there's more he hasn't told me.

I *know* there's more I've kept from him.

"No need. It's been three years."

"You never get over losing someone you love."

"No. You don't. But it looks like I'm finding a way with someone new."

It takes a few beats for me to realize he's talking about me.

Tap tap tap.

The knock on the front door makes me let out a squeal of surprise. Silas looks at his phone.

"It's Duff. Here to take over for me." His eyes dart to my face, looking for me to say something. I remain neutral. It's hard.

"You have to leave?" I ask as I jump up and find my pajamas, shoving them on so quickly, I catch my hair in the tag.

Silas does the same, throwing on his clothes. "No choice."

"What do you mean, 'no choice'?"

"Legal issues." He closes his eyes and takes a long time to inhale, emotion rippling over his face. He gives me a wry smile as he opens his eyes. "Sorry. Habit."

"Sorry... for what?"

"I'm not used to talking about anything. I don't open up. You're being normal and I'm not used to it."

"Normal?"

"You're asking about my day. Questioning when something I say doesn't add up. Inquiring about how I'm doing. It's new." A small laugh escapes him, melting my heart. As his hand covers mine, I turn into a puddle. "It's nice. More than nice." The skin around his left eye twitches. "But it'll take some getting used to. I don't work that way. So I'll need to get accustomed to it. Adjustment and adaptation are my strong suit in the field, but apparently not in the bedroom."

I laugh out of politeness, but his emotional reveal is taking my breath away. "All of this takes time." I lower my voice, turning from joking lover to confidante. "I'm adjusting, too. Second by second, word by word, kiss by kiss."

A radiant smile turns his face into a handsome, strong world I could escape to forever. "Kiss by kiss?" He gives me one, leaning in to kiss my forehead, then the tip of my nose.

"Touch by touch," I add, but before he can match that comment, Duff knocks on the door again, harder.

"Damn," Silas says through a tight mouth.

"It's okay. I understand."

"I'm sorry, Jane. But let's do dinner? Tonight?"

My heart soars. "Yes!"

He gives me a quick kiss on the lips, the kind of casual kiss you give someone you take for granted. It's the kiss you give when you're sure there will be time later. Plenty of time–all of it in the assumed future.

It's a kiss you give someone you love.

I press my fingers against my lips as he leaves, like I'm holding the kiss in place, never letting it go.

Duff clears his throat, sounding like a motorcycle at full throttle. "You need anything, Jane?"

"A time machine."

"Can't submit an expense form to the boss man for that."

"Then what good are you, Duff? Come on. You can do better."

He suppresses a smile and gives me a side-eye glance that isn't part of a conspirator's look. It's a strange, detached reaction that confuses me. "What's on the agenda today, Jane?" he asks, right back to being an emotionless android.

I remind myself that Silas was like this, too, when he started guarding me. What is Duff's inner life like?

"Before I answer that, I have a question."

"Yes?"

"Duff can't be your real name."

"It is. My parents were cruel."

I roll my eyes. "Seriously. What's your name?"

"Seamus McDuff."

"Wow."

"See? Cruel."

"That's... quite a name."

"It's actually Seamus Patrick McDuff. I'm Russian."

He gets a gimlet look from me.

And laughs.

I cracked his shield. This is progress. Something about Duff is familiar and dangerous at the same time. I can't put my finger on it.

"I see why you go by a nickname." Then I realize something. "Your real name isn't any of that. Not one bit." I frown. Is Silas's real name Silas? With military intelligence and special forces, it's possible they're not revealing their true identities.

"Caught," he says, checking his phone while we talk, half his attention on his screen. "My real name is Vladimir Putin."

"I knew it!"

"It's hard being famous."

"It's even harder being infamous," I say softly.

My words make his head jerk up. He looks at me, then says slowly, "I'll bet it is."

A chill runs up me from my Achilles' heel to the backs of my ears. Duff isn't flirting. Not one bit. It's his very presence that freaks out my nervous system. Something in his voice–a clipped end of a word, the careful way he speaks around consonants... what is it? Why is this man setting off all of my alarm bells?

It's strange. And it's creepy. I don't feel unsafe with Duff, though. I just feel like the world is surreal, and if I can just figure out why he's making everything tilt a little, I will be fine again.

Silas trusts him. I trust Silas with my life. Therefore, it's transitive: I should trust Duff. Completely. Fully.

"You being harassed?" he asks, still peering at me oddly.

"When am I *not* harassed? I don't even look at social media anymore. I'm a meme. Stories about me circulate like sexual harassment cases against beloved comedians and entertainment executives. Asking me if I'm being harassed is like asking Kate Middleton if she hopes to be queen one day. The answer is the same: duh."

"I didn't mean online. I mean, are you being threatened?"

"Nothing new." I bite my lip, frowning. "Or, if there is, Silas didn't mention it."

He opens his mouth as if to say something, then shuts it quickly. Silas's college sweatshirt is draped casually across the back of one of the kitchen chairs. Duff's eyes dart over to it, the movement so swift, you might not notice it.

Unless you're looking for it.

And I am.

"Reports say the trolls are napping today, Jane. Grab your free time while you can. Where to?"

"The flower shop. It's on the corner, a few blocks away. Then to The Toast at one p.m. I'm meeting Lindsay."

"The Thorn Poke?"

"That's the one." I wonder how he knows the name of the flower shop, but then again, it's his job to know things. I only know it because we drove past the place and it sounded like a sweet diversion for me.

"What do you need there?" I am in the middle of grabbing Silas's sweatshirt to wrap around my waist when I hear him.

"Flowers," I say slowly. This time, he's the one who rolls his eyes.

"You like flowers that much?"

I brighten. "I do. There's something special about the scent of fresh flowers. It's like you get a reboot on the day. I could use a reboot on the day."

"Sounds like you could use a reboot on the last year, if you don't mind my saying so."

"I don't." I look down at myself. As I take a step forward, my inner thighs brush against each other. I'm sore, and parts of me ache. Sex with Silas is fun and hot, emotional and enthralling.

It is also messy.

"I need a shower," I announce, turning away and going straight into the bathroom.

Where I find a tube of antibiotic cream and a note in Silas's scrawl.

You forgot to do this last night.

S

I blink, reading the words, setting the note down before turning on the shower. Stripping down is fast but getting in the shower is a fearful process. The water stings my skin all over again, thousands of hot knives attacking the spots Silas kissed with his healing attention last night. Too bad kisses can't really fix boo-boos.

I laugh, but I'm sad at the memory of my mother, fixing scrapes with kisses and Band-Aids. Ah, to be that young again. That naïve.

That trusting in the magic of a kiss.

Normally not fast with showers, I find myself hurrying, doing the basics. As I wash between my legs, a thrill of memory from last night makes me swell with renewed need. There is an entire world of sex out there that I didn't understand.

As the water rains down on me, both friend and foe, I find the richness of the shampoo, the gloss of light against water, the feeling of purity and renewal in my cells. Sharing so much with Silas last night and being shared with–it's as if the world righted itself deep in the night.

And all my life I've been crooked without knowing it.

As soon as my hair is rinsed, I shut off the water, my skin throbbing. Every scratch is a pulse. Drying off becomes an obstacle course. Removing the water from my skin and out of my hair is a priority, but doing it without opening barely healing wounds is a challenge.

Like life. You do what needs to be done, but it's never easy, is it?

By the time I've dried my hair, put on new clothes, applied antibiotic cream to my worst cuts, and given up on makeup, I find Duff smiling at me as I enter the living room.

Uh oh.

"What's wrong?" I ask.

His look falters. "Wrong? Why would you ask that?"

"Because you're smiling."

"You take a person's smiling face as an omen of bad news?"

"I do now."

He laughs, the sound deep and free. These men. These protective, defensive, warrior men. Their emotions are origami, folded until they are cryptic, one thing on the outside but completely different when opened up in full.

"I am smiling, Jane, because I have something to show you."

Silas trusts Duff implicitly. I'm trying.

"You do?"

"It's in the hallway."

My brow lowers, his behavior making me curious. "Is it a present?"

"You could say that."

"Am I going to like it?"

"You'd better," he says seriously. "It took a lot of pull to make it happen."

What the hell does that mean?

I walk to the front door and open it, peering out into the hallway. It's empty.

"Is this a joke?"

He reaches into his pocket and pulls out a single key on a purple carabiner clip. "No joke."

"What's that?"

"Come." He leads the way and walks next door, to the right. Duff hands me the key. "Here."

"Won't the neighbor mind?"

"Jane," he says softly, patiently. "You *are* the neighbor now."

Maybe it's the stress of everything that's happened. Maybe

it's the afterglow from sleeping with Silas last night. Maybe it's the fact that no one gives me what I want anymore, but I don't understand him.

"Spell it out for me, Duff."

"Drew and Silas got you your own apartment," he enunciates, the words clipped at the end, his smile loose. "Open the door."

"My own–oh!" Duff gently takes the key from me, puts it in the lock, and opens it. The apartment is an identical layout to Silas's, and decorated in much the same way, the paintings and throw pillows slightly different.

"It's furnished!" I gasp.

"Of course it is. All except the bedroom. For some reason, they don't have a bed for you. Not a real one." I've never heard Duff say so many words at once.

"I can sleep on the couch."

"There's a camping cot in there, instead. A new bed's been ordered."

"It's really mine?"

"Yes, ma'am. Just cleared it all while you were in the shower."

"Is that where Silas had to go this morning? Why he was in a rush?"

The open, friendly Duff powers down into closed-off robot mode. "I can't say."

The combination of my growing elation at having my own place and Duff's sudden reticence about Silas makes my stomach drop and my breathing pick up. Ignoring Duff, I walk into the apartment. It's bare, but mine.

All mine.

"I want to go shopping," I say to him in a voice that makes it clear there's no argument.

Duff stretches his arm toward the door in a gentlemanly gesture. I know it's not driven by courtesy. He does it to make sure he can see out the door and scan the hallway for threats while simultaneously being the last to look in my apartment and make sure all is well. Nevertheless, it's a nice, polite act and I appreciate it.

I tuck my new apartment key in my pocket with a delicious sense of ownership.

I have a place.

Silas and Drew gave me a *place*.

"Still want flowers?" Duff asks.

"Yes."

"Then the plan is clear. The Thorn Poke now, then The Toast at one p.m. Plenty of time."

"Plenty of time?" I ask as we take the stairs down, bypassing the elevator.

"Plenty of time to make your appointments," he says smoothly, guiding me to a black SUV. Duff holds the door open and as I move past him, I smell spices, the kind cologne makers blend carefully to create custom scents.

Before I can ask him if that's cardamom I smell, he closes the door. I'm entombed.

And then I realize we're not walking.

"Wait!" I call out. "We can walk to the flower shop. That's the whole point!"

Duff ignores me and starts the engine, catching my eyes in the rear-view mirror. "No, Jane. The point is to keep you alive and safe. And that means driving you."

"But it's only four blocks away! This is ridiculous!"

"Car bombings, shootings on the senator's private land–*those* are ridiculous. Protecting you isn't."

"Is this an order? Did Silas make you do this?"

"I don't officially report to Gentian."

"Officially. You don't *officially* report to him. Weasel words, Duff. Come on. Is Silas making you do this?" One hand giveth, one hand taketh away.

Silence.

"But, Duff–" It's useless to argue. Duff puts on his mirrored shades and pretends I don't exist in the backseat.

Sigh.

Back to being an object.

No one says I have to be a *silent* object.

"Why do you seem so familiar, Duff?" I ask, overriding my body's weird reaction to him. This isn't attraction. Not one drop of it. And yet my arms and legs, my ears and skin, it's all on edge.

"People say that a lot. I guess I have a face that got recycled in the great DNA dump of life."

His answer is too smooth. Practiced. Like he knew this was coming and prepared for it.

"Where are you from?"

"Philly."

"I roomed in college with someone from Philly. Your accent isn't like hers."

"Lots of accents around Philly. Besides, my parents weren't from there."

"Where were they from?"

"Boston."

"You don't have a Boston accent, either."

"Well, *Jane*, you were raised by a Russian immigrant in Southern California and you don't have a Russian accent or a SoCal accent. What's your point?" He turns the car to the right like we're moving on greased rails, but his eyes scan the horizon constantly.

And then it hits me.

"Do you... can you do an Irish accent?"

"Only when I'm starring in cereal commercials as a leprechaun," he says dryly. "With a face like this, I have a moral obligation to work in Hollywood." He points to his scar.

I don't take the bait. "You sound an awful lot like someone I know. Only you're using an American accent."

It can't be, right? There is no way Duff is my informant. Absolutely no way. All the blood rushes out of my head and right back into it, like someone picked up the car and turned me upside down, then right side up again. My neck starts to throb, the ache making me feel like my tongue is being ripped out of my throat.

I'm losing it.

I'm totally losing it.

"You said I *looked* familiar. Now I *sound* like someone you know. Which is it?"

"I've never met this person. Just listened to him," I falter.

"On the radio?"

"Something like that."

"I never talked to you before the day your car was bombed, Jane. I have no idea who you think I am, but it's not me you're looking for."

"You're in private security. You're trained to lie for tactical and strategic reasons."

"Yes. I am."

"How do I know you're not lying to me now?"

"You don't."

I sigh. "You. Silas. Drew. You're all alike."

"No–they're better looking than me. By a mile."

I can't help but laugh.

"You think I'm kidding? They never tangled with an IED, like me. Don't try to fight an explosive device with the side of your face. You'll lose," he tells me in a sage voice, as if he's Luke Skywalker and I'm a baby Jedi.

"Is that where the scars come from?"

"No, those I got during Barbie Dreamhouse wars with my sister. She plays dirty."

"Did you serve with Silas and Drew?"

"Served with Paulson." He goes mum.

Mark Paulson is an enigma to me, a name I can't help but have a negative association with, considering what my mother did. I avoid him and all mention of him. She handed Lindsay off to John Gainsborough, believing him to be Mark Paulson. The investigation cleared me, but it didn't clear my mom. Did she know? When she told Lindsay to go to the helicopter, did she really know she was sending her to her death?

Or worse? Because she had to know that John, Stellan, and Blaine wouldn't simply kill Lindsay.

They planned to torture her, nice and slowly, squeezing every sadistic drop of pleasure from her pain.

Knowing my mother might have done that on purpose is unfathomable.

I shiver, the full body shake spreading from my core and moving up to my scalp, down to my feet. It's like a full-body shock, the images and thoughts too much. Overloaded circuits come in many forms, and as Duff parks the SUV in a small alley behind the flower store, I take comfort in the fact that unlike my mother, I'm alive. She would do anything to protect me.

And maybe she *did*.

Duff escorts me to the front door. The little bell that rings as we enter the store is an endearing throwback to the past. Most places have electronic doors and sensors, with computers instead of cash registers, but not The Thorn Poke. It's like a store from my childhood, older and quainter, with an ethereal quality the second you step inside and close the door.

I'm transported.

Isn't that the point of flower shops? They're designed to help you *feel*.

"Oh, dear!" says a matronly woman with soft curves and the eyes of an old soul. Her hair is short and the color of honey, curling lightly at the ends. She's about my mother's age. "I am so sorry, dear, but we're closing. We have a big wedding to do this evening and Bowie should have put the Closed sign up. BOWIE!" she screams toward the back. Her change in tone is so jarring, she might as well have suddenly turned into Godzilla.

"It's fine," I say, disappointed but being polite. "I can come back another day."

"Is it–is it a simple order, dear? Do you know what you want?"

That question. Oh, that question. *Do you know what you want?* It echoes through me, stretched like taffy through time itself, messy and threadlike in some places, bulky and unwieldy in others, but sweet and simple, sticky and thick.

"Just, um, browsing," I say, smiling. I stuff my feelings down inside my chest, scrambling to put them in a locked cage where they can't escape and do damage. "I'll come back another time. I love your store."

A little O of surprise and pleasure forms in her expression as her lipstick-covered lips react. "Why, thank you! I feel so bad we're closed, but please do return!"

Duff lifts his chin toward me as if to say we need to go. I turn around and exit the store.

Then burst into tears.

"You were really attached to those ferns," Duff deadpans as he hands me a clean, ironed handkerchief from his navy suit-jacket pocket.

I take it and dab my eyes. Mascara smears onto the bright white cloth. "No. It's the peach roses that are making me cry."

Duff doesn't touch me. None of the men are supposed to unless it's to save or protect me. But his presence is suddenly a comfort. Silas would be infinitely better, but in his absence, Duff will do.

"What now?" he asks.

"Let's go back to my apartment," I say. "I'll work out in the gym."

"From flowers to treadmills."

"Are you ever going to tell me who you really are, Duff?"

"I'm WYSIWYG."

"That's a computer term. I'm a developer, you know. And you are the opposite of 'what you see is what you get,' for sure."

"Artificial intelligence has come a long way."

"You're a robot?"

"When it comes to protecting my clients, that's right. I am. Just remember: we're robots. We do as we're programmed and we follow Asimov's three rules."

"Location, location, location?"

And with that, I finally get Duff to laugh again.

CHAPTER 10

The Toast is the first place I saw Lindsay after she was released from the Island. It used to be this super-chill 1970s-style hippie place, except it was authentic. Real hippies ran it. The pineapple-carrot breakfast muffins were vegan and delicious.

Now The Toast isn't run by hippies, but hipsters. Completely remodeled a few years ago, the coffeehouse is reflective and bright, all stainless steel with color sprinkled in on mosaic tiles, the lighting low and the seating abundant.

I look at Silas as we wait for our lattes and remember seeing him here, guarding Lindsay, seven months ago. He found me, taking over for Duff with a suddenness that confirms we've gone past the professional into the personal.

"No hat?" I tease.

He gives me a deeply confused frown, the skin between his eyes folding in. "What?"

"The first time we met was here. You were following Lindsay. You pretended to be her chauffeur."

He groans and leans down, whispering. "That stupid cap?" His eyes light up with mischief, making his lips curl up with a grin that sets my blood rushing.

"Why aren't you pretending to be *my* chauffeur?"

"Because you're not the daughter of–" His sentence ends like someone clipped it off, like it was under a guillotine.

"Right," I chirp, pretending to be chipper as our coffees are handed off by a barista wearing glasses with white surgical tape between the lenses.

"I didn't mean it that way," Silas clarifies.

"I know. But it's a new reality. Besides, the hat was cute."

"The hat was annoying."

"Maybe I'll order you to wear it," I taunt.

"I can order you around, too. It goes both ways." His breath against my ear makes my skin light up. "Maybe you're the one who should wear the hat. In bed. And nothing else."

"You have chauffeur fantasies?"

"No. But you in that hat, high heels, and nothing else would be quite a sight."

Suddenly, I'm parched. I need the coffee to give me something to do. Something other than blushing, which I'm excelling at.

Silas takes my silence for acquiescence and smiles. "Last time we were in a coffee shop, your car was bombed."

"Don't blame me!"

"I'm not. Just observing." He smirks. "Maybe it's the coffee's fault."

"It will take more than a car bomb to get me to give up coffee." I smile at him before taking another sip. "Thank you for my apartment."

"Thank him." Silas points toward the front of the coffee shop.

Drew approaches the main door, pulls it open with a precise, strong movement. He ushers Lindsay into The Toast, looking around furtively.

"Someone's paranoid," I murmur.

"It's his job to be paranoid. And that's his woman he's protecting." Silas makes it clear he identifies with Drew.

Lindsay comes right over to us, ignoring the place to order coffee, and we're hugging before I can think. It's the first time we've touched since yesterday, since finding out who we really are and aren't. I can feel her pain.

I want to snap at Silas for the "his woman" caveman comment, but the thought fades as Drew and Silas start giving each other the evil eye, then huddle to talk about us.

"He's a piece of flypaper," Lindsay complains. "Won't let me out of his sight."

"He cares," I say, as Drew moves to the counter to get coffee.

Lindsay pulls me away from the guys. Immediately, Drew's head turns, eyes on her, constantly jumping between whatever he's attending to and back to Lindsay. "I can barely go to the bathroom!" she hisses under her breath. "He's relentless."

"This is Drew Foster you married, Lindsay. *Drew*. You know, the guy who is the poster child for the word *relentless*."

"I know! I know. But–he's suffocating me."

"I'm *protecting* you," Drew says to her in a dry, beleaguered voice. He glares at me. "You are never safe anywhere. There's no one you can trust, Lindsay."

"Aside from you," she says softly, eyes filled with a gritty love the two share.

"Trust no one?" I say, brushing off the overt insult from Drew. "Where have I heard that before? You're sounding like a cheesy 1990s paranormal television show, Drew."

"Oh, no, Jane. Whatever will I do? Jane Borokov doesn't approve of me. My reputation is tarnished," he shoots back. His voice is hard to read. Hell, *Drew* is hard to read. I can't tell if this is good-natured but hard-edged teasing, or if he's gone Jekyll and Hyde on me.

Lindsay pulls me to a booth on the far end of the coffee shop. Drew looks like he's about to explode from being a whole forty feet away from her.

"I mean it," she says in a wailing tone, but quietly. "Ever since yesterday, he's even more worried."

"Does he have a specific reason? Is your dad–our dad–uh, the senator–"

"He's still my dad," she says gruffly. "Even if he isn't. We had a long talk last night."

Jealousy turns from green to red inside me. I stuff it down, down, down.

"And?" I venture.

"No one will tell me who my biological father is. Daddy claims not to know. Mom conveniently left the country early this morning for an appearance in China for some children's foundation."

"Monica's so selfless. So giving," I reply.

We share a snort.

Drew appears, carrying two coffees. He hands one to Lindsay, who thanks him with a smile. He sips from the other. "Jane and I will stay here, and you and Silas can do your he-man thing over there," she informs him. She points across the room.

"No. This table is fine." He hip-checks her, sending a surprised Lindsay four inches to the left as he sits in the booth. "This way, I have a full view of the windows and you're protected by Silas on your right," he says calmly, like he's memorized every single contingency and this is the one he's retrieving from memory.

"I want to have a private conversation with Jane."

Drew looks up at her from the lip of his coffee cup as he takes a sip, all eyes and nose. "Go ahead."

"It's not private if you two are here."

"This is the most privacy you're getting from me, Lindsay." He looks at me like it's my fault.

Lindsay's mouth draws tight. "You're being ridiculous."

"I'm being careful."

"You're being obsessive!"

"Then I'm doing my job."

"I'm not your client anymore! I'm your wife!" she explodes.

"Which means protecting you is an even higher priority."

"So is respecting me," she says with a disgruntled *humph!*

"Protecting you *is* how I respect you."

She rolls her eyes and gives me a long look. "See what I have to deal with?"

Before I can answer, her eyes narrow. Then she gives me a tight grin.

"My cramps are sooooooo bad," Lindsay groans. Drew's halfway through his coffee when he pauses, then does that polite thing where you pretend you didn't hear what you actually heard.

Silas looks away, as if either the vase filled with eucalyptus on the next table over or the sugar container is a fascinating work of art.

"Ibuprofen isn't helping, Jane," Lindsay moans. "And the clots! They're grapefruit sized!"

Drew sets down the forkful of cantaloupe he was about to eat out of a small to-go fruit cup.

Silas winces, but says nothing, his eyes constantly moving, unable to look at anyone or anything, increasingly frantic.

"And my breasts are sooooooooo sensitive when I have my period. All I want is salty and sweet stuff. Poor Drew, too. I get so horny–"

"This isn't going to work," Drew says under his breath. "You're not saying anything I don't live with." But his teeth are gritted, and Silas looks like he's about to break out in a sweat.

"Honeymoon over?" I ask Drew sweetly as Lindsay plucks a piece of grapefruit from his abandoned fruit cup and starts chewing away.

Silas tries not to laugh, his knee bouncing with nerves.

Drew's phone buzzes. "Gotta take this," he says, giving Silas an obvious look that screams *Keep an eye on them.*

I touch Silas's hand. "We can get pretty graphic."

"I made it through combat tours. I can handle female–" He waves his hand around my torso. "–stuff."

"How evolved of you," Lindsay drawls.

"That's me. Evolution in motion." He gives her a big grin.

Lindsay leans in and ignores Silas as she says to me, "We really need to talk about how you're being set up. I know you didn't do any of the awful things the press and others are saying you did."

"Others?"

"You know. Talk show hosts. Political bloggers. Op-Ed columnists in the major newspapers. My mom. Half my dad's political circle. Three billion Facebook users who share memes..."

"Oh. *Them.*"

"Right."

"You don't believe them? Really?"

"I did at first. But I know you'd never kill Tara." Light bounces off her eyes, which shine with unspent tears. "I can't believe she died like that." She shivers.

"No. I wouldn't. I didn't. I swear." At the mention of Tara's name, my heart hurts. Silas cleared me, local law enforcement unhappy to have federal agents step in, but there's no evidence linking me to her death, thankfully.

"Someone's setting you up, and they're making it increasingly obvious. I think the whole machine behind this is falling apart."

"Machine?"

"Someone is at the center of a very complicated network of people who have an agenda to ruin my dad–er, your dad–er, you know. The senator. It started with what happened five years ago. They resumed the second I came home from the Island. They were stupid enough–and that bimbo neighbor of Drew's, what's-her-face, was smart enough–"

"Tiffany," Drew calls out.

Lindsay glares at him, as if he's not supposed to remember and she's upset that he does. "–to catch it all on live-streaming video. All the evidence they tried to spin turned into dust. And they're dead."

"But not all of them. It was never just John, Stellan, and Blaine."

"That's becoming more obvious, isn't it? At least I have Drew to protect me." Her eyes dart over to take in Silas, then return to me. "But you have... ?"

"I don't know what I have." Honesty is the best policy when it comes to romance. It's a relief to talk about it with someone. Anyone.

But especially Lindsay.

The weight of Silas's hand on my shoulder makes me smile. He says nothing, but that touch speaks volumes.

"You were my informant, though. You are connected to people who are in a web of some kind. Someone out there wanted to feed me information while I was on the Island. Were they part of John, Stellan, and Blaine's plan? Or someone different?"

"I don't know. Truly. It was a guy with an Irish accent. Older, but not super old. He gave me tips on how to get to you and what to feed you. But at the same time, I was supposed to protect you." I touch her hand. It's cold. "You know how hard it was."

"I stole minutes on the internet when I could. If I'd known it was you, it would have really helped," she says in an stern tone, wounds from the past coming out in her words.

"If I'd told you it was me, we could have both been in more danger."

"I know."

We sit in awkward silence, the seconds knitting broken bones and shattered promises. I can't undo the past, and she can't, either. We're powerless when it comes to everything that's come before this moment.

Going forward, though, we're invincible.

I hope.

"Can you forgive me?" I ask her, Silas's hand tightening, now moving to my arm, helping me to breathe. When he connects his body to mine, it grounds me.

"Of course. Can you forgive *me*?"

"Why would I need to do that?" I recoil in surprise.

"Because I was stupid and believed what everyone around me said." Just then, Drew returns, sitting next to her, looking at Lindsay with an inquiring look. "And mostly because Drew told me you did it."

"Did what?" Drew asks, giving Silas a pointed glare.

"Were part of the conspiracy to kill me," Lindsay answers.

His face tightens. "I'm still not convinced you aren't, Jane."

Never one to mince words, Drew cuts through the good vibes at the table.

"And I'm not convinced you're looking at the big picture," I say calmly. "I'm being set up. It's increasingly obvious."

"If that's true, who's behind it? Why? What does someone have to gain by setting you up? You're already *persona non grata* to most of the country. People hate you." Drew's blunt words cut through me. So many emotions start to jangle inside, like wind chimes in a hurricane. How can he be so direct? How do people look others in the eye and call them liars, cheats, conspirators, murderers?

The disconnect, the lack of caring about my emotions is so cold.

And yet this is his job. His life's mission.

"This-this is doing wonders for my ego," I finally stammer.

"I'm stating the truth," he counters. "You're already an outcast. Why would someone have a motive to make you look like you have your finger in every destructive pie?"

He asks me the question like I'm supposed to have the answer.

Silas interrupts, his voice low and filled with hidden meaning. "Who has something to gain by setting Jane up?"

"My mother," Lindsay says with a snort.

And there it is again. A look between Drew and Silas that I can't figure out. My father and Silas shared a similar look earlier.

What is going on regarding Monica Bosworth?

"Why aren't you laughing?" Lindsay asks her husband, who suddenly makes eye contact with the napkin holder and no one else.

"Because nothing about your mother is ever, ever funny," he says.

"Drew." Silas's tone makes it clear he's not letting this go. The two make hard eye contact, Lindsay raising one eyebrow at me. "Why is someone pointing all these fingers at Jane? She didn't kill Tara. She didn't set up the car bomb and she didn't give the code to the shooter at The Grove. Someone else did."

A look of dawning comprehension spreads over Lindsay's face. "You two know. You know who is setting Jane up."

"No," they say in unison.

"But you have suspicions," I clarify.

They go mute.

Drew sighs, sucking down the last of his coffee then leaning toward me. "I got the report on Tara. Local police department is dropping it. You're cleared." He looks at Silas. "Your timing was impeccable with the body cam on Jane."

Silas gives a slight nod of acknowledgement.

Drew continues. "Our guys are working on figuring out how someone got in there and killed her so quickly and so cleanly."

"She bled everywhere. There was nothing clean about it," I counter, my stomach squeezing at the memory.

"I mean in and out. Not tracked. No video."

"Oh."

"The official story is suicide."

My stomach goes sour and twists, the coffee sitting in there like a pool of blood and acid.

"Thank God," Lindsay says, squeezing my hand.

"Good," I say quickly. "That's one less thing to worry about. But poor Tara. Can you imagine being in the bathroom and having someone slash you like that? Imagine those last seconds as she–oh, God."

Silas leans in, his face so close to mine. I can feel his body heat. "Yes. I can. I imagine *you* being in that bathroom and her killer getting you. I don't want to, but I can. And I'm going to make damn sure no one ever gets a chance to do to you what someone did to Tara."

No amount of coffee can warm my chilled bones. "When you put it that way... "

Drew frowns at Silas. "It still doesn't add up."

"No. But I'm focused on keeping Jane alive. I expect you and the rest of the team to figure out the mystery and get to the heart of this evil beast. We need to find the puppetmaster. Once we know that, we can end the show," he tells him.

"Puppetmaster," I say, drinking a sip of coffee just to break through the numb feeling in my face. "But who are his puppets? I feel like one."

"You're a target. Not a tool," Drew says to me, serious and evaluative. "Or are you? I still don't know which side you're on."

Prickly heat shoots up the back of my neck. In a perfect world, Drew would be one hundred percent on my side. He obviously isn't. I have Silas now, and Lindsay, too.

But Drew Foster could turn out to be a very difficult obstacle in getting my life on track if he doesn't find a way to realize he's being played by the puppetmaster, too.

Silas is about to reply to Drew when both men look sharply to the left. Movement, men in black suits, and the subtle change of atmosphere make me realize someone important is here. The kind of person with an entourage. Maybe a celebrity, or a rapper. Both tend to flock to our little town to get out of the spotlight.

But no.

It's not a celebrity.

It's a politician.

My father.

CHAPTER 11

"*J*ane," he says as he strides to the end of our four-top booth. He gives Lindsay a tight smile and ignores Silas and Drew.

"Hello. Get a craving for a good cortado?" I ask. "I recommend the one without the shot of deception. Tastes less bitter, Senator."

"How are we not blood sisters?" Lindsay asks out of the side of her mouth.

"I want to speak with Jane alone," Harry says to Lindsay, Drew, and Silas in a careful, neutral tone.

Lindsay looks up at him while drinking her coffee, then carefully sets the cup down, blotting the corners of her lips before saying, "And I want to know who my biological father is, but Mom won't tell me. You can't always get what you want, Daddy. Don't you listen to that old rock band?"

I swear he flinches at the word *old*.

"It's not a request, Lindsay. Jane and I need to have privacy."

"Just think, *Daddy*." She's using the term with great affect. "Now both of your little girls are with you, together. Isn't that sweet?"

His features sharpen, his attention on her in full. "Your bitterness isn't going to work. Being direct will."

"I've tried being direct, but let's go for it again. Tell me the name of my biological father."

Drew stretches his arm across the back of Lindsay's booth, a claiming gesture that gets past no one.

"I don't know who it is, Lindsay. Ask your mother," Harry insists.

"She refuses to tell me."

"Then we're at an impasse."

"I am not some negotiating point that is a source of conflict!" She slams her palm down on the table. "I am a human being who has been tortured *for being your daughter*."

My skin begins to crawl, my ears suddenly, furiously hot.

"They would have done that to you either way," Harry says calmly, as if being told such a thing washes all the pain away.

"That's your answer? *That*? You need to hire better image managers, Senator Bosworth," she says in a sharp voice. "Because your answer sucks donkey balls."

His phone buzzes and he pulls it out of his front pants pocket with a pinched look of annoyance.

"Lindsay." He taps on his phone. I'm stuck. I don't think Lindsay's doing the right thing, but I'm cheering her on deep inside me.

He doesn't say anything more, letting her name hang in the air, treating her like a bratty child.

Lindsay rides out the silence, defiant.

I'm in awe.

Harry Bosworth scares the crap out of me now. Knowing he's my father changes how I look at him. Talk to him. Hold myself around him. I feel very self-conscious and incredibly angry, but I don't have a right to my anger. I'm not allowed to feel it.

I'm supposed to be grateful.

I'm supposed to be humble.

But most of all, I'm supposed to be *discreet*.

Lindsay's emboldened, empowered, filled with righteous anger at the paternity testing and its results. She's been raised by two people she isn't afraid of. At least, not now.

And people with power don't like it when the people they manipulate lose their fear. It makes them dangerous.

It makes *us* dangerous.

Prey aren't supposed to be bold.

Prey are supposed to *cower*.

How can you define yourself as the dominant predator if people don't fear you? It's the ultimate betrayal. Victims are supposed to fold. Power brokers don't care about people.

They care about order.

Stay within the lines they draw, do their bidding without question, and sacrifice every piece of yourself so they can prop up their reality. That's all they ask.

Just give us your soul, they say. *Why are you arguing?* they ask. *You're so selfish*, they chide.

The best among them make you agree.

And make you give until all that's left is the memory of your own volition.

And even then, they demand that, too.

Lindsay, though–Lindsay's not buying it. She's not giving in to it. She's not *anything-ing* it. Transgressions from her parents rise so far above the fray. They violate so many standards of decency that she's breaking out of their forced reality.

I'm watching.

And damn it, I'm taking notes.

"Jane," he snaps. "Perhaps you can talk some sense into your sis–"

Lindsay's snort cuts him off.

Drew and Silas are basically ceiling supports at this point, like columns designed to make sure the building doesn't crumble. Ever observant, they just watch. Although Drew's got a vested interest here that is way deeper.

"Your friend," the senator amends.

I know what he's doing. Pivot the emotional tension so I'm the one dealing with Lindsay. Pit us against each other. Turn me into the person smoothing out her edges and trying to make her see reason. And when she doesn't?

Make that my fault.

I struggle to come up with the perfect words, verbal judo that stops him and uses his own power against him. My head is ringing and my skin feels like a suit I put on this morning, baggy in places and too tight in others. No mental playbook has prepared me for this. How do I spar with my own father as he tries to shut down my not-quite-sister, who has every right to challenge him?

I wrack my brain for an answer, and settle on the most dangerous.

"No."

His eyelids lower halfway, jaw going slightly slack. "Excuse me?"

"No," I repeat.

If I wait him out, I can survive this. Panic pours through me like a broken dam, debris traveling along the raging river, sludge and water spilling out, relieved as the pressure seeks to even out and stabilize, spread itself out over the vast expanse of its new space.

Transition is the most difficult stage in labor and delivery, my mother told me once. It's the moment you lose all your confidence and think you're going to die. But it's not reality. It's the body and mind fighting the momentous change that is inches away.

I feel like I'm going to die as Senator Harwell Bosworth stares at me, clearly stunned by my resistance.

Lindsay grins.

Drew and Silas don't react.

The grey at his temples is clipped close to his head, the line between brown and distinguished fade so perfect. It could have been drawn by an engineer with a straight-edge and a pencil. His eyes are the same color as mine. Wrinkles flirt with the edge of skin around his eyes. His eyelashes are short and stubby, while mine are long, curling up like my mother's. He has an aquiline nose and small moles that cluster near one nostril, a light, flat smattering of melanin that gives him character.

I stare. I observe. I collect details. It's all I have of him.

My heart zooms, unaccustomed to being looked at so closely

at by someone with so much power. The senator barely gave me two glances most of my life. His full attention is a threat, an intimidation, an inevitability that says I'd better fall in line.

Or else.

I swallow hard, my throat dry, and ride out *or else*.

"Jesus. You're just like Lindsay. I thought you were more–"

"Invisible?" I accuse.

"Sensible."

"You want me to go away."

"No." He gives me a look filled with a strange compassion mingled with anger. "No, I don't. But I don't have a plan for you. We're inventing the plan hour by hour, minute by minute."

Silas slowly slips his hand over mine, threading his fingers, squeezing hard, then releasing, our skin still touching. His message is loud and clear.

My relief is evident, my body relaxing instantly. I've been holding my breath and tightening my shoulders without realizing it. Now that Silas is here, biology kicks in. It overrides psychology. The body knows.

The body can't be lied to.

"Silas, would you, Lindsay, and Drew leave?" Harry says again.

No one moves.

Silas looks at me, then Lindsay, then back to me, studying my face. "I'll stay."

"No one gave you permission. Get out. And take Lindsay and Drew with you," Harry snaps.

"I can't do that."

"That's a direct order."

"I'm not here on official business, sir. I'm off duty."

Harry's eyes ping quickly between Silas and me. He scoffs. "Drew and Lindsay are bad enough. You two?" He gives Silas a cold, even stare. "Given *your* background and your sister's drug addiction? Marshall is going to need to add an entire team to manage your relationship with my daughter." He lowers his voice on the last two words. It's really, really weird that the senator is doing this in a public place.

So weird, I start to get paranoid. For a man shrouded in secrecy, this feels *off*.

The words *my daughter* make me jolt. Lindsay is his daughter. I'm just Jane. Anya's daughter, Lindsay's friend.

You know. The extra young woman.

The *extra*.

At the words "my daughter," Lindsay gapes at Harry. And then it hits me. This is what it takes to make her leave. He's doing it on purpose. I almost feel bad for her. *Almost*. I'm too busy trying to manage my own internal chaos. I have no energy to help her.

Lindsay and Drew suddenly get up, sliding out of the booth and standing.

And just like that, they're gone, leaving me alone with Silas and my father. My father, who has just hit Silas with one hell of an offensive statement.

"Have some respect," I challenge, speaking over the lump of fear in my throat. "Silas's sister just *died*."

"Of an overdose," Harry snaps. "We can't have that kind of event contaminating you now, Jane. We were barely able to get the Tara issue under control. The media is howling about your role in it. The camera footage makes it clear you didn't do it, so law enforcement isn't breathing down our necks, but Jesus Christ, Jane, you're at the center of yet another spectacle. We don't need to add a drug-addict death to the roster of people who seem to mysteriously die when they're connected to you, however fleetingly." His eyes flit to the main door, emotion trying to escape from whatever crevice in his body it can. I look at his hands. They don't shake.

How do people control their insides? All the internal over-whelm and looping can't be contained in me. It comes out. How does my own father–my flesh and blood–not feel it like I do? Stopping the internal calamity would be akin to God reaching deep inside my chest and suspending every part of me, frozen in a single moment of ultimate power.

Maybe that's what I'm seeking.

A god who can do that. When I was little, my mother could

do that. Make the world stop hurting me. As I grew older, her power diminished.

Or so I thought.

It turns out the world is just more evil than any parent's goodness.

So where is my father's divinity?

I break through my whirling-dervish state and tell him, "You sound like Monica. Now I know where she gets it. I always thought she was the one being cruel and horrible with Lindsay, treating her like a knick-knack you put wherever you want it to try to impress people. But you're part of it, too," I marvel. "I may be your daughter, but I won't let you treat me the way you've treated Lindsay all these years. I am not an object. I am not a chess piece you move around a board at your leisure to gain power."

Silas just watches us, a sentry, a soldier, a presence.

A historian of my journey to uncover secrets.

Harry looks at one of his security people, who immediately walks to a small door I hadn't noticed before, and opens it.

"Jane," Harry says, yet again pretending Silas isn't there. "Let's speak in private." He doesn't wait for my answer, instead going into a tiny room, one that seems to be for conferences here at the coffee shop.

I follow. I'm not sure why, but I do.

Hope springs eternal. Or maybe I'm just an emotional masochist.

Sometimes hope is the most toxic substance on earth.

"Lindsay has been a lightning rod in the middle of a mess created by Nolan Corning," he tells me as Silas and I enter the room. Silas pivots to shut the door without being asked.

Harry is completely unflappable. Not one damn word I just said to him is having any emotional impact. "You have no concept of how complex my campaign really is. Whether you like it or not, you're now part of it," he starts.

"I am absolutely not. You don't get to parade me around and turn me into some–"

"Parade you around?" He lowers his voice. "Absolutely not."

The mimic of my own words is jarring. "It's the opposite. We need to keep your paternity status under wraps. *Tight* wraps."

"Then why would you care about Silas's family? His sister's death? It has nothing to do with me."

"Because if the media ever did get wind that you're my daughter, every person you've ever screwed is about to become an open book. You think you're being pursued *now*? Just wait."

Screwed comes out sounding like an accusation. An insult. A moralistic, condescending word designed to put me in my place. Silas's entire body goes tense at the word, his breath picking up, anger and defensiveness kicking up quickly.

"My sex life is no one else's business."

"It is when you're my daughter."

"I should think you'd be more concerned about your *wife's* sex life," I spit back, all caution thrown to the wind. Mythology books are filled with tales of the children of gods discovering the bitterness that comes with fallibility.

And the reckoning never ends well.

He doesn't get the implication for the first few seconds but when he does, I receive a nasty, caustic look. I probably deserve it. I don't care.

Because my words are true.

"Lindsay's biological father is none of your business."

"Apparently, my *own* biological father is none of my business, either! If you had it your way, at least."

The man has a heart. He does. I wish he didn't. This would be so much easier if I could dismiss him as evil. Turning Harry into a villain would make my life simpler.

But he's not evil. He is not a god.

He is human.

And human beings have a remarkable capacity for complexity. For hypocrisy. For believing two truths that contradict each other, but clinging to those truths desperately.

And of course, for love. Our capacity for deep, abiding love is what makes us so complicated.

So stupid.

So careless.

And so, so worth giving a second chance.

"It wasn't just me, Jane. Anya kept the secret as well," he replies. Even he doesn't seem convinced by his own words, running a hand through his hair as his eyes move rapidly, ever calculating. After checking the watch on his left wrist, he just sighs and looks at me again, as if I'm supposed to have some kind of answer to make this all fit neatly into a box so he can move on.

"Too bad she isn't alive to give me her perspective. How am I supposed to believe anything that comes out of your mouth? You've spent my entire life lying to me. My entire life. *Now* I'm supposed to trust you? *Now* I'm supposed to give you the benefit of the doubt? You have a lot of nerve, Senator."

"I do." He reaches into his suit jacket and pulls out a flask. He takes two plastic cups from the water cooler by the door, and pours an inch of amber liquid in the cups.

Then he holds one out to me. He ignores Silas, who takes it all in stride.

"Drink," he says, following his own command, slugging down the shot.

"No, thank you." I want to stay clear. Keep my wits about me. Not be fettered by alcohol.

"This is one of those conversations better conducted under the influence of a shot or two. Trust me." He gives me a wry look I can't decipher.

I take the drink.

And choke it down.

Harry pours himself another shot, consumes it, then takes a deep breath. All of my interactions with him until this moment have been in groups. Lindsay and me and him. The three of us and Monica. My mom and some advisors. Bodyguards.

Crazy meetings where I am moved around like a box of old yearbooks no one wants, but can't bear to get rid of.

He has no true power over me. Letting the press know I'm his biological daughter is a hand grenade clasped in each of our hands, the pin pulled, our palms sweaty.

That pretty much describes my day-to-day existence most of the last year.

"I want to be clear, sir," Silas interrupts, although no one's talking. It feels like a breach of protocol. He's coloring outside the lines, wildly violating every code of conduct I know his job requires.

Then again, he's off duty.

"Get out of the room, Gentian."

"No, sir. Not just yet."

Now it's Silas my father stares at.

"Are you disobeying an order?"

"I am off duty, sir, so there are no orders between us. Only Jane."

Only Jane.

I'm between them, literally and figuratively, my body the midpoint in a line that stretches from my secret-filled past to my hope-filled future. Silas is putting his career on the line to defend me in this ridiculous meeting with a man who won't accept how much he has damaged me.

Defending me is Silas's purpose.

But what is his goal?

"You're not doing yourself any favors, Gentian," my father declares, working the alpha-dog angle, trying to make Silas conform. Testosterone infuses the air like nerve gas. It's toxic. I can taste it on my tongue, feel it drift along my skin, searching for a way in.

Seeking compliance. Conformity.

Submission.

Silas, though, doesn't play my father's game.

Silas has his own rules.

One set of rules for work.

And a wholly new set I'm about to witness.

"I'm not here to ask for favors. I'm here to make sure that Jane gets what she needs." The set of Silas's jaw, the way he holds his body so loose, yet primed, makes me unable to look away. This is a man comfortable with the physical state of aware-ness and vigilance. This is a man whose DNA has built into it the capacity for violence. This is a man who has trained and honed his muscles and mind to kill for a higher purpose.

In this room, right now, *I* am his higher purpose.

That knowledge makes the chaos inside me go still.

"You weren't hired to meet *all* her needs. Especially the ones you've chosen to start with." Harry's eyes flicker with a curmudgeonly glare, one filled with reproach as he stares Silas down.

"If you're alluding to sex, sir, just say so. No need for weasel words."

Harry looks murderous.

"Don't you tell me how to communicate, Gentian. Don't you tell me how to do *anything*."

"Then I'll ask for the same, sir. Don't gaslight Jane. Don't deny her what she needs from *you*."

Harry turns to me, raw and livid. "And what is that, Jane? What do you need from me?" If anger had a color, it wouldn't be red like in the movies.

It would be black.

The color of an endless abyss.

Like his eyes.

"I need the truth," I plead, voice shaking.

"Which truth?"

"*The* truth."

"You're so young. Naïve. You still think there is *a* truth?" He shakes his head. "Cute. Really cute. No such thing exists. If you haven't learned yet that multiple truths exist and come into constant conflict with each other, you have some severe life lessons coming your way." His voice is so smooth, years of public speaking and private schmoozing turning it into a work of art. If I closed my eyes, I could listen to him yelling at me and find it to be a riveting performance.

Sound washes over me, Harry's voice a weapon of beauty, his words the bullets he loads into his throat, his mouth and eyes aimed at me and Silas, the trigger cocked.

If he were going to shoot, we wouldn't even be here. A part of me knows this.

And suddenly, I have the upper hand.

"More severe than being denied my own father for twenty-four years? Or having my car bombed? Being sent tweets describing how men want to gang rape me on live-streaming television like Lindsay was–but worse? Or being sent pictures of snuff films with my face superimposed over the poor victim? How about losing my mother in the most public and humiliating way possible? Or losing our house, my apartment, everything I own, and being reduced to wearing Lindsay's hand-me-downs? You think I haven't suffered? You think I live with some rose-colored glasses on? You're not as smart as you think you are, Senator–*Daddy*–if you think *I'm* naïve."

My voice carries, growing louder and louder, Silas behind me. I can feel his attention, his praise, his support as an almighty roar of protest grows inside me.

"How dare you!" I shout. "You turned my entire life into a lie and you're standing here judging *me*?"

"I am assessing the situation," Harry says sharply, that cold countenance so pervasive. In an instant, my world distills down to one, singular goal: to knock him out of his privileged state of being so shut off from emotion.

Make no mistake: it's a *privilege* to have power without experiencing emotional consequences.

"You're a stone-cold sociopath who would rather see your own daughters suffer for your goals," I accuse, the feel of steel on flesh palpable as each word enters his consciousness.

All the color in Harry's face drains out of him, his eyes going wide, authentic, unfiltered emotion unveiled as I watch his reaction, my gaze holding him accountable.

"No," he rasps. "That isn't true."

"It's closer to the truth than you'll let yourself admit," I respond. "But it's especially true of your wife. What she has done to Lindsay is unconscionable."

To my surprise, Silas and Harry exchange a look. It's fleeting, but inescapable.

I've touched on some piece of information I'm not supposed to know.

All my anger migrates, redistributing between both men.

"Look, Jane, you're clearly distraught right now–" Harry's manipulation sets off my alarms.

"No. I'm clearly *right*."

He looks at his watch. "I have a meeting in one minute. We'll need to table this discussion for another time."

"You can't treat me according to *Robert's Rules of Order*. I'm not on a subcommittee for foreign affairs. I'm not a bill you're considering. I'm your *daughter*. You don't table your *daughter*." My last word catches in my throat, the emotional impact of saying it to his face too much to hide behind a wall of anger. Silas's eyes grow compassionate but his jaw is clenched tight, body primed to step in and protect me.

Me.

Not the future president of the United States.

I walk to the door and realize Harry was right.

That shot of whisky did make a difference.

"I'm tabling *you*, Senator. Effective immediately. I don't want to talk to you. I don't want to hear from you. I don't want your money. I don't want your pity. If you won't give me information– and that is all I need from you–then you don't get *me*. You don't get to control me. You don't get to tell me where to live or what to do. You spent twenty-four years pretending I wasn't your daughter, propping up a back-room lie without filling me in. And for that, you get what you deserve–this."

I exit the room and slam the door.

Then I run.

Before I can reach the door, I'm blocked by Duff and some guy in a suit I don't know. He's the size of a small mountain and has the deadest eyes I've ever seen. The thump of footsteps behind me gets louder as Silas appears, face a controlled mask, minor muscle movement the only hint of turmoil underneath.

"I've got her," he tells them. They move away from the door and I burst through it, running down the sidewalk, not caring what this looks like.

Keeping up appearances is someone else's job.

CHAPTER 12

I run straight into a wall. A cloth-covered, finely tailored wall.

Drew's body surprises me as I crash into him and Lindsay. She's right next to him, and while I should have seen them as I fled the coffee shop, some part of my flight response doesn't track them in my sight.

I fall backwards as if Drew were made of stone, and as I fall my knee cracks against the broken, crooked sidewalk, pain radiating through my bones. Skin tears and blood rushes to the surface to repair the injury, my language centers cut off for a moment as my mind becomes a screaming red cloud.

Drew's hand goes to the holster on his belt, hovering, as Silas appears, his worried face over mine.

"Get me out of here," I demand as he helps me stand. Duff walks swiftly to a black SUV and Silas helps me to the door, gently lifting me up as I wince in pain. I look at my knee and see a constellation of older bruises around the raw, broken flesh. This is who I am.

A map of mottled wounds.

I'm running away from my father, who is arguably one of the most powerful men in the country.

But there's someone even more powerful in my life, and he's

113

climbing into the SUV next to me, slamming the door shut as Duff peels out and leaves Harry's retinue staring at us. No sign of Harry.

No expectation he would follow me.

"What an ass," I say, working hard to control my breath. "Why would he come all the way to the coffee shop like that, Silas?"

"I don't know. How bad is it?"

It takes me a second to realize he's asking about my knee.

"It hurts. A lot. But I've endured worse."

"I know. I've watched you. I've seen the bruises and the cuts." His face hardens. He reaches into a flat pouch behind Duff's seat and extracts a small first-aid kit. I wince in anticipatory pain from future alcohol swabs. He sees me wince and his eyebrows do this adorable thing where it's clear he knows exactly what I'm thinking.

Silas is giving me anticipatory *compassion*.

"It's going to hurt," he says apologetically as he pulls the antiseptic torture device out from the foil packet.

"Duh. It won't hurt more than anything else I've experienced in the last week."

"Has it really been only a week? Feels like a lifetime."

"Thanks. Glad to know the seconds tick like days when you're around me."

"Time stops when we're together, Jane," he says in a light-hearted voice.

Before I can answer, he quickly presses the alcohol swab on my open wound. I hiss sharply and arch my back in pain, then slowly let out my breath.

"Damn, that hurts."

"Sorry." He's being clinical and calm, the word robotic.

"It's my own fault. I ran into Drew and fell."

"I saw."

"I couldn't stay in that room with my–with Harry–one second longer."

"He didn't deserve your attention."

That statement makes me well up. None of the scrapes or bruises do, but his empathy... oh, how it pierces me.

"Hey," he says softly. "It's okay." He uses the edge of his index finger to wipe away a stray tear, his touch making my cheek stretch up with a smile.

"Where to?" Duff asks from the front seat.

Silas looks at me with an expression that hands me the world.

"Home," he answers Duff. "Take us home."

I lean against him, twitching here and there as he cleans and bandages the wound on my knee, which is now swelling like it's imitating a baseball. I close my eyes and let myself sink into his body, relishing how my head feels against his shoulder, my ear against his jacket, the scent of his warmth and how it all mingles inextricably.

I let myself drift off, comfort and peace in the casual freedom to cross invisible lines between us, and soon there is no pain, no discomfort, no fear.

No light.

I'm running in the darkness, in a cavernous cocoon covered in velvet and slime. It runs along my bare ankles, coating my feet. The sound makes me want to rake my eyeballs, pull out my hair, cut off my ears. Squinch squinch, *it echoes.*

Squinch.

"Silas!" I scream, my voice boomeranging back to me, wet and thick like mucus.

He doesn't reply.

I fall, my knees thick in the black fluid, my lungs pressed flat like pancakes. I can't breathe, but I crawl, my fingernails breaking off as I dig into the slime and pull myself forward, frantic. The slime turns to thick, black dirt, the kind with fertilizer in it, the smell like a flower shop,

My feet turn into roots, splitting with a terrific pain that feels like a thousand razor blades are slitting my bones, turning me into slivers with roots that spiral out like tentacles, tendrils seeking to violate and invade.

As I open my mouth to scream, I see a man in a fine suit, his back to me, hands in his pockets, body loose and casual yet confident in his power.

My heart slams in my chest, then slows, smacking against the wall of ribs it finds, until the noise inside me turns to a slippery, sloppy sound.

Squinch.

Squinch.

Squinch.

"Jane," the man says in a cultured voice, one that feels like ice invades every hole I have, making me scream with lungs so flat, they aren't real. My body tries to breathe but it's forgotten how.

The room goes grey. Mist swirls around me as I click my tongue, my neck laboring to stop the involuntary spasms of my lungs. Pain rips through my throat. The muscles strain and shred in order to bring me oxygen. The edges around my vision start to ripple, like lightning twisted by a blacksmith to track my periphery —

"Jane?" Silas's soft, rumbling voice comes through like we're underwater. He plants a kiss on my temple. "Jane. We're here. Home."

I jolt, realizing I've drifted off, inhaling sharply through my nose as my jaw tightens, suppressing a yawn. Tingling pain shoots through my right leg. It's fallen asleep, the pins-and-needles sensation making me shake it over and over, a little too panicked in my attempts.

What was I dreaming about?

Fear grips me, the sense hard to shake. My muscles don't know whether to be loose or tight, whether to stretch or constrict. I'm coming out of slumber. In the awkward in-between, I have no ability to regulate or calibrate.

Silas does it for me.

Leading me into our building–it's so strange to think that way, but it *is* ours–we take the elevator up, Silas insisting I lean on him for support. As I make my halting way to my apartment door, he continues to his, taking three steps back to touch my elbow.

"My place," he says, his eyes filling with a series of emotions that feel infinitely more complicated than what they are: desire.

"I'm fine in my apartment."

"You have a blow-up mattress as a bed."

"It's on a cot. It's comfortable."

"I'm not inviting you over to have sex, Jane. I'm inviting you to my place because you need to recuperate on a proper bed."

"Why not sex?" I blurt out, unable to hide the disappointment in my voice.

His eyes darken, his smile wide like a predator's.

"I told you. I don't want to be a revenge screw." His smile turns to something more contemplative.

"You're not."

"I don't want you to sleep with me in anger."

"Then we're never sleeping together, Silas, because all I *am* is angry these days."

"Jane."

"If you don't want me, I understand. You heard what my father said. You'll be hounded by the media and–"

His kiss is relentless, hard and demanding, a kiss that takes your breath away at the same time it stokes a flame. My fingertips dig into his business shirt so hard my knuckles ache. The warmth of his chest through his clothes makes me want more. I want to strip him naked and spend the next few days exploring him. I want his bed to become my playground. I want a world where we're the only people in it.

I want a lot I can't have.

But this? From the way he's kissing me, I don't have to just want. I can actually *get*.

My bad knee makes me wobble in his arms, a thick arm around my waist in a split second, holding me up. Suddenly, I'm airborne, in Silas's arms as he walks to his door. Balancing me against his chest while pulling out his keys, he makes me laugh.

"I don't need to be carried like this," I protest.

"Oh, yes, you do."

He kicks the door open, closes it behind him, and I click the deadbolt. Expecting to be dumped on the couch, I realize that's not where we're going.

Heat pools between my legs, rushing fast like raging rapids, making my blood sing. My heart speeds up and I'm aroused, my clothes too tight, too much, my fingertips seeking the skin at the base of Silas's throat.

I need to touch him. Skin to skin. All of it. Every bit.

And from the way he lays me gently down on his bed, stretching his arms and using his legs to lower me until I'm resting on the duvet like a feather pushed by the wind, I'm pretty sure he'd like to touch every inch of me, too.

"Let me get that knee an ice pack."

"How about you kiss me and make me feel better?"

He gives me a searching look. His hair still has that slightly overgrown style that makes him even more attractive, and his chin and cheeks are covered with more than a five o'clock shadow. The scruff gives him a bad-boy appearance. Add in those bright-blue eyes and oh, the scent of him transports me out of pain and into a mood for so much more.

"Are you sure?" His request for consent lights up deep crevices in my soul, more arousing than sex, more worshipful than anything he could do to or for me. "Because I do want you, Jane. I just don't want you to want me for the wrong reasons."

"I don't want to sleep with you because of my father. I'm not like that."

"How do you know?"

"How do I know what?" We're so close to each other, mouths inches apart, that our words are warming the space between us.

"That you're not like that? Everyone changes. We morph and alter ourselves to fit reality."

"Not my essence, Silas. Who I am is rock solid. I have a center that doesn't change." I take his hand and put it on my belly, right above my navel. "And that center wants *you*."

He reaches between us, his fingers finding me swollen, the way he touches my throbbing core a breathtaking augmentation of the sensuality we share. Instant electricity fires through my blood. As his lips touch mine, a sweet gateway opens up, the doors parting like my lips, letting him enter with an open-ended invitation to come, stay a while.

And enjoy yourself.

Our first time in bed was cautious, slow, smooth, and new. This time, we're revisiting familiar territory, but from a place of less hesitation. His command resonates in the way he holds my arm, sliding along the stretch of skin with a palm determined to make it clear I can't escape.

Not that I want to.

There is a possession this time, a fiery authority in the way he kisses me, how his touch is designed to make me lose control, the insistence in the way his breath catches. When our eyes meet as he covers me with his gloriously sculpted body, I see something new.

I see how he wants me.

I see how he wants to *own* me.

A spark, deep in my belly, rises up out of the shameful abyss and ignites an energy field between us that pulses. I match his intensity, my mouth hard against his, tongue drawing him in, in, in. My breasts tingle with anticipation, the line of sensation spreading across my entire body until his touch is exquisite, growing rougher. When his fingers thread in my hair and pull gently, I moan.

I *want* to be owned.

By him.

I want someone else to take command as a result of my own surrender. I need to be cared for, to give in with relief to the authority of someone who cares for me. Dare I think it?

Who *loves* me.

A whirling dervish only comes to rest when the spirit is done. I only come to rest when I am in his arms, safe and sated. Right now, I crave him to the point of madness. I need him to take charge.

"You like that?" he murmurs against my mouth.

"Am I supposed to?"

"There are no rules when it comes to pleasure, Jane. You like what you like. Actually, there is one rule: you have to tell me. You have to tell me what you like so I can give it to you." His free hand glides down my side, cupping my ass, fingers digging in just enough to make my core clench, throbbing.

"I like this. I like it when you touch me like you–" I can't say it, suddenly shy, so I kiss him, long and hard.

He pulls back and looks at me with eyes I cannot lie to. "Say it." Voice dropping, Silas becomes a sharper version of the man I know, immutable and unyielding.

I become one long nerve ending.

"Like you own me."

Oh, that grin. The way his lips move, parting with a movement so richly emotional, so devilishly tantalizing. I didn't know he could look like this, like a wolf about to corner his prey.

"I don't yet. I haven't earned the right. But if you'll let me do the work, someday, Jane, I would very much like to own this." His fingers flutter over my breast, making me gasp. "And this." His grabs my ass, possession turning me into a ball of ecstasy. As he lifts himself up slightly, that same hand slides easily between us, instantly finding the part of me that loses touch with reality, his circular motions driving all thought from my mind. "And this. Let go, Jane. Do it. Do it now," he says, the last word a long, drawn-out whisper that comes with a wet tongue on the pulse at my neck, the twin sensations driving me up, up, up into his hand until I explode.

The world goes tight, then expansive. I grab for him to hold on, to stay here, to make sure I don't shatter into a thousand tiny pieces, his chest my only anchor, the light hair a reminder of humanity, the broad, rounded strength of his shoulders keeping me firmly on earth. I am slickness and rhythm, his body rough against mine, giving and giving in a way that makes me see he's actually taking and taking and *taking*.

By releasing myself to his administered pleasure, I'm giving to him.

So I give. And give. And give...

"I want you," I tell him, the words hard to form as pleasure steals my tongue, Silas quickly putting on a condom, the motion fluid and swift. He understands, gliding into me with a hot relief that makes my hips move up against him, hard, his right hand grabbing both of my wrists and pinning them above me. I squirm, the press of our bodies too much, the sensation exploding with waves of exquisite, overly sensitive touch.

But he does not let me escape my own pleasure.

"Harder," I beg, the deep piece of me inside that revels in this crying out for *me*.

He plunges into me, hammering as I curl myself around him. I transcend all the pain, all the chatter, all the crazy blame and shame of my life. I become my true self as he unlocks a vital part of me, giving no quarter, making me face what he offers with his body, his hands, his mouth.

It's nothing short of perfection.

His body tenses above mine and I know that soon he'll take pleasure from me, too. The thrill that races through my blood meets with the moment he crashes into me again. I am open, nothing, everything, the drop of sweat on his brow, the wild look in his eyes, the tense forearm that holds me up. I am him and he is me and we race off into the wind, moaning at the enormity of what we've created with our bodies.

When I relinquish myself to him, I find freedom. I find sanctuary and rest. I find pleasure and pain that feels so good.

I find me.

Long, slow, important breaths fill the air between us, as if what just happened requires more oxygen than usual. My heart won't stop tap dancing, electric impulses dotting my inner thighs, the sense that my body knows its own set of rules that it won't share with my mind becoming evident. Silas rolls off me, serious, his fingers letting go of my wrists in a way that leaves me more empty than when he slides out of me.

We rest in silence, breath slowing.

"That was..." He lets out a long breath, one filled with wonder.

"Yes," I reply, our economy of words both affirming and amusing. He feels it, too.

Thank God he feels it.

"I want you to know," he says slowly, raking his hair with a steady hand, "that I meant what I said. Tell me. Tell me what turns you on. Tell me what fires you. Tell me your dirtiest thoughts."

"Silas!" I laugh, embarrassed and surprised, turned on and pleased.

"You said you want me to own you." He turns to me, eyes so dark, they're like ink. "How far do you want to take that?"

"As far as you're willing to go."

"That's... far."

I shiver, a quick and sudden move, involuntary but triggered by his words.

He pulls back, sensing he's pushed too far. Maybe he has.

Maybe he hasn't.

"We'll go slow," he assures me.

"Are you getting paid to sleep with me?" I ask him, changing the subject as we rest our naked bodies in bed, limbs flung against each other, chests rising and falling in ever-slowing patterns as our hearts try to find their regular beats again.

"Technically?" Tilting his head, he looks away from me, processing my question, running internal data to determine the right answer.

"There's no 'technically' to having sex. You do or you don't," I point out.

"Then I guess so. Yes." He looks surprised, then *very* pleased with himself. "We don't file time cards. I'm salaried, so..."

"Sex with me is a fringe benefit?"

"It ranks up there with employer-paid health insurance, free gym membership, and my commuter reimbursement."

"Pretty sure it should be your top fringe benefit, Silas."

"I don't know, Jane. My company gym is pretty damn nice." He flashes me a wicked grin.

"If Drew finds out, he'll kill you."

"Drew? Andrew Foster? I don't care if he knows. He's the guy who slept with Senator Harwell Bosworth's daughter while on duty."

I go quiet, holding my breath for a second, my skin going numb with shock.

And then I say:

"*You* are sleeping with Bosworth's daughter, too."

"Damn. That's right."

I let out a tired chuckle. "My life is a *Maury* show."

He thinks about that for a minute. "It's more like *Maury* meets *Scandal*."

"Thanks, Silas. That makes me feel so much better. You have a way with words. You should pitch scripts in Hollywood."

"Too stressful."

"More stressful than being ex-special ops and guarding people surrounding a presidential candidate? And me?"

"Even I have limits."

He gets a pillow in the face.

And I get pinned to the bed on my back, Silas straddling me, his hands holding me in place like restraints, unbreakable. Unshakeable.

Then again, I don't want to escape. Not from him.

As he bends down to kiss me, he slides his legs and hips until every inch of him that can touch me is pressing down, our hip bones grinding, our ribs interlinking. His body hair tickles my smooth skin, his lips full and heated as he kisses me. I open my legs and guide him right in. No preliminaries. No foreplay.

Just the pull of being one, together.

He reaches for his bedside drawer.

"I'm on the pill," I gasp, impatient and needy. His eyes widen with a flash of heat.

"You didn't say anything before."

"I didn't — no. But I am now," I whisper before he kisses me, demanding even more.

This time it's quick, powerful, and hard, our climaxes fast and furious. As Silas thrusts into me, I reach up to grab the headboard, wrapping my legs around his waist like I'm holding on for dear life, like I'm drowning and he's my only hope. I lose my grip on the headboard and he grabs my wrists, pinning them above my head again. The raw power and dominance of that one move makes me come.

Hard.

So hard, I scream and buck up into him, our rhythm erratic until it's not, the perfect motion a sine wave of unadulterated lust. He's no longer Silas. He is inside me, spinning me through new orbits, and I'm no longer Jane.

I am a woman whose soft edges have frayed until all I am is waves of orgasms, carrying me so far away from everything I know that I need the tether of him.

His shout of climax is a victory, the push of his tip against the furthest part of me a battering that feels so final, so serene, so hot and rough. I feel taken.

I need to feel taken, swept away, stolen for this joining.

As he comes inside me, I ride out the waves of complete surrender, floating on an endless sea where this is no moon, no sun, no stars.

Just him.

The erratic brush of hot breath against my shoulder chills me as Silas's short rasps of air reach my sweaty skin. We are sticking together, not just where he's in me, but everywhere. My awareness focuses from a blur to a sharper edge as my orgasms trail off, Silas's body big and gravid over me, his arms caging me still, my hands above the top of my head.

Like a crown.

For whatever reason, we don't say a word. He kisses me on the lips, so softly, so gently, as he lets go of my wrists and rolls away, pulling me into his arms. I curl against his bare chest and inhale slowly, savoring his scent.

Minutes pass. Or maybe it's centuries. Who knows? Time slips away, leaving me be.

Finally, I venture his name. "Silas?"

He doesn't answer. His breath takes on an even sound. It slowly hits me. He has fallen asleep. A huge grin takes over my face, my muscles enjoying the luxury of joy coming out of my pores without inhibition. I couldn't control this if I tried.

Why would I try?

And that is how I fall asleep, in his arms, grinning because finally, finally, I have a reason.

A damn fine one.

CHAPTER 13

*T*he lack of coffee scent wafting through the room and the cold bedsheets next to me tell me everything I need to know.

Silas is gone.

Panic doesn't set in. After last night, he won't ghost on me. Duty must be calling. Silas has a job, a niece, a mom to deal with, after all. I get more of his time than anyone else in the world. Sharing him with his responsibilities is part of life.

I don't have to like it, though.

Duff, I suspect, is out in the living room, working from his phone like all of the security guys. I take a moment to regroup. Yes, it means a delay in getting caffeine in my bloodstream, but as I stretch out on the bed, my fingertips grazing the headboard as my toes splay and my body stretches like a Michelangelo schematic, I relax into the mattress and think.

The sheets smell like Silas.

Inhaling, I let my monkey-mind jump and hoot for a few seconds, settling down until I can organize it.

I'm cleared in Tara's death. Official cause: suicide. Real cause: homicide. Actual murderer: still out there.

I'm Senator Harwell Bosworth's daughter. Official line: I'm

not. Truth: I am, and Monica hates me while Harry tries to control me without giving me information I'm entitled to have.

I'm re-establishing a friendship with Lindsay as she trusts me more and more.

I'm sleeping with Silas.

I have my own apartment, even if my bed is a camping cot. It's *mine*.

Lots of pieces of my life are starting to re-assemble, like a quilt that's falling apart but being put back together, stitch by stitch, seam by seam.

But Drew still doesn't trust me.

"Sounds like a well-rounded life," I mutter to myself as I pull up to a sitting position in bed and sigh. My skin feels so empty without Silas touching it. I press my palm flat against the part of the bed where he slept, seeking out any remnants of his body heat. I'm probably imagining it, but I swear it's there. He's so solid, so strong, so real.

And tonight... what about tonight? How much longer will I have him?

Slipping into his sweats, I walk into the kitchen to find a full pot of coffee with a Post-it note on it. Very messy, hasty handwriting says:

See you tonight. S.

That's one question in my life answered.

I grin as I pour myself a cup of coffee and call out, "Morning, Duff."

"Morning," replies a deep male voice. "Sleep well?" I perk my ears to catch any hint of innuendo about me and Silas, but his voice is maddeningly neutral.

"I did. And you?"

"Like a baby. Which means I wake up every twenty minutes and fuss."

I've heard the joke before. In fact, my mom used to make it all the time when she was alive. But like I did with her, I laugh to be polite.

"Coffee?" I ask him, holding up the pot and peering into the living room.

He shakes his head and returns his attention to his phone. "I'm fine."

"I didn't ask how you were. I asked if you wanted coffee."

"I don't drink–" He waves his hand dismissively. "–that."

I look at the pot in my hand with arched eyebrows. "What am I drinking? I thought it was coffee!"

"It is. I just don't drink it."

"What do you drink?"

"Espresso."

"Oh. I see. Duff the Coffee Snob."

"Something like that."

"I thought cops drank awful coffee as part of the job."

"I'm not a cop."

This conversation is going nowhere. Even though I'm in a fabulous mood, I can tell that if I keep talking to Duff, it'll take the shine off my sense of well being. I cut my losses and go back to the kitchen, searching Silas's fridge for milk.

Coffee in order, I take a seat at the dining table and scan my phone for texts. Ignoring nasty emails is hard. I set up a filter in my email account so that any email containing certain insults, including four-letter words like *slut* and another one that begins with *c*, go straight to spam.

That doesn't mean plenty of other nastygrams don't make it through, though.

Spam. *Spam spam spam.* You'd be surprised how much energy people who don't even know me will pour into diatribes designed to shame me. Or drive me to madness. To make me hurt myself.

The emails don't work.

But they do *create* work. I have to filter it all out so I can get to my actual life. The tiny little preview on each email tends to include only the intro to the rants. I'm the whore of Babylon. I need to have a dick shoved down my throat until I asphyxiate. I should be covered in honey and left to rot on an aircraft carrier.

And then there are the biblical ones, all signed by pastors. Or at least, people pretending to be men of the cloth. On the internet, because of anonymity cloaks, you can be *anyone.*

Some people spend their spare time pretending to be religiously ordained so they can morally excoriate me in the interest of lifting themselves above me.

The hours they spend creating these long rants are intriguing. Not the people behind the rants–the hours themselves. Imagine if we could collectively harness all those hours and minutes and put them in a holding tank, to be doled out for good? What if each minute of rage-filled cathartic writing was instead spent teaching people in a developing nation how to install a well for clean water? Too bad the world doesn't work that way. We should be able to re-purpose time itself.

We can recycle physical goods. We can reorient and change our physical direction. We can change our minds. Why can't we change time?

Silly thoughts, I know, but it's a psychological defense when you get enough troll mail like this. A thick skin is useful, but I need to create some kind of mental defense for the hardiest of shitlords. The sheer volume of hate mail and messages and memes I get means I have to think about alternatives, because if humanity is really this sick, then I give up.

And I won't let them make me give up.

"Whatever you're reading, it's bad for your face," Duff says from across the room, standing and slipping his phone into his jacket pocket, revealing the small holster belt that holds his gun. "That frown is going to freeze in place and then you'll look like most of my clients."

I give him a wry smile, a reflection of my inner state. "What I'm reading is bad for humanity."

I had no idea you could do so much with Photoshop.

My trolls show me *alllll* the new features. That picture in the news of me covered in Tara's blood is pure gold from a media perspective. I'm sure I'm getting more clicks than a cheap ballpoint pen in the hands of a nervous sixteen-year-old taking a written driver's test at the DMV.

"Hate mail again?"

"Again? It's never stopped. Just more of it."

"Why read it?"

"I have legitimate email to read, mixed in there."

"You don't have someone from The Grove scrubbing it?"

"If they are, they're doing a lousy job. Besides, I like to know my enemies and their tactics. It'll take more than bodyguards for me to stay safe."

His eyebrow twitches, the only sign of emotion. "Don't go rogue."

"Rogue?"

"You have the best team in charge of your security, Jane." He's so serious. "They know exactly what they're doing. No one else could have kept you alive this long."

I don't know what to say. How do you comment on *that*?

"You really think someone would have killed me?"

"Was the car bomb a fake? Were the bullets that gunman was shooting at The Grove fake? Was Tara's blood fake?"

"No."

"There's your answer. If you don't understand that without Drew, Silas, and your fath...er, the team, that you'd be dead by now, you haven't been paying attention."

Self-righteous anger plumes through me, like someone injected a bolus straight to the heart. "I do nothing *but* pay attention, Duff." I storm out of the room and slam the bathroom door, effectively trapping myself. Silas's bathrobe is hanging on the back of the door. I reach for it as if he's inside it, my face buried in the light flannel. It smells like him, a heady mix of soap and skin, reminding me of sex last night. In an instant, I'm warm and wet in all the wrong places, needing his body, his mouth, his hands.

Him.

I strip down to nothing and turn on the shower, determined to get out of this apartment and breathe in fresh air. A friendly face is what I need. The act of going out in public without fear feels revolutionary. Rebellious.

Free.

My quick shower is perfunctory, just thorough enough to

make me feel human. As I dry off, I shove my body back into the same sweats I wore last night and move into the bedroom, where a neatly folded set of clothes is waiting for me, as if it patiently knew I'd discover it.

There really is a point where being micromanaged feels like prison.

But this moment isn't it.

I dress, surprised by how the clothing I didn't choose fits me like a glove. A sleek purple sweater, lightweight yet warm, with a V-neck that is modest yet flattering. Pale grey slacks made with some stretchy material that covers my curves like it was tailored for me. My bra–the one I wore here–is folded in the collection. It slowly dawns on me that Silas did this.

Silas picked these clothes for me.

Only a man who had touched my body, admired me from afar and up close, could choose such an outfit. Only a man who paid exquisite attention to my coloring, my shape, my features, my body's architecture, could dress me like this. A thrill of anticipation shoots through me like a live wire.

Imagining my own hands are his, I hug my hips with my palms, riding up from the swell of my ass to the curl of ribs under my breasts. He's white lightning in my mind, the transmission of imagination into skin possible only because he is the center of my fantasy. Tonight, he comes back to me. I know this in my core, his presence now a solid fact in a world of conjecture.

Tonight he comes back to me.

And tonight I give him more pieces of my soul to keep.

This lifeline of Silas tugs at my heartstrings, gratitude allowing the tears to come. Mourning all I've lost is a luxury, but it's one Silas gives me now. The space to grieve is hard fought. He fights for me, though. *For* me.

Not against me.

Not anymore.

My vision is blurred through tears, and as I reach for the dresser to quell my shaking nerves, a small note brushes against my fingertips, fluttering to the ground. I bend to retrieve it and find the same horrible scrawl of Silas's hand.

For you, it says simply. *Wear this tonight*.

My hand goes back to my hip and I feel a small bump along the point where hipbone curls into the delicious start of flesh Silas kissed last night. Fumbling in the small pocket, I find a surprise.

A necklace.

"You bastard," I whisper, laughing until I can't tell the difference between my tears and my grief. The necklace is beautiful, a purple gemstone surrounded by spun platinum, the braided metal custom designed.

Encircling the stone is a series of small holes. The pattern is intricate, designed to look like Celtic knots, gorgeous in the simplicity of geometry.

Behind the gemstone is a very small, solid silver piece.

Which holds a battery.

Silas's beautiful gift is also a horrid reminder of reality. The twin revelations of his romantic gesture and his pragmatic protectiveness fight inside me, outrage and love in a sweaty, twisted battle for dominance.

Everything I experience will be monitored.

And every step I make will involve constant protection.

By him.

Slipping the delicate chain around my neck, I accept this. I accept the collaring of a man who won't compromise when it comes to my safety. I accept the haunting beauty of his multi-layered gift.

I accept the team of guards who will be fierce and careful in Silas's absence. Duff is still wrong, but my anger toward him dissipates as I stare down at the purple stone that rests just above the swell of my breasts.

I surrender to Silas, and only him.

This is how he loves. With beauty and pragmatism. He cannot do one without the other.

Which will be his downfall?

A curious madness makes me rush through getting ready, the need to get out of here such a strong impulse, out of the blue. Living in my own head, even for a short time this morning, is too much. A few minutes later, I walk into the living room, pockets filled with my phone and a small wallet. I leave without saying a word to Duff.

Who simply follows.

Walking into the hallway and stomping down all the stairs, I burst into the sunshine with a heart that feels like a thousand butterflies all folded together. The second I breathe air from the wind that says hello with a light caress of sunshine, I smile.

And I walk.

Wherever I want to go, I go.

My legs stretch with ever-lengthening strides as I gain confidence, remembering a former self who used to have the freedom to take such a simple walk for granted. Four blocks used to be an annoyance.

Now it's heaven.

Duff doesn't argue with me like he did the other day. Even if he tried, it wouldn't work. Sheer force is what he would need to exert to stop me, and Silas wouldn't tolerate that. Fighting me now is more dangerous than ever before. I'm not the same Jane I was yesterday.

I'll never be the same.

And not because I'm Harwell Bosworth's daughter.

Turning the corner, I see The Thorn Poke, an Open sign on the propped door. A light wind pushes the scent from inside out to me, beguiling and welcoming.

Come in, the scent says. *We're here,* it beckons.

Let's be friends.

Because the door is open, no bell tinkles when I enter. It's just me. Duff stands sentry outside, leaning casually against the store's brick wall, his shoulder touching, legs crossed at the ankle as he looks at his phone. He's the picture of a business man in pause.

In reality, he's a trained beast, ready to leap.

"Hi!" chirps a young woman, the exuberance catching me off guard, making me jump a little.

"Oh, did I scare you?" Her hands fly to her mouth in embarrassment, eyes wide, forehead creased with worry. "I am so, so sorry!" She's behind the counter and curls her hip just so as she steps around, the motion so practiced, she probably doesn't realize she does it.

"It's okay," I say, laughing. "You wouldn't be the first."

"That kind of day, huh?"

"That kind of year," I blurt out before I can stop myself.

Her creased brow deepens. "Did... um..." Her entire demeanor shifts, as if she's correcting herself. "Are you here for a memorial or a funeral arrangement?"

"What? Oh. No." I smile at her, trying to remember how to be normal with strangers again. It's liberating and awkward. "I'm just... I'm just being silly. I'm here because I want to buy something cheerful."

"Then you've come to the right place!" Her eyes are familiar, hair the same color as mine is now, the cut really similar. She's giving me the same careful evaluation I'm giving her. It's unnerving.

"I'm Lily," she says, stretching out her hand to shake mine. When we touch, I realize what it is. But she says it first.

"We could be twins," she says matter-of-factly, now openly looking me up and down. "You're an inch or two taller than me, and your hair is shorter and more layered, but wow! Your eyes, your build. It's the same. Are we long lost cousins or something? I... I think we've met our doppelgängers."

I can't process that yet. I'm too stuck on her name. "Lily? Your real name is Lily and you work in a flower shop?"

"My parents own the place." She shrugs.

"Did they name all their kids after flowers?"

"Yep. My brother, Chrysanthemum, goes by Chris. And my sister is Nasturtium. Her nickname is Nasty."

"You're joking."

She starts to laugh, the giggle infectious. "Yes. I am. My siblings are actually Gwen and Bowen."

I laugh with her, slightly embarrassed. "I'll bet people ask you that all the time. Sorry."

"I don't mind." Her shrug is friendly. "It's social glue."

"Excuse me?"

"It gives people something to talk about. Flowers are about feeling good. Or, if not good, feeling better. About social glue and connection. You don't send flowers to people you hate. You send them to express emotion. Complete strangers come in here and when they learn my name is Lily, it gives them something to ask. A common topic."

"You're saying that even if someone comes here to send flowers to a funeral, they can talk about your name?"

"Happens all the time."

"Well, Lily, it worked." I grin at her. "I'm Jane."

"I know who you are."

Oh, no.

"And I think it's just awful what the media have done to you."

Oh, *wow*.

"You–you do?"

"No one could be as evil and conniving as they say you are. No one. Especially someone my age. I'm twenty-three. You're, like, close, right? I know women my age. No way, even if I were a political insider, could I do all the crimes they say you've done. You're being set up."

"How do you know this?"

"Because my tinfoil hat tells me so."

"Is it right most of the time?"

"So far, one hundred percent right."

"Thank you." I soften. "You don't have to say that about me."

"I wouldn't say it if it weren't true! I only lie to people's faces when they make atrocious flower choices but I can tell they're dead set on them."

"What's an atrocious flower choice?"

"The wrong combo. You know. Like fonts."

"Fonts?"

"Font styles can be beautiful on their own, but combine the wrong two and you get nothing but visual garbage."

Through the window in the flower shop door, I see Duff lift his hand to his ear piece. Uh oh. Never a good sign.

"Besides, *everyone* tells me I look like you. Do you know how hard it's been to be teased like that for the last year?" she says seriously.

"I can imagine," I say, but the words come out like I've been breathing helium.

Her face drains of color, the paleness so strange on her friendly face. "Oh, geez. I'm such an idiot. I didn't mean it like that. Compared to what you're living through, my experience is nothing! I'm sorry."

"No need to apologize."

"Is that what you mean about a rough year?"

"Yes."

"And you're here to..."

"Feel better."

"That I can help you with, Jane! Flowers can't cure any problem, but they can make it a little easier to deal with." Her grin is infectious.

For the next five minutes, she takes me on a tour of the store, cheerfully explaining the pros and cons of plants and flowers, teasing out my likes and dislikes. She's so attentive and full of empathy–over flowers.

Flowers.

Little covert glances between us make it clear we're checking each other out, the resemblance too close to be anything but disorienting. I'm definitely the very definition of the term "plain Jane," with boring brown hair (now auburn) and hazel eyes. I blend into crowds. While that is an asset now, when I was younger it made me the extra in any crowd, the dull brown rock in a sea of crystals and gemstones.

But seeing someone else who looks so much like me gives me pause.

Because Lily is beautiful.

"I notice you keep looking at the allium." Her eyes dance

along the edge of my sweater, taking in the purple. "Are you trying to match your clothes?"

I laugh. "No. I just like purple."

She points to my necklace. "I can see that."

And Silas can see you, I almost say. I cover the stone with my hand, suddenly split into two consciousnesses. One is having a lovely time talking about flowers with Lily.

The other feels like a cheap spy.

"That's a lovely stone. It matches the sweater. Was it a present?" She winks. "Boyfriend?" Her eyes take in my bare hand. No rings.

I can't answer that. I freeze. I can't answer her question because I'm suddenly filled with nothing but the stark reality of Silas.

I can't stop thinking about him. As clichéd as that sounds, it is true, yet so much more. I can't breathe without inhaling him. I can't see the world through any other lens than him. He is the air, the stars, the tickle of wind against my cheeks, the damp flush of misty rain that brushes my neck.

I am in a kind of sexual madness. Silas throbs between my legs. His pulse is mine, his sweat-soaked heat warming my skin even when he is gone. I live in a world no one else inhabits but him, and he knows it. Feels it.

There is no way *not* to know, because when the world pinpoints into a tiny space with only one other being, you know all there is to know about them.

Thank God.

My body yearns for him seconds after we stop touching. Attuned to his scent, his touch, his carriage and movement, I wait in the space between our touches, pause in suspended animation, a shell that operates under the most basic of commands.

I speak with people. I buy food and eat it. Drinking coffee is a rote behavior.

Unless we are connected, I am less.

When we are connected, we are everything.

Obsession like this isn't healthy. I know that. The problem

with obsession is that it feeds itself, desperate to stay alive. The wanting isn't rational. It is all-consuming and designed to be so. Highs that come from just looking at Silas, the glance triggering memories of his mouth against my breast, his fingers skimming the swell of my thigh, the boneless relief of orgasms elicited– those highs come from obsession.

If obsession is irrational, then I reject all reason.

Pleasure that comes from obsession is too great to reject wholesale, too divine to dismiss as insanity.

"Uh, Jane?" Lily's hand on my shoulder breaks me out of the exotic spell Silas has me in. "You okay?"

"What? Yes. Fine."

"You're flushed. Are you feeling faint?"

My pulse throbs between my legs. The touch of my bra fabric against my nipples is torture. Shivers take over every inch of my skin like a tsunami storming the shore, pushing up into my veins, sending wild memories of sex and Silas's scent through every nerve ending I possess.

He possesses me, even when I'm not in his orbit.

Footsteps, loud and swift, and a shadow covers the right side of me. A hand touches my elbow.

"Jane?" Duff's rough voice shakes me back to a semblance of normalcy. He glares at Lily. "What happened?"

She glares back. "She got a little woozy. Don't look at me like that."

"Like what?" I ask, confused, struggling to pull myself together while ignoring the untamed impulses setting my body into overdrive.

"Like I would ever hurt you."

Duff is a sentry, an emotionless protector who won't be affected by her.

"Please tell me he's not your boyfriend," she pleads in a voice so unlike her friendly demeanor.

"No. He's not."

"Whew."

Duff gives her a cranky smirk, looking more like an eighteenth-century pirate than a twenty-first-century agent. "Why, sweetheart? Relieved I'm single?"

"You wish."

"I'm fine." I don't want him here, interfering with my bubble. Before I can find the right words to make him leave, he just does. Magically, he slips back out to the small area on the sidewalk, this time sitting on a small bench surrounded by geraniums.

"Who is that? Your bodyguard?" she jokes.

"Yes."

All laughter disappears from her face. "Whoa. Really?" Compassion fills her features. For a brief flash, she looks like a younger version of my mother. "I'm so sorry. I can't imagine what your life is like."

"Trade you," I say with a laugh.

She remains serious. "We could. You look enough like me."

"If this were a Hallmark Channel movie, we'd do it, wouldn't we?" I smile at her.

Glancing at Duff through the big picture window, she gives me an uncertain look. "I'm pretty sure your life is more like a Lifetime 'woman in peril' movie. You know. The kind where the guy she trusts most in the world turns out to be her biggest danger."

If Lily had kicked me in the stomach she couldn't have hurt me more.

Shame fills me. It's an instant horror that takes over the body. I have no control over it. My mind can't rationalize it away. Hormones and chemicals released by cells inside me with no external directive flood all of my receptors. My skin crawls. My eyes flitter and jerk, darting left and right as I try to take in visual input and put it neatly in a category where it belongs, store it in short-term memory so I can take in the next piece of sensory input.

Overloaded circuits shut down.

But humans aren't circuit boards.

Instead, we take it and take it, the pile-on of overload reaching critical mass until we go mad.

Madness is a form of self-preservation.

Madness makes systems protect themselves.

Madness is the most elegant of all entropies.

And madness is the end game for people who overload others.

I'm not mad. Insanity would be a welcome break from it all, but that is not my fate.

"Let's get you a nice table display. How about purple, yellow, and white?" Lily's trying to do what I do. Establish normalcy. Unlike so many others, she's not doing it from a position of panic or denial. She's not being fake to cover the horror of who I am and my reality.

She's being kind.

And in my world, that is almost transgressive.

"Irises? Lilies?" she asks, making fun of her own name.

"You're the expert," I tell her with a shaky smile. "Why don't you pick?"

Her eyes light up. "Really? Because customers never say that. They always want me to put together terrible combinations."

"I don't want to be just any customer. Go for it."

For the next ten minutes she hums and putters, checking in for short questions and zipping off, her constant energy a happy sight. It's like watching a hummingbird drink nectar. Lily lightens my world for these few minutes and I'm grateful.

I'll also be back. Money can't buy happiness but it can buy flowers. It can buy time with Lily and her indefatigable charm.

Whirlwind Flower Chick appears suddenly with a breath-taking explosion of color squeezed into an enormous vase in the shape of –

"Is that a unicorn?" I ask, agog.

"YES!" She looks like Buddy the Elf meeting Santa at the mall. "Isn't it just so perfect?"

"For a five-year-old," I say slowly, imagining little Kelly's face if I come home with *this*.

"We all have inner five-year-olds. Color is young. Color is happiness. Unicorns are sparkly happiness, so even better!"

Leave it to me to find the only flower shop in the entire world with Lisa Frank working in it.

"Lily, that's a bit–"

"GORGEOUS!"

"–much."

"No," she says firmly, as if she's my best friend and I need to be put in my place. "No, Jane, it is not a bit much. It is *muchly* much. It is outrageous and bold and over the top and it sings color. That is why you are taking it home with you. And I won't take your money, so you can't say no."

"Huh?"

"It's a gift."

I eye the supernova of flowers with great skepticism. A smile pulls at the corners of my mouth in spite of myself. It is definitely muchly much. You cannot look at a unicorn stuffed with golden sunflowers and daisies and big, purple spider mums and not grin.

"No!" I protest. "Of course I'm paying for it."

"Your money doesn't work here," Lily says, her voice officious and endearing. "I mean it. Spend a day with that happy blossom party in a unicorn and I guarantee you'll be back for more."

"You just referred to a bunch of flowers as 'a happy blossom party.'"

"What else is a bunch of properly balanced flowers in a unicorn vase?"

Good point.

"Lily, this is a business–"

"I'm giving it to you as a freebie. A taste. Besides, if you pay for it, you'll ask me to change it, and I don't want to mess with perfection."

I look at the arrangement again.

"It's like someone took a glitter bomb, portions of a Harold and Kumar movie, and added an FTD commercial," I tell her.

"NAILED IT!" she cheers, clapping.

Giggles bubble up inside me and spill out. The sound is familiar and old at the same time. "It really is, ah... stunning."

"If it makes you laugh, it did its job."

"Oh, it's making me laugh."

"Then good. You got what you need."

What you need.

Silas is what I need, but in his absence, this will do.

She puts the monstrosity in a large bag with a solid bottom, carefully, craftily fitting it in. The stirring scent of flowers feels like I'm truly breathing for the first time. All the air in my lungs is so fresh, so fevered. Each deep breath brings me back into my own skin.

Lily grabs me for a klutzy hug and looks me in the eye. Her face is a beaming ray of light. An old movie from the 1990s, one of my mom's favorites, floats into my memory. *Sliding Doors.*

I am staring at the person I could have been in an alternate universe.

"I know once you're home with your very own unicorn arrangement, you're going to be so happy. Goofy fun is under-rated, Jane. Be silly. If you can't be a little fun with flowers, when can you be?"

Duff raises one eyebrow and looks at her through the window like she just suggested we perform a seance for a dead pet.

"Thanks," I reply, starting to wonder how a person could be so optimistic, quirky, and unflaggingly happy all the time. I guess if such a person exists–and Lily certainly does–she should work in a flower shop.

Or on the set of a Judd Apatow film.

As I start to walk back to the apartment building, the weight of the flower arrangement becomes increasingly difficult to manage. Duff is a few feet behind me, and before I can stop to adjust my grip on the bag, he swoops in, taking the handles with a masculine grace that doesn't match his exterior.

A whiff of cologne tickles my nose, the scent unlike any I typically enjoy. Every part of him is inscrutable, closed off and barricaded. He's a cipher.

I get the sense that's intentional.

Back at my apartment, Duff leaves the large bag on the floor. I look at my dining table. *Mine.*

Smiling as I extract the flower arrangement from the bag, I

give it a place of honor. Later, I will cook dinner for Silas. We'll eat and catch up on the day, laughing and sharing secrets, and then he will take me to bed and peel back another layer of my armor, showing me more of myself.

That's my assumption.

Within hours, I'll be proven very, very wrong.

CHAPTER 14

*A*nother morning of no coffee scent.

And, as I sit up in bed, my reflexes jerky with surprise, no Silas.

"What?" I gasp, covered in chenille, the burgundy cloth like cold skin against my body. I leap to my feet in a panic, confused and disoriented, trying to reconcile a lack of Silas and a lack of a bed with my half-awake state.

I turn and find a strange man staring at me.

He takes one step, then a second, eyes wide with curiosity, lips parting to speak.

I scream.

He lets me.

"Allow me to introduce myself," the man says, his voice accented. Something Eastern European, the kind of voice actors in old Dracula movies used to have. It doesn't calm me.

At all.

"SILAS!" I scream. "DUFF!"

"My name is Romeo Czaky and I work for Drew Foster."

I stop screaming.

"Romeo?" I squeak. "Your name is *Romeo*?"

Dark eyes with lashes so plentiful, he looks like he's wearing eyeliner, probe mine, the eye roll well practiced.

"Yes, Romeo." The R rolls slightly, enough to sound silky, like a cat's purr. "It is a common name."

"You're–you're from the agency?"

"I am."

"Where's Duff?"

"He had to step out."

"And Silas?"

"I do not know. I am only scheduled to relieve Duff." He says the name like the U is pronounced "ew."

My pulse is beating so hard, it feels like I'm shaking the wall I lean against. "How do I know you're not lying?"

"I have been here for the last four hours, Ms. Borokov." Unlike Americans, he says the V like an F. "If I wanted to harm you, I had my chance."

The calm way he delivers such chilling words has a hypnotic effect on me. He's right. He could have killed me in my sleep. He didn't.

Therefore, I trust him.

Strange thought pattern in a functional life, I know.

Dysfunction is all I know. When you live in a dysfunctional system, the dysfunctional is functional.

"Okay. But why am I asleep on the couch?"

"Ah. Duff said you were waiting up for Gentian."

"He never came here?"

"No."

"Maybe he's next door."

"Ah, no. I can confirm that he is not."

I frown. "Where is he?"

"I do not know."

"But you know he's not next door?"

"I've been instructed to give you that information."

Oh, please. Here we go again.

"What other information can you give me?"

"What do you want to know?"

"All of the information you're *not* supposed to give me."

A sneaky smile appears, only there for a second. Romeo sets his mouth to a firm, tight line. "You know I cannot do that."

"No. I don't."

Surprise flickers in eyes the color of hot chocolate. "You don't?"

"I know you refuse to tell me. Not that you're *unable* to."

He's underestimated me. He's realizing it right now, in real time. My advantage is slim and narrowing by the second. Not an enemy, not an ally, Romeo is just another guy in a suit with defensive training and better electronics than most of the bad guys. He probably served in some country's military forces, like Drew and Silas, and now he's doing private security for people like me.

He's seen and not heard.

Like I'm supposed to be.

"I am only following orders, Ms. Borokov," he says apologetically, but the glint in his eye betrays him. This is a game.

I turn away, impolite and impatient. When he's on my detail, Duff humors me, never giving more than he is allowed, but he always *respects* me. This guy is a whole different world. For the first time since I've lived under constant surveillance, I'm uncomfortable with my guard. Not worried he'll do anything improper–I wouldn't stay in the room with him if I had an inkling of that.

But I don't like being treated like my demand for information is *cute*.

I grab my phone and check messages. Three death threats, one rape threat involving shoving dynamite up me and lighting it on fire while I'm tied up, two spam texts for refinancing student loans and two personal texts.

Be back when I can. S

and

Jane, I know this is weird, but can you meet me somewhere today to talk?

That text is from Mandy.

The room spins.

Who's next? Is Jenna going to tag along? With Tara dead and the news in a tizzy over me, I can't even pause long enough to absorb it all. The trip to the flower shop was a breath of fresh air.

Literally. And now Silas is gone, I've got a condescending ass for a guard, and *Mandy* wants to see me?

Sure, I type back, anger making me rebellious. *When? Where?*

Not in a bar bathroom, she writes back.

I gasp at her brutal honesty, the dark humor too soon, too coarse. My focus shifts and I'm back in that copper-filled ladies' room, Tara's blood draining out of her, my shoes soaking, my horror rolling out in real-time seconds as I watch someone I once cared for dying before me.

Three dots on the screen, and then one word.

Sorry.

That's a first. Mandy, Tara, and Jenna never apologized to Lindsay. Never said a word to me after the attack nearly five years ago. Never acknowledged my existence after Lindsay went away.

Never.

And now Mandy's apologizing for a distasteful joke? How about apologizing for ruining Lindsay's life–and now mine–with her lies all those years back?

For what? I type back. Poking her is stupid.

I don't care.

Can we talk? In person? she writes. *Please?*

For Mandy to cough up a *please* means whatever is going on is bad. Really, really bad.

Only in public, I say back.

Outdoors? she replies. *At the big park by the beach?*

Our town is small enough to have only one major park near a beach. I know exactly where she's talking about. It's perfect, all open space, no corners or closed doors.

Yes, I answer.

In an hour? she asks.

I look at the clock. I slept in later than I expected. It's just past ten. No wonder Silas isn't–

Oh. That's right.

He never came home last night.

Jane? the text says.

Noon, I say.

And then I turn off my cell and go take a shower.

It's a quick one, my skin still smarting from the tiny scabs that are starting the healing process. A fast, hot shower helps, and once I'm dressed and go to make some coffee, I find myself pleasantly surprised by a guard shift change.

Silas is sitting in a folding chair at my dining table, admiring my unicorn.

"Where have you been?" I ask, coldly contained as I make a full pot of coffee. I might be angry at him, but I would never deprive the man of caffeine.

"Working."

"All night?"

"Since when did you start playing twenty questions?"

"Since you didn't come home."

"Home? Is this my home?"

"No." I'm flustered and spill coffee grounds all over the floor. "It's mine. And I–" My breath catches in my throat as if it's snagged on a loose nail, a jutting splinter, a sharp branch on a crooked tree. The path to Silas is riddled with obstacles. One of the biggest is that I don't know where I stand.

Client?

Lover?

Friend with benefits?

"You what?" His voice drops to a hush as he steps forward, the shadow he casts like a dark warning, a twin self with sinister motives. Willing myself to stay put, I wait until he closes the gap between us, hands at his side, eyes tired but watching me with a growing hunger.

"I don't know what this is," I admit, too tired to try to play games.

"This?"

"Us."

"Us?"

He's taller than me, chin tipped down, and as his breathing picks up I can feel the barest edge of his hot breath as it reaches me, so diluted, it has no meaning. Nothing he says, in his words or with his body, tells me what I want to know.

Need to know.

Can't bear *not* to know.

"Yes, us," I reply, chin jutting up. "What are we?"

"Human."

"Silas."

His head tilts, just enough to show me how much emotion he's masking under the calm exterior. "What do you want us to be?"

"Whatever it is, I want clarity."

"How do you define clarity?"

"It sure doesn't involve conversations like this."

"You're defining it by what it isn't, Jane. But I'm asking you to tell me what it *is*."

My chest is ready to explode. The crosswinds inside me are too swift, too strong, too hard to fight. "Are we together?" I reach up and finger the necklace he left for me. Not missing a beat, his eyes catch the movement, widening.

One finger touches my cheekbone, sliding down the plane of bone, looping the necklace chain. "As a couple?" His voice makes me shiver.

His touch makes me wet, an ache rising within me that I've never felt before.

"Yes," I tell him, ask him, *beg* him. I would do anything for him, right here in this endless moment where anticipation turns me into someone I don't know. Someone who wants him with every fiber of my being. Someone who can't help but move millimeter by millimeter until that hot, intense breath is warming my nose, until the world is nothing but his lips, his tongue, his hands.

On me.

"You," he says, blowing lightly on my closed eyes as his wall of heat comes closer, "tell me. Are we a couple? I know my answer. What's yours?"

I use my mouth to respond. But not with words.

The kiss isn't polite. Raw and filled with long hours of wondering, it's the kind of kiss you don't expect because you can't control it. It takes over completely, dominating the space between us, turning the absence of touch into an abomination. I bite his lower lip and he sucks in mine, the flick of his tongue a preview of softer, lower flesh he plans to minister to. In the holy sanctuary of our bodies pressed together, we *sing*.

The melody requires rhythm, Silas's hips pushing against my belly, his body seared against mine by the time I break the kiss to breathe. Nothing else matters. Not coffee, not his absence, not the layered mess of my identity. We're bonded by this and only this, his hands pulling my shirt up, mine reaching for his belt buckle and finding his thick bulge.

Bzzzzz.

Our phones vibrate in unison, unrelenting and demanding.

He groans. It's a sound of resignation. I step back and let him deal with the war inside him. Sometimes I win. Sometimes I lose.

He frowns at his phone as he reads. I grab my phone and see a message from Lindsay about getting together, then all the earlier messages from Mandy. I look at the clock. In twenty minutes or so, I need to get going.

"Silas–"

I know my phone is being monitored by many layers of government intelligence, so by the time Silas is done with his work text, he already knows.

"Hmm?" he asks, eyes going unfocused, coming in for a kiss.

"Mandy texted me and wants to–"

"No."

I didn't ask permission. It's clear Silas isn't offering support, either. His body goes rigid, hands in fists.

"You sound like Drew."

"Good. Lindsay's *alive* because of Drew." His face is a shade of red I associate with arousal–or anger.

"Mandy wants to meet me in a park. A public place. It's not like Tara. We'll be outside the entire time, completely in view." What a shift. From nearly having sex on the living room floor to arguing about my turncoat friends.

"A sniper could take you or her down," he points out.

"A sniper could have killed me a long, long time ago, Silas."

"Just because they haven't doesn't mean they won't." He crosses his arms over his chest, taking a deep breath, making himself bigger.

I open my mouth to reply, but then his words hit me so hard, I feel sucker punched. "But–"

"My team will surround you."

"Fine!" I can choke that out because it's easy. Processing is hard.

Reacting is so, so simple.

In fact, it's so basic, I can't control it.

"Why do you want to meet with her at all? These women handed Lindsay–and you–over to those bastards. Ruined Lindsay. Went to the media and destroyed her reputation. Why would you want to let them into your life, even a crack? Look at what happened to Tara, damn it. That cannot–*will* not–happen to you!" Silas's whole body is one thick mountain of tension, all his muscles on high alert, arms still crossed, eyes dark. I can see him imagining the worst, the pain of future possibilities reflected back at me, but he's haunted by something else.

"I'm looking for information," I say through clenched teeth, my hands sweaty and pressed against my hips. I've never wanted to kiss *and* slap someone at the very same time. He's making it impossible for me to remain rational. All my anger turns into a deadly beat that takes over my body until I need to scream or come.

Or maybe both.

"That's *my* job," he says as he grabs my shoulders, hard, and pulls me into a kiss that's meant to tame me, to shut me up. As his tongue fights mine for primacy, I realize this isn't a kiss that says anything more than that. Civility is long gone, and all that is left is lust.

Lust it is, then.

On tiptoes, I reach around his shoulders and slide my hands up under his shirt, pulling it over his head with a full-body rush that makes me so ready for him.

"Hey, hey," he laughs, grabbing my wrists gently and stopping me. "Trust me, I appreciate the sentiment, but I can't." He pulls me into his arms and kisses me like a man who doesn't know the meaning of the word *can't*. "I don't have time." Regret infuses his words. "I'll have to take a raincheck."

I groan, my blood filled with lust to the point of exploding my body into a million tiny pieces of need. "Seriously? You started it by kissing me!" I grab his hips and pull him against me, rubbing up, feeling his thick erection through his clothes. "What about a quickie?"

"You're killing me," he says in a deep, throttled voice. "But I don't have time."

"I thought guys liked quickies?" I rub against him again, wondering where on earth this version of me came from? I don't do things like this.

Then again, I've never had the opportunity.

"I do indeed like quickies."

"Then prove it."

"Jane," he growls.

"I've been baaaad," I whisper, looking up at Silas through my eyelashes, pretending to be coquettish and coy.

It stops him in his tracks, his reaction unnerving. I've never seen Silas's face look so wolfish. So predatory.

So dominant.

"You're determined to go, aren't you?" His question comes out of the blue, like someone poured crushed ice up and down the length of our half-clothed bodies.

"Yes."

"I don't want you to see her."

"I—I know." His abrupt change is throwing me off, my body's signals so confused.

"I mean it."

"I *know*."

"You have to promise me you will cancel."

No, I want to say. *No*, I need to tell him. *No*. All my *nos* I haven't been allowed to assert come crashing into the back of my teeth, scraping along the scalloped edges of the tongue that presses against the pearly curves of my bite.

No.

"Okay," I say instead, buckling under, wanting to please him. "I'll cancel," I lie. I hate the lie. Hate it.

Yet I need it, too.

His chest lowers, sinking with relief. My fingers brush against the light hair on his chest. "Good." Silas gives me a perfunctory kiss on the forehead. "Glad you see reason."

Reason? As long as I do what I'm told, I'm reasonable? As long as I agree with him, I'm rational? There can be no other opinion?

As he stands, I see reason, all right.

A big old reason why I'm going to make sure I damn well *do* see Mandy.

As Silas showers, a plan takes shape.

Quickly, I compose myself, pulling my clothes into place, finger-combing my hair. As far as I know, Silas is my only detail. When he's in charge of me, he's it, unless we have a standing driver.

That means this is my chance.

I grab my phone, then pause. If I have it, Silas can track me. I look at the clock. 11:10 a.m.

I could take an Uber, but they'd find me. Fast.

I can't walk there in time, and the bus or train is unsafe.

My eyes are drawn to my beautiful centerpiece, the unicorn's glitter-covered eyelids telling me the answer.

A girl named Lily.

* * *

"Jane! I told you the unicorn—"

I round the counter's edge and pull her gently behind the small door that separates the back rooms of the business from the customer-facing section.

"What's wrong?" she gasps.

"Do you have a delivery van?" I'm breathing hard from running. Once Silas realizes I've disappeared, he'll find me quickly. I don't have much time.

"Yes."

"Can I ask for a huge favor?"

"Sure. Anything. What?"

"Can you drive me to the park? The one by the beach?"

"That place? Why?"

"I need to meet a friend." My chest aches from the unexpected sprint and air is trying to get in my lungs. It feels like I'm breathing through cotton candy.

"What about your bodyguard? Or, like, an Uber? Why can't you–*ohhhh*." Her face registers complete shock, then her eyes narrow, canny and sharp. "You don't want your bodyguard with you, do you?"

"No."

"I understand. He was kind of an ass–"

"I don't have time, Lily. Can you please drive me? Or can I borrow the van?"

"God, no! My mom would kill me if I lent out a business-registered truck!"

"Then can you take me?"

"Depends. Why? You're not doing anything illegal, are you?"

I give her a nasty look.

"Don't judge me! I just need to make sure. Mom says if we use the truck for personal trips, it can pierce the corporate veil or something. Mom is a rule follower. She asks permission."

"Then you'll need to ask forgiveness if something goes wrong," I tell her.

"You don't know my mother at all," Lily mutters, but she peels herself away from me, goes to the front of the store and flips the sign to Closed.

"Twenty minutes. I can give you twenty," she says as we sprint out the back door to an alleyway. A green van the color of grass, wrapped in photo images of colorful flowers, greets us. I get in the passenger's seat and instantly feel like I've had the best night's sleep on top of drinking three shots of espresso.

I snap the door shut and so does Lily. "Wow!" I gasp.

She grins, her smile lighting up her face. Normally, she looks like me, but not now. I've never, ever been that relaxed, so happy and sure.

153

"It's great, isn't it? Like rolling around town in your own little rain forest." Lily starts the van and peels out of the alley. She pauses at the end before making a hard right.

"I assume you're doing this to meet a hot guy," she shouts as we barrel down the street.

"No. I'm doing it to *avoid* a hot guy, actually," I explain.

The van slows down slightly, then speeds back up. "You mean, some guy is in hot pursuit? We're in danger?" she squeaks.

"No, nothing like that. I would never ask you to put your life in danger for me, Lily. Never. I just need to get away from my guards and meet an old friend."

"Why don't you want them there?"

"*They* don't want *me* there. Overprotective. It's tiring being told what to do and where to go all the time. Sometimes I want my freedom, you know?"

"Oh, yes. I still live at home with my parents. I work in their store. My little brothers are still at home. A freshman and a senior. I get told what to do *all* the time."

My silence makes her words fade out.

"Oh, damn, Jane! You mean you're controlled by your security guys? 24/7?"

I nod.

"That's just wrong!"

"It's for a good reason."

"Which is?"

"To keep me alive. Someone tried to blow up my car and shot at me just this week."

"Are you sure escaping from your own guards is such a good idea?"

"I just need an hour. Ninety minutes, tops."

"Why?"

"Because he told me *no*."

"Who?"

"My, uh..."

"The hot guy?"

"Yeah," I sigh.

"You're dating some hot dude who tells you when you can see your friends?"

Weird way to put it, but... "Yes."

"Oh, man. Now I get it. Screw him."

I blush.

She laughs.

We drive.

Within three minutes, my nose feels like I'm a bee sipping nectar and we're at the spot in the park, right on the edge of an enormous sea of grass leading down to the beach. Crabgrass edges the "lawn," if you can call it that, and kids are playing Frisbee. Mandy's a nervous mess of legs and folded arms, looking up at every car that pulls into the parking lot.

When I climb out of the green florist's van, she gives me a squinting look of revulsion.

Ah, Mandy. Never change.

"Thanks, Lily," I say sincerely, moving fast. "Go back to the store. I'll be fine getting home."

"How?"

"My hot guy will find me. I won't have a choice."

"But I gave you a head start, didn't I?" She puts her closed fist out for me to bump.

"Yes," I say, bumping back.

"Sisterhood!" she calls out as I jog away.

"Is that an undercover van? FBI? CIA?" Mandy asks.

"I can't answer that question," I tell her.

"Young agent," Mandy replies, eyebrows up. "I guess they recruit right out of college."

"Are we going to stand here and talk about my driver, or are you going to explain why you wanted to meet? The last time one of you reached out to me, I ended up on the cover of every tabloid, wearing her blood."

"Jesus, Jane. Have some compassion for the dead."

"I'll do that when you show a shred of it for the living."

The skin around her neck begins to redden. "I knew you'd throw that in my face. It was only a matter of time."

155

"Five years. Five *years,* and you let Lindsay, and then me, be tortured. Long time," I spit back.

"Is this how you talked to Tara when she reached out to you? Because I'd slit my wrists, too, to get you to shut up about it."

"Don't even joke." I look furtively around us. "You have no idea what I had to do to get here. So this better be worth it."

"I don't know if it's worth it to you, but it is to me. I'm trying to survive." Her eyes dart everywhere, assessing. "We're terrified."

"We?"

"Jenna. Our families. Tara's family. We know there's footage proving someone else killed her and not you, but maybe you made him do it."

"You think *I* have that kind of power?"

"The media make it seem like you do." Her casual shrug makes me want to strangle her.

"You're not that stupid, Mandy. You know it's not true. And besides, get to the point. Fast. When my guards find out I ditched them, they'll come roaring up."

"You came here with no guards? Are you crazy?" Eye bulging, she gives up all pretense of being calm and cool.

"I'm motivated."

"I assumed you'd have a detail! I only picked this place because it seemed safer. I figured your guys would protect us! That's the whole point!"

I shrug. "Sorry. We'll have to take our chances. Make it quick."

Squinting in frustration, she looks at me with disgust. "You evaded your own bodyguards. I always thought you were the smart one in our group. What a stupid, stupid thing to do. They're killing us all. One by one. Why would you–"

"Tell me something I don't know."

Planting her hands on her hips in defiance, a very pissed-off Mandy says caustically, "You were the goal. Not Lindsay."

All the muscles around my lungs stop working. Mandy stares at me, her features full and sharp, as if I'm seeing her through an increasingly focused lens.

"What?"

"You, Jane. Didn't Tara tell you?" Her affect is nasty. She knows her words hurt me.

That's the point of saying them.

I rifle through memory, as if those few minutes I spent talking to Tara at the bar were a stack of photographs and I need to search to find the right one.

"Blaine wanted you. Alone. We were supposed to leave Drew and Lindsay and you there. But you were so damn stubborn." Fear makes her blink rapidly, her eyes darting everywhere as I watch her. "You wouldn't listen. So we took you with us." Her face tightens, almost crumpling with tears.

Almost.

"If you'd stayed, it would have been easier. We didn't know how bad it would get," she adds.

"If I'd *stayed*? If I'd stayed at the house because Blaine wanted me there? You mean when they raped and tortured Lindsay?" I can't keep my voice from rising. "Do you hear yourself, Mandy? You're saying I should have stayed behind so they could do the same damage to me!"

"I'm not saying that," she says emphatically, shaking her head. "But Blaine was so, so pissed at us. It made everything harder when we had to lie."

Matter-of-fact tones don't blunt her words. They worsen the impact, in fact.

A distant alarm starts in my body, ringing a slow, ominous bell that tolls for me. Silas's warnings aren't just about shitlords and crazies, or political operatives ten levels deep.

Mandy is a literal threat.

To me.

Blasé about what she did five years ago, talking to me now as if *I* were the cause of her pain, Mandy is the epitome of every soulless part of this network that controls me.

She's *sad* that I didn't fall into a trap Blaine set for me five years ago. Sad because my actions made *her* life harder.

"What do you want from me, Mandy?" I ask, the words rolling out of me, slow and ponderous.

"Protection. You're so lucky," she whines. "You have a security detail. We told the investigators everything after Stellan, John, and Blaine died, and they gave us nothing. Left us hanging. And look at Tara. I don't want to die like that! So gruesome. So gross. No–I need a bodyguard. I *deserve* one. I want what you have."

I want what you have.

Tires peel behind us, the long, high shriek of rubber on asphalt insistent and violent. I close my eyes and count the seconds. One, two, three...

"JANE!" Rough hands grab my arms, the sudden shock of Silas's violent yank combining with Mandy's words to make me rattle in my skin. Pulling me away from Mandy, Silas practically drags me a hundred feet from her, hissing in my ear.

"Don't you ever, *ever* do that again. Do you have any idea what you've done?" He's shaking me, his hands on my biceps now, brutal and reactive. As I open my eyes and look over his shoulder, I see Duff in the driver's seat of yet another nondescript black SUV, mirrored shades and all.

Mandy looks Silas up and down, evaluating him like he's going through an employee performance review. A family walks between us, the mom pushing a stroller, a preschooler behind her with an outstretched hand holding a bottle of bubbles. The sun makes the gentle waves in the distant ocean seem whiter, foamier, more opaque and less clear. Seagulls caw in the distance as I struggle to bring myself back to my angry–

My what?

Boyfriend?

Lover?

Bodyguard?

We never did settle that detail, did we?

"I am here because I get to have a choice," I say slowly, the words unrehearsed and halting as Silas stops shaking me. Mandy gives me a raised-eyebrow look, moving slightly to the left, her hand rising like a visor to her eyebrows as she watches us.

Silas tries to pull me closer to the parking lot. Scanning the horizon, he lasers in on me. "Your 'choice' is going to get you killed. Not to mention get me fired. I've never lost a client before."

"I'm your first?"

"Yes."

"Then good. We're even. You're my first, too. Just in a different way."

His eyes go hooded and the full intensity of every part of him comes right at me through pupils that constrict, like a fist being pulled back before a blow.

"I came out of the shower singing. *Singing*. Son of a bitch! It took me longer than it ever should have to realize what you'd done. Once I figured it out, I chased you here." He's furious.

In the distance, a stoplight clicks over, engines revving, cars moving. The baby in the stroller starts to fuss, the dad of the family busy spreading a quilt on the ground with the preschooler, who runs underneath the sudden swell of the blanket as a gust of wind blows it high.

Their giggles contrast sharply with Silas's words.

"Jane? Is this going to take forever?" Mandy calls out, her finger tapping her phone in the universal gesture for *I am more important than you*.

"Ignore her," he orders me. I'm happy to obey. "And listen to me. I've kept you out of more restrictive settings. I'm the only reason you're not rotting in a room at the Island. Or worse," he rasps, his anger coming out of him via osmosis, his grip on my arms a sting I can't shake.

"Prison is prison, even if the guard is nice," I shoot back, licking my lips.

Anxiety makes me hear everything acutely. A dripping water fountain becomes water on a drum. A child's laugh becomes mocking cackles in my ear. The ocean's waves in the distance are like a train engine, the Doppler effect in full gear.

Except that's *not* a train.

The mom with the stroller starts screaming, every second turned into a sliver as I look at Silas, whose eyes widen, his arms wrapping around me as he bends slightly at the waist, then shoves us to the right, a hard lunge that sets our entwined bodies airborne. Confusion makes me fight him, writhing to escape, not knowing why he would shove and hurt me like this.

The impact as we fall makes my shoulder crack, a black spinning tire running over the tip of my loose shoe, gasoline exhaust coating us in unbreathable smoke. The heat of the big truck's engine sears me. Revving hard, the truck moves with tremendous speed as I watch it from my crooked point of view, my temple on the grass, my shoulder screaming obscenities through my blood.

With a sickening thud, the truck's grill hits Mandy's body dead on, driving it back into the thick palm tree at the edge of the parking lot.

Rag doll, I think. *She looks like a red rag doll.*

Except rag dolls don't have their intestines fall out as a truck shifts into reverse and backs away, peeling into the parking lot, slamming into a row of motorcycles that topple like dominoes. Rag dolls don't fall, limbs twisting like pipe cleaners.

Rag dolls don't bleed waterfalls.

And the truck–*it's red with a white bumper sticker and a grill full of Mandy's intestines*–gets away.

Just like I got away from Silas.

CHAPTER 15

*T*he black SUV pulls out of the parking spot, the red and blue police lights reflecting off the beige interior, the pattern turning everything purple if I don't pay attention.

What feels like hundreds of emergency vehicles and media satellite vans surround us, the crime scene sadly familiar. Yet again, Silas has to explain my position in this mess. Yet again, he's my alibi. Yet again, a friend of mine has been killed under suspicious circumstances.

Yet again, I'm being set up.

Pressure builds behind my eyes, the bridge of my nose expanding. My brain feels like it's swelling inside my skull. My body reacts in all the "normal" ways it is supposed to respond to trauma. I shake. I throw up. I ache. Processing the images of Mandy's broken body takes all the energy I'm capable of producing, and then some.

There is a breaking point. Bodies aren't designed to experience never-ending, unpredictable threats like this.

I'm literally in combat.

Except this isn't a war zone.

It's my *life*.

Duff drives us on roads I don't recognize, the endless blur of color and motion outside the windows no longer lulling.

Nothing can calm me down. Covert and overt looks from Silas tell me he's worried, on edge, and angry.

He should be.

He was right.

My mouth opens to say something, but the words don't come. What can I say? Every step of the way, he's been right. Tara is dead. Mandy is dead.

I am supposed to be dead.

"Airport," he instructs Duff, who takes a sudden left turn. I'm sure we're going to Alice's.

I don't even ask.

We zoom right down the block where the flower shop is located. A glint of green metal from the same van Lily drove me in catches my eye.

"We need to stop," I say, hand already on the door.

"Why?"

"I, uh, need to use the bathroom," I lie, pointing to The Thorn Poke.

Silas's side-eye barely registers. "You mean you want to see your partner in crime."

"Lily did nothing wrong."

He ignores my words but nods to Duff, who eases the SUV into a parking spot right behind the store. "You can go in, but one of us is with you the entire time."

"What a nice change."

"Don't even test me, Jane. For God's sake, what you just did put yourself in jeopardy. It gave the enemy a chance to kill you."

"But they didn't."

"They came damn close. Too close. Look at your shoe."

I look down. There's a tire track on it.

"Did you smell the exhaust like I did? Did the heat of the tailpipe's blast make you feel like you were in a desert wind? Did the grass kick up from the van's spinning tires and get in your mouth?" He's livid, voice low and furious, his face twisted in anger.

At me.

"Two out of three of your former friends are dead. Dead

during meetings with *you*. Meetings in public places where murders like this just shouldn't happen, but they do, damn it! These people aren't messing around! You can't take your own safety so lightly. No amount of stubbornness can defeat a determined killer." He slams the seat in front of him with the heel of his hand.

I know he's right. I do. Part of me accepts it. Internalizes it.

But another part needs to be in denial. Denial is my friend sometimes. It's how I keep going.

"You're my bodyguard, Silas. You're my lover. You can't treat me the same way as my bodyguard when we're also growing closer. You can't order me around and expect me to be an obedient little girl who does as told. You can't simultaneously awaken me and deny me agency."

Air passes through his teeth and into his throat as he looks at me, mouth open, his features conflicted.

"You *can't*," I insist.

His eyes narrow, grip lessening on my arm, sliding down to my elbow as he holds it with a gentler presence. "You're right. I can't."

My shoulders drop, the conflict shifting into a safer emotional space.

"Are you telling me I have to choose?" he asks.

"Choose?"

"Choose between being your lover and being your bodyguard."

The thought had never occurred to me. "No–I never said that."

"You didn't. I'm asking it now. If I can't connect with you," he whispers, his hand moving down to thread his fingers in mine, thumb softly rubbing the web of my hand, "and guard you, then it sounds like I'm in a double bind. There's no way out. Not a good one, at any rate."

"I want you for... both."

"Then you need to do as I say when I'm guarding you, Jane. If you don't, you could die."

"And if I keep living a life where I have no freedom, I'll die, too. A different kind of death, yes, but it's like being snuffed out slowly."

I don't know how to have conversations like this. I do the only thing I can think of.

I go into the shop to find Lily, leaving Silas to ponder.

"Jane! Oh my God! It's all over the news!" She glances at Silas and does a double take. "You weren't kidding about the hot guy."

A green cloud of jealousy pours over me, but clears quickly as she adds, "You look like you need a hug. Can I give you one?"

"How can you be so upbeat all the time?" I ask in a daze as she comes around from behind the counter and we embrace.

"I work in a flower shop. It's in my contract. If people are sad and it's because someone died, be respectful and somber. Otherwise, people are here to be cheered up."

"That hug was just part of you doing business?"

"Oh, no. That's because I'm a hugger and I think you'd make a good friend."

I laugh, the sound of bitterness and decay.

"The news says a woman was crushed to death by a van. That it was intentional. Were you there?"

If I start crying now, I'll never stop. I can't talk about what just happened. My mind needs to compartmentalize, to categorize, to put trauma in boxes where it can't touch the parts of my life that still need to function.

"Yes. I'm fine."

"Did you know her?" Lily pulls back and gives me such a kind look.

"Yes."

"Oh, Jane. I'm so sorry." She looks down, then catches my eye. "Did you know? That someone would try to kill her?"

"No."

"Do you think he was trying to kill you?"

"I'm... Lily, I'm not really thinking right now."

"Jane." Silas is behind me, in the shop. The cloying scent of all the flowers, the very freshness that I found appealing an hour ago, is now making me queasy.

So is the look on his face as I turn around.

"We need to go." He looks over my shoulder at Lily and just blinks, exactly once. "Now."

Lily grabs me and squeezes, hard. "I wish I knew what to do to help you," she whispers in my ear.

I squeeze back. "You already have. Thank you."

And with that, we leave.

The ride to the airport is a lonely experience, even in Silas's arms. Long stretches of silence give me time to think. It's only in silence that the rabid rush of thoughts becomes clear, separating out from the crowd effect of being crammed into too small a life.

"Duff," Silas says, breaking the hush. "Turn on the radio. We need to know how this is being spun."

I close my eyes. All I see is dead ragdolls.

I open my eyes and bury my nose in Silas's lapel.

"Sources close to Amanda Witherspoon say that Jane Borokov initiated the meeting, requesting that they meet at the—"

"LIE!" I choke out. "That's a lie! I have the texts to prove it!"

"*Shhh*. I know," Silas assures me.

"In a series of text screenshots provided to us by sources close to the deceased, the evidence appears to corroborate the claim."

"Faked!" I insist. "It's all fake!"

"I believe you," Silas says. "I do."

Duff catches my eye in the rearview mirror. His expression is neutral.

"How do they do this? Who has the kind of power to fake electronic records like that? Why are they twisting the news coverage so quickly? Is it to paint me as the villain up front?" I ask Silas, pleading for him to give me a coherent explanation. In the pit of my stomach, I know there isn't one, but this is where denial comes in.

"It's not hard if you know how to use computer tools and feed the media machine at the right entry points."

"Entry points?"

"Give the click-bait sites the information you want to have spread. Make it salacious and juicy. Give them what they want and they'll spread it far and wide. The truth doesn't matter," he says, almost as an aside.

"It matters to me."

"Me, too." He kisses the top of my head. "We'll sort it all out later."

"At Alice's?"

"Yes."

"*In a related case, the grisly death of Tara Holdstrom has been ruled a suicide by the—*"

"She didn't commit suicide," I say with a long sigh. "I know I should be relieved I'm not being charged, but the lie." I sit up and look at Silas, feeling feral. "You said—"

He nods, turning his head toward the speaker.

"*—family members describe a woman with a long history of anxiety and suicidal ideation, leading to an attempt in 2011 that was unsuccessful. Although her parents sought treatment for years, in recent months, since the Bosworth and Borokov case blew wide open, Tara Holdstrom had grown increasingly erratic in her—*"

"Turn it off, Duff," I call out.

A snap of Duff's wrist and the sound ends.

"They're doing it again," I say, my words like barbed wire on a newborn's skin. "They're setting it all up. The spin is just lurid enough to go viral. Tara was never, ever suicidal. Her parents must be going along with this because they have no choice."

"Or were bought off," Silas mutters.

"Before the van came, Mandy begged me to have Drew's team protect her."

Silas frowns. "She did? Tell me everything she said."

I close my eyes and send myself back a few hours, remembering the family, the kid in the stroller, how that van could have done so much more damage.

And then I see dead Mandy, hanging half crooked from the tree as the van's grill pulled her.

My stomach clenches, gag reflex kicking in.

"Jane? You just turned four shades of white and now you're green." He turns and grabs a small bottle of water, opening it and handing it to me. "Drink."

"I'm not thirsty."

"Drink anyhow." His voice is soft concern mixed with steel.

I follow this order. He's right. I feel better instantly.

And I don't close my eyes again.

"She said she wanted what I have."

"What you have?"

"You."

"Me, specifically?"

"No. A bodyguard. Drew's team. She said that after Tara's death, she realized how bad it is. Tara told me the people behind all of this threatened her family with fake crimes. Said they would plant false child pornography on Tara's father's computer. Stuff like that–it's what they did to make Tara, Mandy, and Jenna lie about Lindsay and say she begged for rough sex from Stellan, Blaine, and John."

He reddens with anger. "You told me."

"And Mandy was terrified. Absolutely terrified."

"She's dead," he says under his breath. "She was right to be afraid."

Bright lights flash in the distance as we get close to the airport. I know the drill now.

Going to Alice's is my only escape.

Want what you have. Mandy's words haunt me.

Because I do have something she doesn't have anymore.

A beating heart.

yphoid Jane! the headline screams. *She's not infectious, but she's lethal to be near.*

"Put that down," Alice insists. "Who on earth brought the *New York Post* into my studio?" Plucking the newspaper out of my hands, she hands it to Silas, who is sitting in a rattan chair at the edge of the room, sipping coffee from a tiny espresso cup. "Here, Boy Scout. Don't let her see that again."

"Don't blame me. She sniped it from the pilot when we flew here. Besides, it's about Tara. Mandy hasn't even hit the news yet."

"Did you now?" Alice asks me, her smirk showing her real reaction.

"I need to know what people are saying about me," I protest.

"No, you don't." Silas and Alice are equally emphatic as they turn into verbal twins.

"I do! It's a coping mechanism."

"*I'm* your coping mechanism," Silas says as he leans in, his voice making me jolt. "I'm what you need. Your friends are what you need. You don't need headlines and shaming."

"What friends?" I ask, tears filling my eyes.

"Me, for one," Alice says. "And him."

"He's not my friend."

"I'm not?" Silas's brow drops.

"You're my..."

"Bodyguard?"

"Silas, you know what you are."

"Maybe he does, but I don't. Come on, Boy Scout. What are you and Jane? Don't make me go get my Win 94 and poke it out of you." Alice drinks the rest of her lemonade and looks up, standing slowly and walking unsteadily to the kitchen. She looks so old and frail suddenly. As she pours more vodka, I wonder how much of a head start she's had on us in the alcohol realm.

Some deeper worry plagues me. I can't name it. Can't give it a label. It just *is*.

"Don't even joke about threatening an agent with a gun, Alice," Silas says dryly, shaking me out of my darker place.

"Wouldn't be the first time," she sweetly replies.

"Or the last," I mutter.

"You're getting impertinent," Alice chides me, but she's grinning.

"I always was your best student," I reply.

We laugh. It feels good. Silas pretends to ignore us, but he can't help but grin.

"I know you know this, Jane, but none of that was your fault. Whoever is at the heart of this mess is responsible. You're damn lucky the van didn't get you."

"It might have if Silas hadn't been so fast."

Silas shakes his head. "No. He wasn't aiming for you."

"How can you be sure?"

"He could have altered his path. Taken us out, then Mandy. He didn't."

I try to swallow but can't.

"Mandy was the target, then?" Alice's face tips up, giving him her full attention. "You know this?"

"As much as someone in my position can know it, yes."

"Then it's as good as fact, as far as I'm concerned."

We sit in silence, my coffee liberally flavored with a warming Irish cream that Alice slipped in there. I suspect a quantity of vodka has been added as well. The flight here was abrupt and bumpy, turbulence turning my gut inside out. Nerves can only take so much before they become overstimulated, always working because the signal to rest has been broken.

Drew ordered me here. I heard the conversation. Said I wasn't safe for anyone to be around. I'm sure he got rid of me so Lindsay wouldn't comfort me. Support me.

Be anywhere near me.

It's just as well. Alice's place is an oasis and this time, no one is making me leave. Alice gave me the same room I had before. Her paint supplies are fresh, set out by the covered, unfinished painting of me. *Think of this as a work trip*, I tell myself. A haven. An asylum.

A prison of my own choosing.

Silas clears his throat, takes a sip of coffee, and winces. "We've, uh, learned other information."

Alice looks at him. "And?"

"Tara left a suicide note."

"Bull!" I gasp. "That's complete bullshit. Just like the radio report when we were driving to the airport with Duff. This is spin, and none of it is true. I'm no fan of Tara's, but it's all a lie!"

"You saw the headlines about Mandy, but I take it the Tara stories are already on page twelve," Silas explains with a sigh. "The PR spin on Tara is that she was mentally unstable, 'never really the same' after Lindsay's attack, had a history of anxiety, and the suicide note clinches it."

"But that's not true!" I protest.

"Same old same old," Alice says sadly. "Not much has changed since the 1950s. Paint a woman as hysterical and unhinged and you can justify the worst crimes."

"Tara didn't commit a crime."

"I didn't mean Tara. I meant this is standard operating procedure. It reeks of agency involvement. Make the victim look like she did it to herself," she explains.

I give Silas an appraising stare. "Is that true?"

He shrugs.

Oh, that shrug holds a lot of secrets.

"Then it's a clue," I muse. "Tara and Mandy really were

inside jobs." I start to ask about Jenna and whether anyone is protecting her, but Alice interrupts.

"It's all one big inside job, sweetie." Alice pats my cheek and sits down, eyes watching me carefully. "And when are you going to tell me all about Harry?"

"Harry?"

She knows.

"Yes. Your–"

I finish the sentence for her. "Father. Alice, you knew? All these years?"

"I suspected. I heard the rumors. And when you came to Yates, I had a financial aid counselor look at your record. All of the tuition was paid by the Bosworths."

"What? No! I had a full-tuition scholarship. An academic one, based on my high school record."

Alice's eyes fill with pity.

"No!" I gasp, hoarse and empty. "You can't tell me that wasn't a real scholarship. That it's all been–that I–"

"Sweetie, I don't want to tell you, but I have to. Your scholarship from the college was small. The rest was paid for by Harry Bosworth. It was a well-kept secret. Around Yates, people just thought of him as an ultra-generous, giving man to help his staffer's daughter like that." As she swallows, her throat tremors. Her hand lifts to the base of her collarbone. It's shaking.

I frown and start to ask if she's okay, but Silas speaks first.

"But not you," Silas asks her.

"No. Not me. Men like Harry aren't generous in that way. They give to gain stature, power, favors, or more money. They don't give without a good reason."

"And being my father was good enough?"

"I can't speak to his motives, but I guess so," she says softly. "I guess so."

I gulp the coffee, which has gone lukewarm, and give myself a full-body shake, as if exorcising demons. "Even my proud achievements aren't mine," I gasp, absorbing it all. "I've always thought of myself as someone who did this on her own. It's–it's part of who I am." Sobs take over my breath. I give in, speaking around them. "He's taking too much from me. He lied to me my entire life. My mother gave him her life. He made her lie to me, too. Who the hell am I if my entire life has been nothing but a lie?"

Silas reaches for me. Alice's look is filled with empathy. I stand up, pushing him away.

"You spent our first few days together being a complete dick to me," I say to him. Clearly, he didn't expect to hear *that* based on the look he's wearing.

"You told me why. I get it. But you took all this fake evidence and these twisted field reports that someone planted and you and Drew believed them. You believed nothing but lies. And knowing that you *know* it was all lies–and that there are even more lies that aren't about me, but can hurt Harry–what do you do?" My question is an accusation.

"What do you mean?" Silas asks, chin rising, body tense.

"What do you do when an entire case turns out to be wrong?"

He doesn't hesitate. "You assume everything is a lie and figure out the truth piece by piece."

"And how do you do that?"

"You dig. Relentlessly. You roll over every rock. Methodically and with great care. You reconstruct the truth out of the pieces you find and verify."

"And then?"

"And then *what*?"

"What do you do after that?"

"You trust the next level in the system and hand it all over to them."

"Is that what I'm supposed to do? I just learned that my life–my very existence–is a lie. How do I find all the pieces of truth to assemble a whole that I can pass on to the next level, Silas?"

He looks stricken.

"Tell me!" I beg, my throat hoarse from crying, my neck aching from the pain of holding so much in the voiceless part of me that never knew she could say what she feels.

"I don't–you're not a *case*, Jane."

"I'm not?"

"No. Not anymore."

"Then what am I? Who am I?"

Alice steps forward. "You are Jane. And that is enough."

"No offense, Alice. I love you dearly, but what the hell does that mean?" It's always hot in Texas, but it's hotter than usual in the studio. I start to fan myself and pace the room. I'm unraveling. My skin feels like long bands of noodly ribbon. All the lies flay me, turn me into exposed nerves and bleeding vessels.

I need to be centered.

I need to be anchored.

Mostly, I just *need*.

Just then, a *tap tap tap* at the main door, followed by the creaking sound of it being opened, cuts me off. A round, smiling woman with black hair in a long braid enters, carrying a tray of food.

"Miss Alice? We have some snacks." The woman smiles at Silas, then gives me a completely unearned dirty look.

I'm stunned into silence.

"Thank you, Delia. Just leave it there." Alice points vaguely at a coffee table. Delia removes the top of the tray to reveal cookies and some small sandwiches.

Delia leaves as fast as she can.

"What was that about?" Silas asks, beating me to it. "If looks could kill, Jane would be twice dead."

"Oh. That," Alice says as she reaches for a chocolate cookie. "Delia doesn't like Jane."

"You think?" he says.

"She's convinced Jane did it all. Says there is a secret group on the internet that connected all the dots. Then again, Delia thinks the Westboro Baptist Church caused the twin tower attacks on September 11, so take her opinion with a grain of salt." Alice munches happily. "The woman may be a loon, but she's an extraordinary cook and baker."

I ignore the cookies and just sigh. "You were talking about enough. What's enough? How am I enough?"

"I can't answer that for you, Jane. You'll have to figure it out for yourself." Alice's words have a finality to them that makes a surge of panic rush through me.

"Don't I already have enough to figure out? This isn't fair," I counter.

"Life isn't fair," Silas says in a voice dripping with sympathy.

"And platitudes aren't fair, either. That doesn't help!" I turn on him, lashing out, needing an outlet for all these feelings welling up inside.

"Why are you mad at *me*? What did I do to piss you off?" he asks.

"Nothing! You've done nothing! I'm just angry! I have a right to my feelings! I have a right to my freedom! I have a right to my identity! No one gives a damn about any of *my* rights!" I explode.

"We do," Alice says, putting her hand on Silas's forearm as he gives her a confused look. "That's why you're venting to us right now, Jane. Because we're safe."

"Safe?" I gasp.

"Child, you never showed any negative emotions during those three years at Yates. Not one single time. Other faculty members admired your poise, your positivity, how such a young woman could be so nice. And that's who you were for so long, Jane. You were nice."

If I was so nice, why does the word sound so awful the way Alice says it?

"You know what nice people do, Jane? They stuff their feelings. No one ever did anything remarkable in this world by being *nice*. No one ever invented a revolutionary device or idea that changed society by being *nice*. No one ever became rich and powerful by being *nice*. And no one–not one damn soul in all creation–ever met their own needs by being *nice*."

My crying stops. All I can do is stare at her.

"*Nice* is a cover. It's a threadbare cloak we throw on and pretend it's a mink coat. It's what we settle for when we can't have better. Jane, when did you ever argue with a professor or a boss?"

"What?"

"Argue. You know. Tell someone your opinion differs from theirs and when challenged, hold your ground."

"I–ah–I do that all the time."

She points to Silas. "With him. Sure. Because he's good. But how do you defend yourself against the people in your life who suck your soul and regurgitate it back to you, expecting praise?"

Silas watches her, wholly engrossed in Alice's words. The actual words she's saying are divorced from the reality I'm feeling. Dawning horror and extreme denial are battling for supremacy inside me. She's right. She's wrong. She's insightful. She's crazy.

She's old.

She's *Alice*.

"People don't exploit me like that," I scoff.

"No, they don't. You invite them in, make them a cup of tea, and offer up your *nice* self to them to use and abuse," she replies, eyes narrowed as she stares straight into my soul, her wrinkled skin folding in on itself like lifetimes layered on top of each other.

"That's enough," Silas says, interrupting. "Jane's had a horrible day, and this conversation is nothing but–"

"Truth." I cut him off. "Every word Alice is saying is true. I am nice. I really am. Jane is so nice. Jane is so pleasant. Jane is so sweet. Guess what? Sometimes I don't want to be. And I have no choice. No one in my life has allowed me the space to be anything but nice."

"Take that space, Jane. It's yours if you want it."

"All the people I want to take it from are dead except for Harry!" I shout. "And he–he–"

"He what?"

"He didn't love me enough to step forward and be my father!"

Silas moves to me, enveloping me in a warm, big embrace. I struggle for a few seconds, the thick wall between myself and the world my final shield. Some part of me can float right through it, though. The trusting center inside me lets Silas comfort me.

"You don't have to be nice with me anymore," Silas whispers. "I just want Jane."

"I don't know who that is."

"We'll find out together."

"What if... what if you don't like who I become?"

"You won't become anything I won't adore."

"How do you know?"

"I just do." He's staring at a fixed point, just past my head, and I track his eyes to the large painting of me, the one Alice is working on. It's covered, but a small section of one corner peeks out. After staring for a few seconds, he turns his attention to the masterpiece from my college years. Alice's work fills the room, my body simple.

And telling my true story.

"Alice," I call out in a voice so firm and true, it feels alien. "Are you in the mood to paint, by any chance?"

She grins. "And if I said no?"

"I won't be nice about it." I pull out of Silas's arms and walk to the small dressing area. As I undress, he makes strange sounds of emotional struggle, a weird assemblage of disapproval, incredulity, and frustration.

Perfect.

"You can't," he finally says, calling out from his spot across the studio, voice echoing into my heart.

"Can't what?"

"Can't pose for anyone other than Alice."

"I can't? Says who?"

"Me."

"Is that an order?"

"No. But it is a statement of fact."

"And if I don't want to be nice?"

"Then I'll go full caveman on you."

"What the hell is 'full caveman'?" Alice asks, her laughter crawling across my skin as if it's refreshing the pores.

"Don't test me."

"Is it like the Incredible Hulk? I wouldn't like you when you're full caveman?"

"Seriously, Jane. Promise me," he demands.

"I haven't posed since college, Silas. I'm not about to run out and take my clothes off for strange artists just because I'm breaking all the nice rules."

"Good."

"But even if I did, you couldn't stop me."

"I'd have to try."

I don't even bother wearing the robe, strutting out from behind the folding screen, barreling down on him with my finger in his face.

And then I freeze.

Because I've never been naked, posing, in front of a man who has been inside me.

Oh, the difference.

My body has new meaning when it's exposed before someone who has made it sing. Openly, possessively, his eyes crawl over my hips, the small patch of hair at my mons, the curl of my calf, the breasts that rest patiently like small globes, cradled against my ribs like ripe fruit on a tree. His gaze makes my experience in my body take on a completely new meaning.

"Please, Jane. Sit," Alice says.

I do, assuming the pose in the half-finished painting.

She looks at me for longer than is comfortable, her head tilting as she studies light. This I expect.

What I do not anticipate is the amount of attention she gives Silas.

Who is watching only me.

"Look at him," she says to me, making me jolt.

"What?"

"The way he's looking at you." Her voice is contemplative and otherworldly. "I want you to look back."

Slowly, I look at him.

There is a hunger in his gaze that makes me want to be consumed.

And for the next thirty minutes, he devours me with his eyes.

Time stops. Seconds do not pass. Minutes become centuries, universes, vortices where cross-forces negate each other.

Nothing in Silas's eyes is neutral. The stakes are laid out as he gives me what no other man has ever given me.

His full and complete attention.

We breathe together as Alice paints. We blink, but do not look away. The room is a low, steady hush, the only sound our breath, light movement, the paint turning the electrical arc of passion between us into art. Alice's hand is steady, though she squints, studying me more than usual.

After thirty minutes, she pauses.

"I am tired," she announces. "More tired than usual."

Only then does Silas break the spell. His chest expands with large, fast breaths. He goes to the kitchen, out of sight.

"Jane," Alice calls out, her voice already down the hallway. "I am going to bed. I won't be back in the living room tonight." The precision of her words makes me shake my head.

If we were in a dorm, this would be a sock on the doorknob.

I reach for the small pile of my clothes, searching for my panties, when suddenly a warm hand is on my bare ass. Lips close in on my naked shoulder. The disconcerting brush of clothing against my bare back intensifies as he wraps his arms around me, gently grasping my breasts, and bites my earlobe.

I moan, the sound like wildfire.

"You are unbearably exquisite," Silas tells me. "I've never seen anything like that before. I want to weep when I look at you. I want to thank God. I want to run into the wind on a sunny beach. I want to make love with you in a wildflower field. I want to climb mountains and write sonnets and compose music for you, Jane, when you let me look at you like this. Let me do something else," he says into my ear, the power of his words making me shiver. "Let me touch you in ways that don't involve being nice at all."

I try to turn around, to look at him and kiss him and say *yes* with my bruised body and battered heart. He tightens his grip on me.

"Not yet," he demands. "I watched you, the curve of your spine as you turned to the right. The way the air loved your ribs, displaying the gentle slope of your breast against bone. How the light honored you like the queen of the sun. You became pure beauty when you let me look at you. Your eyes aren't just mirrors of your soul. Your entire body makes me realize my eyes have spent my whole life gazing at shadows. You're the only person who is real. Alice's painting captures that," he says, his throat tight, his hands tighter against my torso, "but I want to make you even more real. Let me do that, Jane," he continues as he slowly pivots my body until I'm facing him, my breast grazing against the buttons of his suit.

I answer him with a kiss.

In the middle of our tongues playing with each other, his taste like ambrosia, he lifts me into his arms and carries me down the hall, open and victorious, until we're in the guest bedroom Alice had ready for me when we arrived. He sets me down on the bed and I stretch, arms wide open, nipples tight and needing more than his gaze.

So much more.

He reaches for his belt buckle, releasing the end of the leather belt, shrugging out of his suit jacket. With open pants, he changes course and gets out of his business shirt.

It's my turn to watch.

Suits are, by their very nature, conservative. They are neat packages of conformity, designed for the man wearing them to blend in. That's why special agents and bodyguards wear them. A suit conveys authority. Power. Structure.

Watching a man remove the symbol of public dominance is a delightfully sensual sight. The prospect of naked, private dominance leaves me breathless.

Broad, bare shoulders reveal themselves as he strips out of the fine white cotton, folding the shirt neatly over the back of a wooden chair next to the bed. He stands there, bare chested above his pants. Hands on hips, he pauses and lets me enjoy the view.

Less than a minute later, he's nude, stretched next to me on top of the made bed, one knee between mine, one of my legs already around his waist, wanting him more than I've ever wanted anything or anyone in my life.

And for once, I get what I want.

For a fleeting second, every single critic pours into my mind, undermining what Silas and I have right now. All the tweets, every Facebook threat, emails and blog posts and doctored images and memes run like a horror film behind my closed eyelids, a flicker palace of pain and shame. It's overwhelming and constant, a long, unyielding death march through the worst humanity has to offer, all in the name of judgment. At times like this I can't shut it off. Trying to compartmentalize it only feeds the beast.

Love is the antidote.

Do I have enough?

"Hey," Silas says, sensing the swirling void of inhumanity inside me. "Let go, Jane. They'll drag you down if you let them. Don't let them."

Tears fill the corners of my eyes. I fight them, but his words give me another avenue, one I hadn't considered. "I'm not the one clinging, Silas. They are. They won't let go of me."

"Give them nothing to hold onto. Hand yourself over to me. Every part. Every piece." His kiss lands in the valley between my breasts, a sweet press of lips that brushes a sigh from me, the sound rasping like a cleanse, a surprise spring shower, a rainfall during the April mountain melt.

"How?"

"I don't know the *how*. I just know the *why*. Do it because I love you."

I know I'm breathing. I feel it. My body works, pressed against his. But did I just hear what I thought I heard?

His chin rests where his lips just were, eyes on mine as I look down and see my future in those beautiful swirling blue irises, framed by long lashes that beckon. "Yes. *I love you*. Give yourself to me so I can keep them at bay. They don't deserve you. Not your body, not your heart, not your mind. And definitely not your memory. Don't let them do that to you. Destroyers live for the space they can take up, for the lives they can end, for the love they can vanquish. They can't create. They don't know how.

And in their frustration at their inability, they only have one weapon: annihilation."

Riding up the planes of my bare skin, my nipples dragging along the dusting of hair at his chest, he comes to rest on me, thigh bones long and lean, belly tight and soft. Those big arms cage me in, fingers brushing stray hair off my face. Soulful eyes meet mine, the air between us redolent with our sex, our unique imprints. Inhaling deeply, I breathe in his truth.

"They only know one way, Jane. You have universes to explore with your capacity for love. Don't let one limited world define you. Don't let it contaminate *us*."

And with that, my heart snaps in two.

"Never," I say fiercely. "Never. I don't want them inside my head. I don't want this, Silas. Please make it go away."

"You have to trust me."

"I do!"

"Then show me."

"How?"

"By letting me show you that I am trustworthy. Give me your body, Jane. All of it. Every bit." He kisses me, a full and thorough kiss filled with decadent promises, a kiss that pushes every boundary and asks for more space, more freedom, more license.

Just more of me.

"You have it. All of it."

"I want your thoughts, too. When I'm in you, I want to fill you. I want you to be completely and utterly mine. No one else's. Mind, body, soul, memory, heart–"

"I love you," I confess, the words so heavy. So true. I need to say it back to him, to complete the open circle between us.

As he kisses me blind, his fingers find me soaked for him, one stroking down to my deep wetness, gliding back up to make me gasp and grind against his hand. Two fingers make a slow journey down and suddenly I'm at his whim, my body crying out for release, my mouth against his as he takes me, captures me, completes me with wordless, endless power.

"Heart. Soul. Body," he says against my open mouth. "All of you." His fingers stop, the pause like a heartbreak. "All of you."

"Yes," I gasp, the plea evident. "All of it. All of me. Take me, Silas. Please. And if I don't know how to let you take me, take me anyway and teach me."

A silent roar rises up from his body as he swells, bigger and broader over me, his fingers playing a dangerous game as I seek the perfect friction point to writhe in his arms, my hands useless, the world centered on all of the ways he is cracking me open to find my truth. Each nerve ending dances on my tongue as he kisses me with a demanding edge that says all I have to do is let go of whatever's holding me back and he will catch me.

So I do.

His hands encircle my waist and pull me up, as I gulp air, trying to get hold of my body, which is coming and coming and coming as he touches me. Suddenly, I'm on my knees, his hard thighs pressed against my ass from behind.

"What are you doing?"

"I want you to come."

"I am," I say, my voice a low purr.

"I want you to come without a kiss, without me in front of you. I want you to come in a way that is fully focused on you. I'll make you come. You need to make yourself let go. I can't give you that permission, Jane. Only you can."

"I have no problem," I choke out as he unrelentingly touches me, like this is a game, a race, a pleasure marathon.

"I want you to take from me. I want you to give yourself to me. You need to empty yourself so those voices that plague you have nothing to grab." He squeezes one breast, his hands suddenly on me, both nipples teased until I cry out. "This is about you," he urges as one of his thick thighs shoves mine aside. Air, cool and dangerous, breezes across my open ass and a tingle of fear and arousal makes me swell with even more need.

If that's possible.

The second he enters me, my wetness more than enough to make the feeling divine, his fingers are stroking me between my legs, the twinned sensations making me lower my head, biting the pillow. Oh. My. God. I didn't know I could feel like this.

I didn't know a man could make me feel this.

Silas's slow, controlled thrusts are like a staircase of pleasure, each move inside me another step climbing higher and higher, and then all I see is red, explosions of color and light behind my closed eyes, my body shaking in full, walls clamped down on him so hard, he moves with effort, his breath on my shoulder blade a reminder he's there.

Because I disappear.

I fade into nothing, the release so strong, it's almost antimatter, his bold control fraying as he pushes harder, deeper, soulfully into me, our bodies now all about carnal pleasure. No sound matters. No movement is too much. I obey his command:

Give in.

Oh, how I give in. Free fall feels so, so good.

As he comes inside me with a series of pushes so hard, I cry out again and come, I pull him in through sheer force of ecstasy, making him stay inside, turning the tables. Silas has no choice for a few seconds. I won't let him go.

I won't.

I have all the power.

And then I collapse.

The sound of my breath comes from thousands of miles away, yet it is enough. The feel of his delicious body blanketed across my back and ass is enough. The push of my hair against my ear as he, too, finds his breath is enough.

This is enough.

Nothing else matters.

A phone buzzes. Silas groans against my shoulder.

"Go," I tell him.

He pulls off me, the cold air like an ass slap. He reads his phone. He winces.

"Damn. I have to–" The consummate professional, he's already dressing as he starts to explain.

"I understand." I'm reeling, but I have to let him go.

"I wish you didn't have to." I watch him as he dresses, the quick work he makes of it nothing like the slower undressing from earlier tonight.

Blissed out, I don't want this to end, and yet... it has to.

184

"I wish I didn't, too." He's already halfway out the door when he circles back and gives me a quick kiss on the cheek.

"We'll talk more later," he says. His eyes carry so much more meaning.

"Yes," I say, and then I drift off, completely gone.

Safe. Sated.

In the sanctuary of us.

CHAPTER 17

Old-fashioned coffee makers can be programmed, and that means I awaken to my favorite scent.

As I turn over in Alice's guest bed, I inhale, breathing deeply from the pillow where Silas rested last night.

Coffee is now my number two scent.

He had to go back to his assigned guest room. Decorum is in place for a reason. I understand, but at the same time I miss him. How quickly I've grown accustomed to having him in bed, naked, his presence a reminder that I'm a human being and not a scourge.

Birdsong fills the air outside my window. Sunlight streams into the white-walled room, making it feel bright, like I imagine heaven to be. I take a moment to inventory my body. Being in my head is easy.

Staying connected to all of the pieces of me that move me through time and space is much harder.

Drew's team is hired to protect my body. No one helps me to protect my mind, heart, or soul. It's not Silas's job, but then again, sleeping with me isn't exactly in his employee manual, either.

My phone says it's nearly 10 a.m., which means Silas should

187

be up by now, surely. I let myself stretch slowly. Last night was remarkable.

It takes time to settle into the crevices of my skin.

The room is so quiet.

Peace comes to us in many forms. Visual peace means clean lines and harmonious light. Tactile peace means freedom from unwanted touch. Auditory peace usually means silence.

In the naked silence I find a serenity.

And a strange, foreboding fear.

As I stay in bed, on my back, I look up at the white ceiling, the light coming in just so, turning the room into a warm asylum, far from the madding crowd of amateur shame artists. It's an art–it truly is–to find and exploit the soft spots in people online.

As I sit up, I smell him. Smell *us*. The sheets are thick with the musk of desire fulfilled. It's a pleasant scent, so private. So hidden. You have to be one of the participants to savor it, to let it inhabit you and turn scent into memory.

Conjurers and wise women know that kind of emotional alchemy.

So, too, do we now.

All the day's insults and injuries float through my head as I stand, assaulting me with thoughts of the outside world and the calamities brewing and exploding in a whirlwind around me. This reprieve has been wonderful.

But reality means Mandy's death is a press event, and I'm at the heart of it.

This is the tragedy: Mandy's death.

There is a secondary tragedy, too: that I cannot properly mourn her. Or Tara. Or my mother.

I'm given no time to weep. All I'm allowed to do is deny. Run. Submit.

Silas has given me another space. A space we create, where I have more choices.

I choose him.

I dress quickly, quietly, eager to get a morning cup of coffee and to sit in the playful light with Alice. The hallway is dimly lit, an interior corridor untouched by natural light. As I walk into the big, open studio, I find myself smiling.

Twenty minutes later, I've had two cups of coffee and all the solitude I want. Craving interaction, I peek outside. A dusty wind blows in the space between the studio and the main house. Shutting the door, I pad around to the bedrooms, wondering where Silas and Alice might be.

As I walk past my guest bedroom, I hear my phone buzz. When I reach it, a text from Silas simply says: *In the main house. Duff's outside the door facing west. Will be back soon.*

Well, there's one answer. What about Alice?

She's not one to sleep in so late. Her bedroom is next to mine in the guest wing. I softly rap on her door.

No answer.

The front door opens, a woman's voice humming softly under her breath, a jaunty tune with a beautiful, low melody. A person could dance to that song. My hand is on Alice's doorknob but I release it and walk toward the kitchen, nearly colliding with the housekeeper, Delia, who holds her hand over her heart and gives me a wide-eyed stare.

"Oh! Ms. Borokov. Sorry," she says, the humming stopped abruptly. She's all business. I wonder if she's an undercover agent, pretending to clean. "I didn't know you were still here."

I smile at her. "Am I supposed to be gone?"

"No, ma'am." Her pinched face makes it clear she wishes I would leave. "Just that Miss Alice didn't call for lunch to be made, so the staff assumed y'all were gone off somewhere."

I frown and look at Alice's door again.

As Delia walks past me and goes into the room where Silas slept last night, humming again as I hear the sound of fabric being fluffed, I reach for Alice's doorknob.

Tap tap tap.

Trepidation sets in like gravity, a deep and heavy burden I take on because I truly cannot turn away. Turning the knob, I tell myself I'm being silly. I tell myself Alice is fine. I tell myself all sorts of fantastical things because in the end, I know.

I just *know*.

She's in bed, the sheets peaking at the fine edges of her bones, her head tilted to the right, mouth open just enough to see the lines of her teeth.

And the sheet does not move up and down with the steady breath of the living.

"Oh, Alice," I say, the words coming out in a long, mournful sigh, her name a whisper on a spirit's wind. Peace may come in silence, but death does, too.

And death, unlike peace, is merciless.

I don't have to touch her to know. I don't.

But I have to touch her for another reason.

Love.

Her hand is cold but still soft, the gnarled knuckles a roadmap of a long life. They hold the history of so many adventures. The synovial fluid stores memories of paintings, Alice's heart spilled out onto the canvas and smeared with a brush made of vision and art. Her mouth is open slightly, the skin of her face slack. Death looks safe on her. Alice wasn't a safe woman. Risk personified, she would have hated knowing she looked so restful, so serene.

I'm crying before I realize it, my hand clinging to the dry, papery surface of her palm. We're programmed to expect other human beings' bodies to act in specific ways when triggered. A dead body cannot react. Maybe that's the very definition of death: the inability to respond. Perhaps ghosts are just dead people who can't let go of action and reaction. Who still harbor impulses to follow the laws of physics.

All of these thoughts race through me as tears run freely down my face, onto my shirt, one perfect wet circle landing on Alice's vein-covered hand.

"Alice," I whisper, hoping that whatever part of her lingers in the room can hear me. If I can only make her know how important she is to me. If I can somehow reach her in this in-between, then I can let her go. I don't want to. Her love has been such a touchstone these last few weeks.

The problem with death is that all agency is stripped away. You truly have no choice.

"Alice, thank you." I lift her hand and kiss it, my lips wet from my own salty tears, her skin cold. "Thank you for teaching me how to look inward. Thank you for teaching me where to find beauty. Thank you for showing me love when the world just wanted to plant hate inside me."

Footsteps grow louder until I hear them right behind me, a tiny scream making it clear that it's a woman behind me.

"What happened? What did you do?"

I turn around to find Alice's housekeeper holding a set of bedsheets, all neatly folded, in her arms.

And then she turns her head toward the main house and starts shrieking: "HELP! HELP! SHE KILLED MISS ALICE!"

CHAPTER 18

ngel of Death Jane Borokov Does it Again

Calamity Jane

Watch Out, Jenna! Jane's Coming for You

The website headlines aren't innovative–or surprising–but no matter how thick my skin is about being made fun of and threatened on social media and in the press, it always gets to me.

This time it's deeper. Worse. Alice is gone. I can't hear her wisecracks about the news coverage. She'll never shake her head and smirk at the Post or the Times headlines. Her body is at a funeral home while everyone here treats me with kid gloves. She was ninety-two and not feeling well last night.

Alice died of old age.

But not in the media spin. For them, it was me. I killed her.

Delia's screams didn't help, Duff rushing in to find the housekeeper on her knees, pointing at me, calling me names in a language I don't know. He radioed quickly, Silas coming fast in a group of suited men who pulled me away from Alice's bedside.

I cried in Silas's arms until he had to let me go to strategize, give orders, make plans. Duff set me up in the main house, in a solarium decorated with fresh Southern charm. Flower-patterned fabric and bright whites predominate, white wicker ruling the decor. Lily would like this, I thought. It's a cheerful room.

Not a place to mourn.

Then again, in my life, every place is for mourning. Grieving. Processing all that's been taken away. Alice was my last rock-solid champion. I do have Silas, but it's complicated. New. Exploratory and tentative.

Alice was just... Alice.

And now she's not.

I look over at her studio. It is swarmed with local law enforcement vehicles and an ambulance, all the lights flashing, sirens off. As red and blue flicker and spin, I turn away. The memory of her cold hand in mine makes a fresh batch of tears rise soundlessly in my eyes, my throat, my heart.

She's truly gone.

Like my mother.

My phone buzzes. It's hundreds of notifications, all chattering away. But checking my texts, I see a few from Lindsay. I read them and cry some more.

Then one from Harry.

I am so sorry. I know she meant a lot to you. Now you need to come back to The Grove. Immediately. For your own safety.

I navigate to Notifications. I'd rather read about my own debasement than deal with the emotional fallout from my father's text.

For the next ten minutes I steel myself and read headlines, tweets, Facebook musings, and more. I'm being painted as Alice's killer.

This hurts more than Tara or Mandy's deaths.

"Stop reading," Silas says with a sigh, gently prying my cell phone out of my hand as he walks soundlessly into the room. He replaces the phone with a mug of fresh coffee. "Over-caffeinate yourself instead."

"That's not healthy, either."

"But it's better for the ego."

"Truth." We sip in companionate silence as I try yet again to weather an unexpected storm.

"There's a limit, you know?" I finally say, controlling my emotions better than I thought I was capable of doing. "I can only take so much. At what point do people break to the point of no return?"

He watches me attentively, so focused that I suddenly feel self-conscious. Most people don't actively listen to other people. Silas does.

At least, he does with me.

"I don't know. I've never reached that point, so I can't speak to it."

"Have you ever come close?"

A shadow forms in his eyes. "Yes."

"In... when you were deployed?"

"There, and here at home."

"What made you not break? Because I'm pretty sure the only reason I haven't snapped in half and bled to death is because of you and Alice."

He shakes his head slowly, meeting my eyes over the edge of his coffee as he takes a sip. "I don't know. If I knew, I'd tell people so they could use the information and insight to help people who do snap. But I have no idea."

I sigh. "Right."

"I'm being honest. I really don't know."

"I'm not doubting you. It's more that I'm resigned to the fact that I'm never going to have some magic path to take to make sure I don't shatter. Disintegrate until what makes me Jane is just *gone*."

"I won't let that happen."

"It's really sweet that you think you can stop it."

"I know I can."

"How? Seriously, Silas–*how*? You don't know what the qualities are inside you that kept you from breaking. How can you be so sure you can stop me from breaking, too?"

"I just know."

"That's... sweet."

"You don't believe me."

"I think you believe that."

"Not an answer, Jane."

"Actually, it is. It's the truth."

"There is always more than one truth."

"Now you sound like my father."

"Is that a compliment or an insult?"

"Neither. It's just," I shake my head and snicker. "It's truth. And the truth is that last night, I posed for Alice. Last night, she talked to me and gave me advice and support and cracked jokes and now she's just gone. Gone." I give him a pleading look. "I swear, Silas. I didn't kill her."

He recoils. "I know that. Jane. You don't have to say it."

"I feel like I do."

"I don't. I watched how you were with her. How much she loved you. You were like a daughter or a granddaughter to her. She found your essence and made you see it, too. She was more than a mentor to you. She loved you, Jane. You loved her. And I know you well enough to know you'd never, ever hurt her."

"Yes." I stare across the room, eyes fixed on a small bowl of rocks and seashells. Some part of me shifts from thoughts that can convert into words to a nonverbal place. The words float like clouds in my mind, blending and splitting, graceful but meaningless.

Silas is very good at sitting in companionate silence. Not many people can do it.

After a while, my mental drift gets the better of me. I stand and walk to the screen door, opening it. Silas follows, coffee in hand, and we stroll through the gardens. We walk on the stone path, the interplay of different kinds of rocks a form of art. Even Alice's landscaping has an artist's eye.

Of course it does.

"It's about to get worse," Silas finally says. I appreciate the honesty. Being shined on or ignored is getting old.

"I know."

"Alice is... was an institution. She was Mogrett's daughter. This is going to get full-guns coverage by all the establishment media. You name it, they'll have long-form articles and you'll be at the center of those."

"I know that's supposed to be more intense, but they aren't more than a few steps away from the click-bait websites with Photoshopped versions of me in memes that makes the rounds on Reddit and 4CHAN."

"They're better than that," he argues. "And they have deeper pockets for investigative reporters to dig."

"True on both counts. But the bottom line–how they position me, as a person–is surprisingly similar."

"I suppose you're right," he adds grudgingly.

"Does that–does that change how you feel about me?"

"What? Why would it?"

"Because if we are going to be together, this is who I am. The version the press spins. I'm Jane Borokov, evil mastermind. Willing pawn. Scheming bitch. I'll always be *that* Jane."

"That is *not* who you are!"

"No. It's not. But to millions–maybe billions–of people, it is. Perception is reality for most people, Silas. You know that. Are you prepared to spend–" I cut myself off before saying *the rest of your life*.

"I'm prepared to love *you*. The real you. The *you* Alice captured on canvas. The *you* who played Candyland for three hours with my orphaned niece, who didn't know her mother had died. The *you* who loves fresh flowers and coffee and who is smarter than you show people. You, Jane. Not the facsimile that some headline editor creates for clicks."

"That's easy to say, Silas. It's easy to be the honorable guy who does the right thing. But you're talking about," I say, pausing. Say it, Jane. Say it.

"Talking about what?" he presses, watching and waiting.

The rest of your life.

Duff appears out of nowhere, face drawn down with a look of doom. "Gentian. We need you."

Silas gives me a pained look. "We'll talk later," he says, turning away as he and Duff disappear around a corner.

Leaving me with the unspoken burden of expectation.

CHAPTER 19

*M*y apartment is quickly becoming a flower shop.

When we walk through the door after leaving Alice's ranch, the scent of fresh flowers fills the room.

"Oh, right. I forgot to mention that Lily had these delivered. Duff texted me while we were gone and asked for permission to bring them in."

A surprisingly tasteful vase of pink peonies is sitting next to my dying unicorn display.

"Huh. No unicorns."

Silas gives me a strange look. "Unicorn flowers?"

I point to the older vase. "Lily. She's a hoot."

"Sounds like she's becoming a friend. That's good. You need more."

"Yes."

"Just tell her never to be your driver again when you're running away from me."

"It wasn't her fault." I finger the card on the new flower arrangement. My name is on the front, and inside, a simple message.

If you need an ear, please call me. My deepest condolences. Lily

I close my eyes and inhale slowly. Silas is right.

I do need more friends.

Just then, my phone rings. The actual ringtone goes off.

I hold my phone up for Silas to read the display as it rings. "Hedding, Stuva & Bollinger?" I read. "Sounds like a law firm."

Silas motions for me to take the call. "That's a major firm in DC. Answer it."

"You sure?"

He nods. I accept the call. Too late, though–I get dead air.

"I'm sure they'll leave a voicemail," I say, but Silas isn't listening. He's frowning, deeply.

At my phone.

"Why in hell would Hedding Stuva call *you*?"

I shrug. "Maybe I'm being sued? Wouldn't be the first time."

"No–they'd call Harry's lawyers for something like that. All calls related to anything legal pertaining to you go through them. Hedding Stuva is a white-shoe, genteel DC firm for the ultra wealthy. It doesn't make sense."

"Maybe Harry hired them?"

"I would have been told. Did they leave a message?" He peers at my screen.

I look at the blinking notification on my phone. "Yes." He doesn't have to ask. I navigate and hit Play Message.

"Hello, Ms. Borokov. This is Nathaniel Stuva from Hedding Stuva, a private law firm. We need to speak with you concerning one of our clients. Could you please return this call at your earliest convenience?" He gives a number.

Silas's lips are parted, eyebrows up in a look of extraordinary astonishment. Leaning in toward the phone as if it will tell him some secret not yet disclosed, he says, "What the hell?"

"Why is this so troubling?" I ask, perplexed.

"Because the last time I had any interaction with people at Hedding Stuva was the El Brujo case."

My turn to be perplexed. "El Brujo? You mean the drug dealer who died? The one who was a dean at Yates University and no one knew?"

"Yeah."

"What did this law firm have to do with him?"

"Turns out he was laundering money through some offshore

investments. Hedding Stuva handled some of the taxation paperwork. It was a big stink. They don't deal with dirty money. Old money, slimy money, robber baron money–they're fine with that. But not drug money and *definitely* not sex slave trafficking dollars."

"Why would they call *me*?"

"That's what I'm wondering."

I pick up the phone. "I'll call them and–"

"No," he says quietly. "Don't. Let me talk to Drew about this first. I can't think of any good reason why Hedding Stuva would call *you*. This smells like a set-up."

I know better than to argue. Frankly, I don't want to argue. This is so out of the realm of normal. Not the odd call from a law firm I don't know.

Silas's reaction.

"We need to bring Paulson in on this," he says as if talking to himself.

"Mark Paulson?" A chill runs through me as I say his name. "Why?"

"He was a major part of bringing El Brujo down. And now you're being contacted by a law firm that was part of a drug and sex slave dealer's empire. He knows more about the whole web than anyone else. I want him in on this."

"Do we have to?"

Silas seems taken aback. "You have something against Mark?"

"It's not fair, but yes. I do."

"What is it? Why?"

"He's the reason my mom handed Lindsay over to those guys, on the helipad."

"Mark had nothing to do with it," Silas says calmly, but he's defensive. I wonder how close they are. "John Gainsborough pretended to be Mark. You know that."

"I know. But emotionally, I don't know. Some part of me on the inside still thinks of him as the reason my mother is dead."

"That's one hell of a leap."

"I never said it was rational."

"Fair enough. He's crucial. Mark has a mind that rivals Drew's for this kind of work. His training is so complex. And with his experience with El Brujo kidnapping his fiancée and–"

"Wait. What? Say that last part again?"

"Mark's fiancée, Carrie, was kidnapped by El Brujo's men. She was snooping around and found a way station for sex slaves they smuggled into the U.S. from Mexico. She also found her friend down there."

Memories of everything from my time at Yates spill over, making it hard for me to speak coherently. "Carrie Myerson is Mark Paulson's girlfriend?"

"You know Carrie?"

"I know of her. You can't go to Yates or be an alum and not know what Dean Landau did. That he was El Brujo." I let out a small gasp and realize I'm barely breathing. "Mark Paulson's fiancée is *her*?"

"Yes."

"Then being set up as the fall guy for kidnapping Lindsay is twice as bad. I heard the rumors at Yates about how they really killed El Brujo. How he cut off arms and legs of women he kidnapped." I shiver.

"That's why the call from Hedding Stuva is troubling," Silas declares. "I'm bringing Paulson into this."

"Okay. I understand. Not that you need my permission."

His eyebrows rise with amusement.

"Glad to have your blessing."

I look around the apartment. Nothing's changed other than the new flowers. The dead ones need to be thrown away and I'm starving. Dispatching the decaying blossoms into the trash, I wash my hands and turn to the task of making something we can eat.

Only to confront an empty fridge.

My phone buzzes. I look.

I freeze.

ENTER TO WIN! Halloween SWEEPSTAKES! TEXT 21334 to UNICORN for a chance.

That's not a spam text from a candy company.

That's a message from my informant.

Silas settles in on my couch, reading from a folder Duff handed him earlier. He has his personal and work phones on the seat next to him, face tight with concentration.

Tell him, my conscience begs. *Tell him.*

But another voice, that seductive, sabotaging inner voice, says something quite different.

It says one word.

No.

I turn away, giving Silas my back, and pretend to make coffee. Meanwhile, I text 21334 to UNICORN.

The reply is a riddle. It must be. We had no choice all those years. Who knows how long my electronic life has been under surveillance? My knees turn to wet nerves as I realize I've likely been monitored my entire life.

Being Harry's daughter has made it so.

I stare at the screen and hold my breath as I read the reply.

All witch hunts have a warlock.

CHAPTER 20

"*J*ane?"

I scream, jumping in the air just enough to lose my grip on the phone. It falls onto the kitchen floor.

Silas is in the doorway in a flash, folder clenched in one hand. "What's wrong?"

"You scared me."

"I did? Why?" Bending down, he retrieves my phone and looks at the screen. His face takes on an astonished expression.

Oh, no.

"Your screen. It spidered. But it still works." Tracing the thin cracks, he reads the message. "Joining sweepstakes?"

"You know. Stupid thing. I got free chocolate a long time ago and they keep sending me these stupid messages," I babble.

"Yeah. I know. We've seen them in the reports on you. You enter a lot of contests. Ever win any?"

I scramble to find the right lie.

Silas's phone saves me. It rings.

"That's my personal phone. It must be Mom." He places my broken phone on the counter, screen down, and rushes to the couch.

As I hear him talking to her about Kelly and some legal

paperwork, I let myself reel. *All witch hunts have a warlock.* What does that mean? Cryptic, sure. But all the past messages I received this way were more elaborate. Designed to evade being discovered, yes.

Impossible to decipher? No.

"Hey," Silas says suddenly, back in the tiny kitchen and smiling. "I'm starving. That piece of chicken on the plane was a close cousin to rubber. Your cupboards are bare. My fridge has nothing but beer, maple syrup, and old lettuce. Let's go out to lunch."

"In public?"

"Duff scouted out a solid restaurant. Besides, it's on the way to The Grove."

"The Grove?"

"You know you have to face your father, Jane."

"I know, but–so soon?"

"After lunch. Dealing with his campaign's reaction to Alice's death will be much easier on a full stomach."

"You sure about that?"

"No. But it sounds like the right thing to say." His stomach makes a gurgling sound.

"You're just hungry and want to make me go out to lunch with you."

"Busted."

My phone rings again. It's Hedding Stuva. I ignore it.

"You're popular."

"It's Harry," I lie. I don't know why I lie. As he looks at me with an air of expectation, I feel so ashamed. I shouldn't lie to him. The man has literally been inside my body. Once you invite someone that far, don't you owe them the courtesy of never lying to them, ever? Seems like a small privilege to extend, given the intimacy.

But I don't. I don't give Silas the truth. And I'm not quite sure why.

"How is your mother? And Kelly?" I ask, hoping he doesn't notice I'm changing the subject. Given what Silas does for a living, it's likely obvious. If he notices, he doesn't let on.

"Mom says she's doing as well as can be expected. Right now, we're dealing with lawyers and custody. Tricia hasn't even had a funeral." He lets out a shaky sigh. "Mom had her cremated. We'll do a memorial service someday. Not yet. Mom needs to be named primary guardian so she can move with Kelly back to Minnesota." Silas pivots past me and pulls the coffee carafe out of the machine, rinsing it in the sink and starting to fill it up to make a pot.

"Minnesota?"

"Where I'm from. Where Mom lives." His voice is so even. I watch him as he makes coffee. The simplicity of his movement is enchanting. Arousing. How can I find such domestic tasks so appealing?

"I know. It just seems so far away."

"It is. Someday I'll take you there and you can see for your-self." He smiles at me and shuts the coffee machine lid, turning the little red light on to brew.

"Someday," I whisper, my mind running free like a child in a wildflower field filled with butterflies.

"I can't now, but–"

"No, no. No rush. It's just–it feels good to think about 'someday.' I haven't been allowed to have a future." I lean back against the countertop and look at him. Waiting, I wonder why I feel like my very existence has changed forever, as if I've discovered a completely new layer to life that's been there all along.

"Let's talk about it on the way to lunch."

"Why'd you make coffee if we're about to leave?"

"It's 10:11 a.m., Jane. We have plenty of time." Did we really leave Texas just five hours ago? It feels like a lifetime. I stifle a yawn.

"Oh." I watch him. He watches me. I crack first, starting to giggle.

He doesn't join me.

"You have a right to one, you know."

"A right to what?"

"A future."

With you? I want to ask, but it's too much. "Oh. Right."

"That's it?" He gives me a faltering smile. "Where's feisty Jane, yelling about her rights?"

"I am not feisty!"

"Then what are you?"

"I'm... authoritative!"

"And feisty."

"Little yappy dogs are feisty. Women aren't feisty. That's demeaning, Silas."

"Doesn't make it not true." The coffee's ready and he reaches up into a cupboard to get two mugs. I admire the view from behind.

"Feisty, huh? That means I'm a fighter."

"Of course you are." Nudging my coffee mug toward me, he motions with his chin to the fridge. Without needing clarification, I go and get the milk out. We're a well-oiled machine when it comes to coffee.

Can we learn to be like this in life?

"It's tiring, though," I confess as I pour enough milk into my coffee to get it to my perfect, drinkable shade. Silas doctors his and looks at me over the edge of his mug as he sips.

"Fighting is never restorative," he finally says. "By nature, it takes a piece out of you."

I finger my bangs. "So far, flesh is all accounted for, but my enemy got some hair."

"You're damn lucky that's all they got."

"Not lucky. Well protected."

I'm in his arms, his mouth sweet and caring as he kisses me, our bodies moving closer as the contact spurs more. He pulls back slightly and tightens his grip as he readies himself to speak.

But before he can reply, his phone buzzes, followed by an immediate knock on the front door. Questioning eyes meet mine as he asks without a word who that might be. Across the room in a flash, he checks the door's peephole, frowns, then opens the door.

Kelly stands there, holding the hand of an older, greying woman with bright blue eyes.

"She insisted, Silas," the woman says, her tone apologetic. "Said you had the best-smelling bubble bath and she–"

"JANE!" Kelly screams as she spots me. In an instant, my shins are covered by a clinging little girl who is squealing my name.

"She really hates coming here," the woman deadpans. She looks at me politely. "Hi," she adds with a wave. "I'm Linda Gentian."

"Jane Borokov," I say through laughter.

Kelly settles herself on one of my feet and mutters, "Play giant, Jane!"

"I know who you are," Linda says to me softly, eyes troubled, smile neutral.

My stomach sinks.

I take three or four steps with Kelly rooted on my foot, until we collapse at the couch into a pile of giggles. I can pretend Silas's mother didn't just set me off into a spiral of shame if I just focus on little Kelly, who hugs me with sweet little girl arms and whispers, "Uncle Silas told me your mommy is dead, too. Can we start a club?"

My already-aching stomach now feels like someone kicked it with steel-toed boots.

"What kind of club, sweetie?" I ask, looking her in the eye. I am holding it together on the inside only because the alternative isn't fair to this darling little girl who obviously needs a mommy.

Just like me.

"A club for people who are sad," Kelly whispers. "You're sad your mommy died." She nods slowly, her soulful little face tearing me apart. "Grandma says it's normal to feel sad. I don't want you to feel sad, too, Jane. Maybe if we're sad together we won't feel so alone. That's what my teacher says. When you make a friend, you don't feel so lonely."

Silas turns away, his hands going flat on the counter, shoulders hunching. Linda's hand flies up to her throat, fingering her necklace, eyes gleaming like the clear blue ocean on a hot day.

"Yes," I say, working hard to keep my voice even. "I'd love to be in your club with you. I don't want you to feel sad, either."

"Do you miss your mama, too?" she asks seriously.

A vision of my mother in jail makes me blink hard, over and over, as if I'm trying to erase it from behind my eyeballs. "I do. I miss her a lot."

Silas turns and gives his own mother a look of such appreciation, it sears me.

Kelly's eyes spill over with tears. She throws her arms around my neck and cries softly against my shoulder. "I didn't want Mama to go. You didn't want your mama to go. Why did they go away? I want Mama. I want Mama. I want Mama!"

I want my mama too, kid, I think as I dissolve into tears right along with her. Kelly's weight sends me down to the ground, and I pull her into my lap and cradle her in my arms. She's pure emotion, wailing and shaking, sniffling and keening. I join her in my own quiet way that adults are allowed.

We don't have permission to just feel, like Kelly. We aren't sanctioned to open up our hearts and show the contents to the world. We're prohibited from crying out like animals in mourning for the dead.

We're told to bottle it up. Keep it polite. Control our emotions within the etched boundaries society draws for us.

Pretty soon I'm not sure who is holding whom as I dissolve into tears in her arms. We weep for so long, the sound of Silas and Linda in the background one of presence, not judgment.

Finally, Kelly stops sobbing, the front of my shirt soaked with our mingled tears. Big, round, red eyes meet mine. "You're warm and soft like Mama, but you don't smell like her."

"What does she smell like?"

"Cinnamon. Like donuts. Mama wore perfume like cinnamon. I like cinnamon."

"You do?" I ask, Silas catching my eye, mouthing the words *thank you*.

Linda takes a few tentative steps into the kitchen, handing me a box of tissues. I smile at her and pull a few out, patting Kelly's face with one.

"I like cinnamon. That's the kind of donuts Mama got sometimes on Sunday mornings." She turns to Linda and asks, "Grandma, can we get cinnamon donuts?"

And with that, Linda joins the crying fest. Silas grabs a tissue and hands it to his mother, putting his arm around her for comfort.

Kelly looks up at her grandmother and uncle and asks, "Why is Grandma so sad? Grandma, are you in the club, too? Did your mommy die, too?"

I swear Silas looks like he's about to cry. He can't cry. He's the only person in the room holding the world together.

Silas clears his throat as Linda gives Kelly a deep look of love. Before she can reply, Silas says, "I'll go get some cinnamon donuts." And with that, he walks out to the front door. Hushed male voices make it clear Silas is getting one of the security guys to go buy donuts for us.

As Kelly stands, Linda bends down and places her hands on her granddaughter's shoulders. "Yes, honey. My mommy did die. Remember how we talk about Mawmaw?"

"Mawmaw was your mommy?" Kelly looks confused. "But I thought she was Mama's grandma?"

Linda lets out a slight laugh. "She was."

"Grandma! That's silly. How can Mama's grandma be your mommy, too?"

And just like that, the moment shifts. Linda straightens up as Kelly walks to the fridge and opens it, pulling out the milk and standing on tiptoes to put it on the counter. Reaching for a mug, Linda drains the last of the pot of coffee while Kelly looks at her.

"I want milk, Grandma."

I stand and search for a glass, setting it next to the milk carton.

"Not that one," Kelly says, scrunching up her nose. "I want a purple cup."

"Those are next door, honey," Linda says patiently as she raises her eyebrows and gives me a look of camaraderie. "At Silas's apartment."

"Can we go get it?"

Silas comes back into the room, tense and emotional. "The donuts will be delivered next door, Mom," he says.

Linda's eyes bounce between me and Silas, trying to read whatever's going on between us. Silas stretches, the long, methodical movement of an elite athlete trying to endure. I'm not sure what he's enduring, though. Maybe everything.

Including me?

"Kelly, how about we get that bubble bath from Jane and go next door. Silas has milk there," she says more to him, arching an eyebrow of maternal judgment, "now that we bought some, your purple cup, and by the time your bath is over, the cinnamon donuts will be delivered."

"Yay! And our club can make a fort in the living room and eat donuts in it! Joey might come in there with us if we feed him pieces of donuts. I'll bet Joey's mommy is dead. Do cats have mommies?" She beams at me, then Linda. "Now we have more people in our club. And maybe a cat." Kelly frowns at Silas. "Sorry, Uncle Silas. You can't be in the club. You have to have a dead mommy."

Linda recoils slightly at that.

"It's going to be a long, long, *long* time before I can join your club," Silas says, giving Linda a pointed look. "And also, sweetie, Jane can't come over for donuts. We have a meeting."

"A meeting?" Kelly gives me a confused look. "You work with Uncle Silas?"

"Sort of," I say. It's close to the truth.

"Then where's your gun?"

"Gun?"

"Uncle Silas always wears a gun so he can kill the bad people if they get too bad."

Linda's face goes tight. She takes Kelly's hand in hers and steers her toward the front door. "Let's get the bath going so you are all done in time for donuts," she announces in an overly cheerful voice.

"But Jane! Don't you want a cinnamon donut? They're so goooooooood!" Kelly moans.

"If I'm not there, that means more for you and your grandma," I say, forcing a smile. All I really want to do is take her up on her invitation and spend the day eating donuts and drinking milk out of purple cups while hiding in a fort made of sheets, blankets, and furniture.

Instead, I have to go to The Grove and face my father.

And my grief over Alice's death.

I want to be five again.

"It was nice meeting you, Jane," Linda says politely, her voice filled with emotion. "Silas said you were very sweet with Kelly. I can see what he means." Her words carry more to them, a thin thread of approval that warms my heart. I passed some kind of test, I see.

"Nice meeting you, too," I reply, smiling. With that, Kelly gives me one more hug and then they leave, Silas walking them next door, their quiet voices engaged in conversation.

I make another pot of coffee. We're going to need a lot to get through the next few hours.

Yet again, my phone buzzes. I don't need to deal with more texts from my informant, and certainly not ones about witches and warlocks. Between Alice's death, my father, whatever this new relationship is with Silas, and Tara's bloody death, I'm done.

My hands start to shake so badly, I can't control the carafe. It rattles against the faucet head until I force myself to set it down in the empty sink before I shatter it.

The front door closes and the light behind me changes, Silas coming up to my back, his hands wrapping around me, arms squeezing. I lean into him, head abuzz.

"That was hard," he says.

"You have a knack for understatements."

"And you have a knack for being absolutely wonderful with Kelly."

"I'm not doing anything special," I protest.

"Oh, yes. Yes, you are. You turned my mother from a skeptic into a believer. I had to listen to her rave about you while trying to explain to Kelly how my mom's mom could be Tricia's grandmother."

I let my shoulders drop with relief. "That's promising."

He kisses the side of my neck. "I mean it. You're really good with little kids."

"Kelly makes it easy."

"Nothing about Kelly is easy right now." His voice goes rough, his neck moving against my ear as he swallows. We breathe together for a few moments, then he turns me around in his arms.

"I'm so sorry about Alice."

"Me, too. She's the closest thing I had left to a mother."

"I'm grateful I still have mine."

My tears were already shed when I held Kelly. The part of me that grieves for my mom is penned up tight right now. All I can do is step into the kiss he offers me. It has to be enough.

It is.

I'm comforted by his touch. I'm relieved to be in his arms. I'm terrified by my texts. I'm horrified by Alice's death. I'm plagued by uncertainty and fear, but as Silas gives me his tongue, his lips, his protection, his attention–I'm certain of one rock-solid fact.

I'm his.

And nothing will change that now.

CHAPTER 21

*L*unch never happened.

We're in the SUV, Duff at the wheel, as Silas fields what seems like a hundred different phone calls at once. His Bluetooth looks like an extra appendage. He's mastered the art of low talking, dulcet tones barely concealing a firm anger.

The code for Harry's private gate was accessed by high-level hackers who broke into the most shrouded of all computer systems for The Grove.

And Silas and Drew are dealing with the fallout.

I've spent the last hour munching on hastily grabbed to-go cheese and veggie trays, the SUV stuck in traffic, Silas burning through call after call. Plugging my earbuds into my phone, I decide to screen the sixty-seven voicemails left on my system over the last four days. I know someone–some vague, shadowy "someone," has pre-screened out the death threats, the rape fantasies, and the plain old weirdos. What's left are the press requests, personal voicemails, and business issues.

I go by most recent to least recent.

First message: Lindsay.

Hey, Jane. Drew won't let me out of his sight, but let's hang out. Call or text me.

Next message:

Harry here. Call me immediately.

Next one:

Hello, Ms. Borokov. This is Lottie Crenshaw from Hedding Stuva, a law firm in Arlington, Virginia with offices in Los Angeles as well. We need to schedule an in-person meeting with you as soon as possible concerning a critical legal matter. Ms. Alice Mogrett requested this specifically. Please call us back at...

At the mention of Alice's name, my heart speeds up. Alice? A legal matter? What could this be about? Silas's comment earlier about Hedding Stuva being a "set up" and how he wanted to bring Mark Paulson in on this case makes my ears ring. If he thinks Hedding Stuva is somehow connected to the mess with Stellan, Blaine, and John, and El Brujo... this all just got crazier than I ever imagined.

Add in Alice and we've tipped over into bizarro land. I close my eyes and will away the sudden wave of grief that comes.

As we inch our way to the main exit to The Grove, I realize there is no downtime for Silas. Ever. We've been up since 4 a.m.–central Texas time–and we're both starting to droop. You can't tell in his reflexes, but there's a shadow on Silas's face. Maybe it's grief over his sister. Maybe it's the stress of making sure Kelly's okay and his mother's custody of her is all settled.

Or maybe it's me.

Can he tell I'm hiding secrets from him?

Paranoia sets in, making me close out my voicemail and stare at the scenery as we drive. I should tell him. I should get it all out. I should confess everything I've been hiding so he can trust me. So he knows.

So he doesn't leave.

Maybe this is too good to be true. Through all the pain, all the death, all the destruction, I'm finally seeing a little ray of light. Silas is making me feel better than I thought possible.

And now I'm risking it all for–what? To keep my secret informant a secret?

Why?

We turn into the driveway at The Grove to find more armed guards than you'd find on a base in the middle of a combat zone. Men in black military gear carry automatic weapons at the gate. My gut tightens and chills run up and down my spine like tiny bugs.

"What's going on?" I ask, marveling at the sight.

"New reality," Silas says in his work voice. "We had to up the security level."

"To this?"

"Are you kidding? An armed intruder made his way onto private grounds using a hacked code. You damn well better bet Drew's upping security to *this*. Be prepared to be searched."

"Searched?" Maybe it's my tone of voice, but something about me softens him. He reaches for my hand and takes a deep breath, watching me.

"A formality. But one we have to go through, nonetheless."

"As long as I'm not being searched by that doctor, I'm fine with it." I look him right in the eyes and lie. "I have nothing to hide."

"Of course you don't. I trust you."

Do you? I want to ask. I bite the words back.

We climb out of the SUV and Duff pulls away, two guys with wands coming over. No one actually touches me. It's all done electronically. Silas shows them his gun.

Guns.

He's wearing three.

"Why hasn't someone given me a gun?" I ask him as we walk to the office wing of the house.

"Why would you need one? You're sufficiently protected at all times." He sounds offended.

"Why *wouldn't* I need one? If I'm separated from you, or Duff, or that creepy dude Romeo..."

Silas pauses mid-step. "Creepy dude? What's wrong with Romeo?"

"He's creepy."

"You'll have to be more specific than that."

"He's *super* creepy."

"That makes all the difference, then." He frowns. "Did–when you say 'creepy,' was he..." Silas's hands curl into fists.

"No! No, nothing untoward. Just condescending."

"That comes with the job."

"*You're* not condescending."

"I don't need to be. Some guys, though, can be." He shrugs.

"Well, *he* was."

"I'll make sure he's not assigned to you again. What did he do?"

"Refused to give me information."

"Jane. Come on. That means he was doing his job."

"He didn't have to do it so *creepily*."

Silas stifles a laugh as we reach the main door. A gentleman, he opens the door for me. I walk in and run straight into Monica Bosworth.

Whose glare is so icy, she might as well be the air conditioning system for the building.

We don't say a word to each other. All three of us file into the conference room. Lindsay and Drew are already there, some kind of fruit smoothie in tall, clear glasses in front of them. I look around the room to see an assortment of drinks on a small buffet table. Aside from coffee, I haven't had much since we flew back this morning.

Silas moves to Drew, their heads close as they whisper. Lindsay pats the seat next to her and smiles at me. I get a fruit drink and sit down, achingly aware of Monica's eyes on me as she texts someone on her phone.

And then she looks right at me and grins.

You ever see the Cheshire Cat in the old animated *Alice in Wonderland* movie?

I'm staring at the human version right now.

I shift in my seat as I take a sip of the cold fruit concoction. It settles in my mouth like a lump. Forcing myself to swallow, I inhale, then exhale, acutely aware of every microsecond I'm existing. As my skin crawls, it feels like my organs are moving of their own volition under my skin.

I can't name it. Can't place it. Can't describe it, but something is changing as I sit here. Lindsay gives me an expectant look.

"We seriously need to go out for coffee," she whispers as I try to manage the deep sense of unreality that is invading me. It's not Monica's weird smile. It's not Alice's death. It's not one simple thing I can point to.

Or maybe it is.

I give her a weak smile and say, "Yes, definitely. How about after the meeting?" as I cast my glance toward Silas and Drew.

Their faces are drawn into deep, wretched frowns.

Silas looks up and catches my eye for a split second, looking away as fast as he can. He turns his head, chin dipping down, words whispered furiously with Drew in a verbal tennis game, the tight, clipped way they are speaking filling me with a growing sense of horror.

Something is wrong.

Everything is about to change.

"Harry will be here shortly," Marshall announces as he arrives and takes a seat near the projector screen. "We can begin to cover some of the topics before he arrives."

"Topics?" Monica scoffs. "There aren't topics. There is only one topic. Her."

No one asks who she's talking about.

"What are the topics?" I ask Marshall, ignoring Monica. I expect Drew and Silas to join us, but they stand near the door, continuing to talk quietly. Lindsay looks back at them, a small frown folding the skin at the bridge of her nose.

I follow her gaze and work to quell the growing panic in me.

Did Silas figure out the sweepstakes text? Does he know I'm hiding that from him? Instant regret washes over me. I should stand up and walk over there to tell him. I should spill it all, right now.

"Alice Mogrett's death is turning into a scandal of its own," Marshall starts, snapping me back to attention.

Silas and Drew stop talking.

"Jane," he says, leafing through a folder of documents. "Have you talked to Hedding Stuva yet?"

"No. They've been leaving messages, but Silas said–"

"You'll need to take care of the paperwork, and Harry wants you to move all estate work out of their firm. The Mogretts kept their connection to Hedding Stuva for far too long after that mess with El Brujo."

"Could you explain that in plain English, please?" Lindsay asks, glaring at Drew as if it's his fault she doesn't understand it.

"Alice Mogrett died. So far, it looks like simple old age. Natural causes. Jane and Silas were present when it happened. Not the actual death, but they were house guests. Alice Mogrett left her entire estate to Jane."

I hear the words. I do. But I feel Silas's eyes on me from behind.

They burn.

"What?" I squeak. "Alice *what*?"

"Oh, don't play dumb," Monica says in a scathing voice. "You know damn well you helped her to die so you could get her money."

"WHAT?" I stand, then sit quickly, my legs unstable. "Alice left me *what*?"

"She made you the sole beneficiary of her family's money," Harry says from behind me. All eyes turn to him.

"Nearly nine figures," Monica adds in a catty tone. "Nice payday for whatever you did to her."

I spin around to find Silas, to connect to him, eyes grabbing like he's a lifesaver.

Instead, I find him turned toward Drew, face in profile, jaw tight.

"Alice. Oh, no," I moan, sitting down hard, my head in my hands. Lindsay presses a flat palm between my shoulder blades, sitting quietly with me, the only person in the room who seems to care about my grief.

"As you can see, it makes for a PR mess," Harry intones, with Marshall making a small, coarse sound of agreement.

"Alice's death is more than your public relations snafu,

Daddy," Lindsay chides. "Can't you see Jane's in pain? Don't you care?"

Monica makes a dismissive noise. "We care about the fact that she's got an even worse tornado of complication around her."

"I'm sorry," Lindsay whispers, but her voice turns urgent. Excited even, as she leans in and says, "Think about what this means, Jane. You're free. It's your money. You have all the power now."

You have all the power.

Alice. Oh, Alice. You clever, wonderful, inspiring, devious woman.

I stand, my skin like iron shavings in a dusty wind, the boundaries of my body no longer distinct. "I'm her heir?" I ask no one, everyone.

"Yes," Marshall says. "It doesn't look good, but–"

Ignoring him, I pick up my broken phone and slide out of the way, walking behind Lindsay's chair, leaving the room. Monica makes a sound of outrage, but I don't care. I pull up the voicemail from Hedding Stuva and as the phone rings, I wait.

I wait.

I wait until eternity passes by and laps itself.

"Hedding Stuva," the voice says.

"I'm Jane Borokov, returning–"

"Just a moment, Ms. Borokov. I'm patching you straight through to Ms. Stuva. Mr. Stuva is not here, but Helen will take your call."

"Ms. Borokov," says a sophisticated older woman. "Thank you so much for returning our call. I'm Helen Stuva, one of the senior partners here. First, I am so sorry about your loss. Ms. Mogrett was a fine woman of character and strength."

"Thank you."

"We have a matter of legal importance to–"

"Is it true I'm her heir?"

A pregnant silence fills the air. "It would be best if you came to our office and–"

"I will. Trust me, I will. I just need to know if it's true."

"I can verify it's true, yes."

"Can you see me later today? You're in Los Angeles?"

"My day is free for you, Ms. Borokov. And yes, I am here."

"Fine. 1 p.m.? Thank you."

I hang up. I grab the wall for support. It's not strong enough to hold me. Sinking to the ground, I sit on the carpeted floor. Duff is suddenly at my side, leaning down.

"Jane?"

"Yeah?"

"You okay?"

"No. Stop asking me that. I'm never okay."

"Fine. You need help?"

"Another stupid question, Duff."

"The senator wants you back in the conference room."

"The senator can go screw himself, Duff."

"The senator," says the man himself, "does not think the laws of physics would allow that." I look up to find Harry standing there, hands in his pockets, an exasperated look on his face.

"Why am I here?" I ask Harry as Duff helps me up. I look behind him, toward the open meeting room door.

No Silas.

"Because we need to make sure we have a plan for–"

"No."

"No?" Harry acts as if he's never heard the word before.

"No."

"No to what, Jane?"

"No to everything. I'm a pawn. You controlled me because I needed help. I don't need help any longer."

"What do you mean? Of course you need help. You–"

"You heard Marshall," I say as we stand in the hallway, Silas finally poking his head out, Drew and Lindsay's faces visible next to him. "I'm Alice's heir. Hedding Stuva confirmed it." I wiggle my phone.

Harry's expression hardens. "Hedding Stuva isn't the most reputable of law firms," he begins.

I interrupt him. "But it's true. I'm her heir."

"Yes," he concedes.

"Which means I have all the money I could possibly need to hire my own protection."

The reality of what I'm saying sinks in slowly, his face morphing into incredulity as the implication hits him.

"Oh, Jesus, that's not–"

Silas and Drew walk up behind him, Drew's demeanor more closed off than usual. He looks at me as if I'm a piece of dog poop on the bottom of his shoe.

"What's going on?" he asks.

"Jane's exercising some control," Harry starts to say.

"I'm ready to fire all of you," I say flatly.

Four men look at me, agog. Even Duff's jaw drops, and I get the sense he's not easy to shock.

And with that, I spin on my heel and walk outside.

To come face-to-face with a guy in black, wearing a machine gun, peering at me.

"Hold on," Silas calls out, jogging after me. "It's not that easy."

"Oh, yes, it is. I have my own money now. I am independent. Alice wanted this."

"That's not what I mean."

"Then what do you mean?"

"Drew gave me a briefing. A bunch of new information came in over the last hour. Information about you."

Oh, no.

"Like what? I'm sure the media are swimming in 'news' about me, Alice's death, the inheritance, the–"

"We have credible tips that you were part of my sister's death."

"WHAT?"

"And the people you're working with were part of the plots to kill Drew's parents and Mark Paulson's mother and stepfather, too."

"You're not making any sense, Silas."

223

"I'm making *plenty* of sense." Silence hangs between us after his words, like an all-too-patient vulture.

"You can't be–you can't really think–*what?*"

"Give me a reason not to believe it all, Jane." His voice is so, so hard.

"Why on earth would *I* want to kill your sister? A sister I didn't even know existed until you told me? Do you really think I'm capable of that? How? You've been watching me every single day for the last two weeks!"

"The source is credible."

"I don't care! I'm *more* credible!"

"Are you?"

I blink. I hold my breath. My heart stops.

There it is.

How he really feels about me.

My reply comes out as a shaky whisper, anger driving my voice to highs and lows. "I am. I know that. You obviously don't. And it's not my job to convince you anymore. I'm done doing that. I shared my body with you, Silas. I don't regret that. But the part I do regret is sharing my heart. You told me to trust you. I took you at your word, Mr. Honor. Mr. Dignity. Mr. Remorse. And this is what you do to me the second someone spoon feeds you a bunch of fake evidence against me? Really?" My voice is thin and filled with an anguish that is a thousand times stronger than my body.

He says nothing. Just captures my eyes with a long, excruciating look of indifference.

Which is so much worse than anger.

"Go to hell, Silas. You don't deserve another second of my time."

I march across the courtyard, straight for Duff. "I want Gentian off my case. Effective immediately."

Duff's expression doesn't change as he looks at me, then Silas, reaching for his earpiece. "I thought you were firing us all, Jane."

"Not yet. Just Silas. I'll figure the rest out after I've met with my lawyers and sort all this out."

Silas turns away, hiding his face, his shoulders tense, his body rigid. All I can see is his back, a wall of denial.

An impenetrable wall.

My God, I realize. I've been a fool.

This is all nothing but a lie.

A shameless little lie.

CHAPTER 22

*Y*ou ever see your naked body all over the PBS station's news show?

Me neither. Until right now, four days after Alice's death, as I pull my frozen dinner out of the microwave and curl up on the couch, watching as the news cycle spins in front of me, moving from a story about North Korea to–

Me.

Did I mention the naked part?

Alice's paintings are a visual feast that takes away my appetite. The scent of microwaved spicy chicken turns my stomach into a twist tie. There I am.

Naked and broadcast to the world.

After months of being doxxed, having every personal detail spilled all over the internet, having all my Facebook messages and private forum scribblings revealed for the world to see, you would think this wouldn't be so embarrassing. I should have a thicker skin. I know it.

Those paintings are the real me. Not the fake me that the media creates.

That's *me*.

The light on my skin is the same light that graced Silas as he gazed at me. The strokes Alice used, the blends, the perfect imperfections she catalogued–that is me. The way my throat goes concave for a brief stretch of inches, giving my neck a kind of ethereal curve, is me, too.

The world doesn't deserve to see what Alice created.

The world doesn't deserve much of anything right now.

Especially my contempt.

They get it, though.

Clearly, someone found their way into Alice's studio and snapped pictures of the paintings. Larger than life, they boldly take up the screen, hungry for space. That's my breast on screen, the size of a cantaloupe. That's my belly on screen, winking at me with my navel as the eye. That's my jawline, the size of a dinosaur's, reflected in the soft light of Alice's studio.

That's me.

I flip the channels. I'm everywhere. If I wanted attention, this would be cause for celebration.

Instead, I'm alone in an apartment I didn't rent, living next to a man I thought I could trust, and I'm eating over-salted crap as I click through my humiliation on over one hundred channels.

Losing Silas is the part that eats away at me. It's been two days since I saw him last. Duff and Romeo alternate their coverage of me, standing sentry outside my door or finding places to hide. I won't let them in my apartment.

And I'm ignoring all the calls and texts from my father.

Tap tap tap.

I jolt, the remote flying out of my hands and landing in my microwaved noodles.

"Go away!" I shout.

"I have ice cream and lattes. I can't go away. That's a major violation of Friend Code," Lindsay calls back from the other side of the door.

Lindsay? What the hell is Lindsay doing here?

I open the door, because hey–who turns down free ice cream? Especially when it's delivered to your door with your favorite coffee from The Toast and a compassionate smile that makes me want to cry.

Good cry. The kind that gets out locked-up emotions. The kind that softens ice cream and thorn-covered hearts.

Duff catches my eye as Lindsay marches in. I close the door, ignoring him, and she declares, "This place looks like the model apartment at every bland planned community."

"You say that like it's a negative. That's the point," I explain, instantly crushed by her hug. "We're trying to be boring."

"You're succeeding. Wildly."

"We can't all be married to hotshot security firm owners and live a life of luxury."

She snorts. "If by luxury you mean practically being leashed by your own husband, that's me."

"I really didn't need that mental image, Lindsay. Your sex life is your sex life."

She throws a cookie at me. Cookies? There are cookies in that bag, too?

Her eyes land on my remote control, resting in my dinner. "You have really strange taste buds."

"It was an accident. I wasn't expecting anyone to knock on the door. Startled me."

"Is everything okay?" Her voice goes sharp.

"Uh, have you watched the news? Looked at your phone? Been on social media or a basic news website? My naked body is on display across the globe."

"Oh. That."

"That. Yes, *that*." I gesture down at my sweats-covered limbs. "You know. My boobs are on CNN."

"Eh." Her nonchalance is starting to anger me. Then I realize what she's doing. For Lindsay, my exposure really is 'eh.'

Because the parts of her body that have been captured on video and streamed and downloaded, pictured and shown, are worse than what I'm going through.

"I'm sorry," I say. "You're right. It is 'eh' compared to what you've gone through."

"I didn't mean it that way." She seems genuinely surprised by my comment. "I was just trying to make you feel better. I know how much it hurts."

I start to breathe quickly, as if air is a rope and I need to swallow it in one long line before choking. It's as if hearing her say it gives my body permission to feel the pain.

"You okay?" Lindsay asks, fingers on the latte lid as she hands it to me, paused in mid-move.

"No, but I will be. Someday. Maybe when I'm dead," I reply as I take the cup.

She looks at me sharply. "Is that some kind of cry for help?"

"Not in the sense that I'm suicidal. I can't die. Who would they write click bait about if I'm gone? Staying alive is a crucial public service on my part."

Lindsay spews coffee mid-sip. "Jesus, Jane!"

"Oh, I'm sure the media is telling America I killed *him*, too."

She give me a funny look, then laughs. "I totally know where your head is right now. It's like being forced to be in combat at all times, only someone replaced your brain with extremely sensitive cotton that hurts when touched. So you go through life on edge nonstop, but you never have all your wits about you when you need to fight."

I stare at her. The coffee burns my palm, but I can't stop staring.

"And you start to feel like you have no future."

I outright goggle at her.

"Because why should you? You're a piece of trash in the media's eyes. No one believes you, you're only good for drama and controversy. You're not allowed to have a future. In fact, if you tried to imagine having one, you'd take away their toy."

"Toy?"

"You. You're a toy now, Jane. You're just something they play with when they need stimulation."

"Ewww."

"I didn't mean it that way." She screws up her face in concentration. "But it fits, too."

"I just want it all to go away. If I could move to England or Australia, I would."

"Why don't you? Once some of the estate money from Alice comes in, you can."

At the mention of Alice's name, a big hole opens in my chest and starts to spin in a circle.

"Plus, that money means freedom. You can tell my fath– er, *your* father," she amends slowly, "to go to hell."

"What's Harry got to do with Alice and her estate?"

"You know he's been supporting you."

I bristle. "And?"

"That means he's been controlling you. Now you can shake him off. Fire him."

"I never hired him! He's been this invisible hand behind the scenes, driving so much."

"Invisible father is more like it," she says giving me a saucy look, like she's on my side and ready for a rumble with him.

"Yeah. That, too."

"How messed up is your life that having an invisible father who turns out to be a presidential candidate deserves a 'that, too'?"

I try to laugh. I can't.

"I came over because I know you and Silas broke up."

"Did we?" I snort. "Were we ever together?"

"You slept with him."

"Yes."

"I know Silas. That definitely means you were together."

"How would you know? A guy like him probably sleeps with plenty of women." It physically hurts to say those words.

"No. Not since Rebecca."

"Rebecca?"

"His fiancée. Drew says he hasn't dated or been with anyone since she died."

"Silas told me that happened *three years ago*," I gasp, incredulous.

She shrugs. "Just passing on what I know."

"Three years? He's... *no one* for three years?"

"How many guys have you slept with in the last three years?"

I hold up one finger to indicate Silas.

"Same," she says with a strange laugh. "One guy. Drew. And

no one else, ever." She clearly doesn't include what happened to her that infamous night.

I wouldn't, either.

"Sure, but... it's different for Silas. Right? I mean, he's so powerful. Smart. Big. Perceptive and clever. Women must be all over him."

"It doesn't matter if women are all over him. What matters is which woman *he* wants to be all over, Jane." Lindsay looks like she wants to tell me something more. I keep talking, though, more out of nervous habit. Absorbing what she's saying about Silas is hard.

"Well, that's not me now. For sure. He thinks I had something to do with his sister's OD."

"I know. That's why I'm here," she says with a sigh. "Drew's convinced it's true, too. Whatever tipster is sending them information, they're credible enough for Drew to snap back into his 'Jane is public enemy number one' mode again."

"I'm sorry. I don't want to put you in a position where it's awkward with Drew."

She does a double take. "Who said it's awkward?"

"You just–"

"Oh, no. Not awkward. It's actually really basic. He's wrong. I'm right. I think you're being set up. Someone is scorching all the earth around you. He's convinced you're still lying about some things." Her eyes narrow. "Pretty sure he's right about that, but not the things he thinks."

"Silas really thinks I got people to force his sister to OD? I would never, ever, in a million years do that. I wouldn't know the first thing about *how* to do that. And I certainly had nothing to do with Drew or Mark Paulson's parents' deaths!"

"I've been saying the same thing. Stubborn ass. But he's convinced you're not sharing what you know, and that makes him suspicious."

He's right.

"I–remember the texts and the messages we used to get? The ones about sweepstakes and book reviews? Back when you were at the Island?"

"Sure. It's how we communicated in secret. You'd leave a fake book review on a website and I'd decode it. You told me about the sweepstakes texts." Her eyes get really big. "You got one? Recently?"

I figure I have nothing to lose confiding in Lindsay. I show her my phone.

"All witch hunts have a warlock," she reads, giving me a puzzled look. "What the hell does that mean?"

"No idea. All my old messages from that informant were coded. I had to figure out the riddle."

"This isn't some simple riddle. Do you know some witches and warlocks?"

"Um, no."

"Maybe it's a metaphor. Like there's something else. What do witches do?"

"Fly on brooms. Wear black. Cast spells. Have black cats," I say in a voice that's angrier than it should be.

"Maybe it has to do with people who own black cats? Pointing you to them?"

"I don't know anyone who has one."

"Did Alice?"

"No." I snicker. "Does your mom?"

She smiles. "Wouldn't that be appropriate? If we're going to talk about witches, no conversation would be complete without mentioning her, right?"

"Right."

Tilting her latte cup up, she finishes it off and stands, walking into the kitchen. I hear cabinet doors opening and closing. "Time for ice cream."

"It is?"

"It's always time for ice cream."

"True."

Two spoons and two pints later, I realize that while the ice cream tastes good, I have no appetite. Talking about Silas makes me feel shaky. I was ready to hunker down and eat crappy frozen food while watching junk television tonight, not explore Silas's past and wonder why he went three years without dating or sleeping with anyone.

And then chose *me*.

No amount of chocolate or peanut butter in ice cream can make *that* go away.

"You seem distracted," Lindsay says through a mouthful of chocolate goo.

"Want to go for a walk?"

"Now?" She looks outside. "It's getting dark."

"Let's make Duff work for his paycheck."

Reconsidering, she swallows, then smiles. "Yeah! Good point! Where to?"

"My favorite flower shop."

"You want to go to a flower shop? Like a florist?"

"Yes."

"You could choose a dance club. A bar. A coffee and wine house. A restaurant. You could choose anywhere you want, and you choose *a flower shop*?"

"It's special."

Lindsay cleans up the ice cream, dumps our spoons in the sink, pops the lids on the pints and puts them away. Then she looks at me.

"Any chance there are witches at the flower shop?"

"No, but they have Lily." I hold up one finger and jog into my bedroom, fishing through my drawers for jeans. In under a minute I have respectable clothing on, and run a comb through my hair.

"Of course they have lilies. All flower shops do." The way she corrects me makes her sound just like Monica. It's jarring.

"No, Lily. The woman who works there." We grab our purses and open the door to find Duff there, calm and collected.

"Where to? The flower store?" he asks.

Lindsay laughs.

"Yes," I tell him. We make a beeline for the elevator. Duff murmurs into his earpiece. I hear Drew's name.

"We're walking, Duff, so–"

He cuts me off as we start down the stairs instead. "I'm sorry, but no. Strict orders from Drew. Lindsay can't."

Lindsay's hard stop is so sudden, I crash into her back and Duff smacks up against me, pulling back quickly. She turns around from her position on the stairs a few steps below me and looks up, angry. "He said what?"

"His exact words involved obscenities over your unwillingness to listen to him," Duff begins.

"I like it so far," Lindsay cracks.

"But that open-air walking was a hard line. No public bathrooms alone. No small spaces. No open air."

"Basically, I can live in a cage, then," Lindsay grouses, giving me a sour look. "See what I deal with?"

"I know what you live with. Minus the husband part."

Lindsay ignores the SUV parked right at the door of the stairwell and starts walking away, Duff on her tail. I scramble to catch up.

"You're going the wrong way."

She does a one-eighty. "Fine."

"It's not a big deal to take the car."

"It is. You'll understand more after you live with a husband who's a freak about security."

"Not going to happen."

"I think Silas will come around."

"You do?"

"I hear what he says when he comes over and works with Drew."

"What does he say?"

"He mentions you. Defends you. There's a look on his face when you come up. It's adorable. And intense. It's the look Drew has sometimes when he's being open with me. It's the look of a man head over heels in love, Jane."

Duff's behind us as Lindsay holds her head up high. I'm surprised we're not being physically grabbed and thrown in the black SUV, but to my surprise, Romeo appears next to Duff, both of them walking behind us. Within seconds, Duff moves in front of us. Lindsay smirks.

"I'm gonna catch hell from the boss for this," he tells her.

"The boss is catching hell from me, Duff, if it's any consolation," she replies.

We reach The Thorn Poke quickly, the lights on in the shop as twilight steals the rest of the day's light. Lily's working, arranging some hot pink and yellow monstrosity. Duff holds the door for us and we walk in.

Lindsay lets out a low whistle.

"It's beautiful, isn't it?" I say.

"Uhh…" As her voice drops, I turn to see what's wrong.

She's staring at a rack of magazines in the corner.

I'm on all the covers.

And Silas and I are on a few.

Some lucky paparazzi got a long-distance photo of us at The Grove, kissing.

"Oh, no!" I half scream, half moan, the N in *no* caught behind my teeth. The kiss in the photo is hot and heavy, the kind of embrace you have with someone who wants you so badly, they'll risk all to grab a few stolen moments of intimacy, urgency carrying the day.

"That's… not good," Lindsay says as Lily rushes over to me. Her face looks so guilty. She's seen it all.

Hell, half the world has seen it all.

"Silas! He's–we're–caught." I end my sentence with a clunky bang, regular speech out of my grasp right now. All those Tarzan jokes over the years are coming true.

Me Jane.

You Silas.

We screwed.

Lindsay's phone rings. She makes a face, but answers.

Testosterone pours out of the speaker.

"No!" she says, pulling the phone away from her ear as Drew lets out a stream of self-righteous male berating. "No, Drew, I don't care what you ordered Duff to do! I'm a grown-up, and I–"

More testosterone.

She's upset. I'm jealous. Yes, *jealous*. I'm sure being hovered over by her husband is a pain, but it beats not having anyone care. Silas disappeared from my life three days ago. He's avoiding me.

I'd give anything to have him yelling at me, protective and pissed, right now.

I look at the rack of tabloids. We're on five covers.

Pretty sure he's at least pissed at me.

One for two.

"Are you in trouble, too? Sounds like your friend's getting yelled at by her boss for not being careful enough."

"That's her husband yelling."

"Did she invent time travel?"

"Huh?"

"Because you'd have to go all the way back to the Paleolithic era to find a caveman like that."

"No public bathrooms? What do you want me to do, Drew? Pee in the street?" Lindsay shouts, standing in front of a collection of mylar balloons with pink and blue booties on them.

Lily's eyebrows go up. "Nice guy, huh?"

"A little overprotective."

"You think?"

"He has reason to be. I didn't get a chance to introduce you. That's Lindsay Bosworth."

"Am I supposed to know her?" Lily looks at her, then me. "Wait a minute. That name rings a bell."

"Senator Bosworth's dau– daughter." I stumble on the word.

Lily's face goes pale. "Wait–*the* Lindsay Bosworth? The one they say you helped get tortured?"

"The same."

"You guys are friends now?"

"Yes."

"You are really complicated, Jane."

"Yes," I admit, too tired to fight the characterization. "Yes, I am."

Lindsay ends the call, clearly ready to throw the phone at a window or someone's head. Drew's head. But he's not here.

"He says that Daddy is insisting on firing Silas for 'taking advantage' of you, Silas is off duty and not answering his phones. Drew doesn't appreciate my 'insubordination.'" Fire shoots out of her eyes. She looks like a very angry X-Men heroine.

"Insubordination?" I give a small golf clap. "Congratulations. That's quite the accomplishment within a marriage."

"It's not funny."

"No," I say, smothering a smile. "It's not."

But Lindsay cracks, just a little, and snorts. "He's such an ass."

"Harry, or Drew?"

"Both. Drew says Silas's job is seriously on the line."

"Harry already tried to ban me from dating Silas."

Lindsay's gaze jerks to the left, sharply, as she notices Lily standing there, listening. "Do you mind?"

She sounds *just* like Monica.

"No!" Lily chirps. "Not at all!"

"Lindsay, meet Lily. Lily, meet Lindsay." I give Lindsay a pointed look. "This is the woman I wanted you to meet."

Lily giggles at the word *woman*. "Hi! Nice to meet you. I'm so glad they figured out you weren't a slut like those awful friends of yours said you were."

Lily could use a few social skills lessons.

"Thanks." Lindsay looks like she's smelling a sewer. "I guess."

"Oh! That was a compliment," Lily assures her.

"Good to get clarity," Lindsay snarls.

Duff enters the store, sizes up Lily, ignores her, then turns to Lindsay. "We need to go. New orders."

"But we just got here," she whines.

He shrugs. "Boss. You know." A glance at the door makes me turn and look.

To find Silas standing there.

Staring at the magazine rack.

CHAPTER 23

"*I*'m not leaving," Lindsay says defiantly, giving Silas the same lip she gives Drew. "Jane and I just got here. And I've been introduced to Lily, who is fascinating."

"Drew's orders, Lindsay," Silas says with a sigh, like they've been around and around on this issue before. He smells like soap and limes, wearing a polo shirt and dress pants, a light jacket obscuring his gun belt. Tight anger and professional alertness shape his features, jaw hard, the skin under his eyes pulled up tight, face carefully neutral. The epitome of the stereotypical Hollywood bodyguard, he plays the role well.

Except this is life or death. And very, very real.

"Why?"

"My job isn't to ask why," he replies.

Lindsay pointedly looks at the wall of magazines. "What, exactly, is your job, Silas?"

I want to fall into a hole in the ground and be smothered by raw sewage.

"It's to do what I'm told."

She gestures at a magazine with a picture of us kissing. "You were told to do *that*?"

"I'm not talking about me. I'm talking about you, Lindsay."

"Oh, we're definitely talking about how you and Drew are too stupid to see you're being played."

Blazing eyes, so blue, they're almost clear, meet mine. "Trust me. I know I'm being played."

"Not by me," I snap. "By whoever's behind this." I force myself to look at the magazines. "The same person who gave the gunman Harry's private code is probably the one who got those pictures taken."

"That's not part of my job right now," he says coldly.

"We're back to this, are we, Silas?" I hiss the end of his name. "You believe the lies about me and I get treated like–like you swore you never would treat me, ever again."

"That was before new information came to light."

"You *lied*."

"I told a truth based on *your* lies, Jane. You don't get to turn me into the bad guy."

This is killing me. I can feel parts of my body dying swift, painful deaths, yet still wanting to touch him, to be close, to go back to what we had just a few days ago. It feels like decades have passed, attitudes ossified, the hope and eagerness of just a few days ago some kind of quaint naïveté.

I was naïve, all right. Naïve to ever think he would truly love me.

Duff hands Lindsay a phone. I can hear Drew's voice. Lindsay starts to argue, then stops abruptly, her mouth an O of shock.

"Okay," she says in a meek, stunned voice. "I will." A shaky look comes my way. "I have to go, Jane. Can I take a raincheck on hanging out?"

"Of course." I walk to give her a hug, her body tense. Whatever Drew said to her must be bad. "Everything okay?" I whisper.

"No. Be careful. Please," she says as she squeezes me extra hard. "We can use the book reviews to talk more."

"Why? We can't just text? "

"*Shh.*" She lets go and turns away, Duff walking her to yet another unmarked black SUV.

"I'll take you home," Silas says in a hostile voice.

"I'll walk."

"Like hell you will."

"That's awfully unprofessional of you."

"Drawing clear boundaries."

"Oh, don't worry. Your lines are painted with a steamroller, Silas." I go to leave. He blocks me with his body.

"I mean it, Jane. You need to ride, not walk."

"What I need isn't your problem anymore, Silas. I already had you removed from my case. Romeo can take me home. "

"Romeo's gone." He opens the door and holds it with a taut, furious gesture, expecting me to comply.

"I'm not finished here. You're off my case. Go away."

"Um, Jane? Do you need me to call the police? Is he harassing you?" Lily asks, voice rising in anger on my behalf.

The first flicker of real emotion aside from anger makes its appearance in Silas. "No need for police."

"I will wait until *Jane* answers. You're acting like a controlling asshole who might hurt her if I let her leave with you," Lily informs him. In one hand she has a smartphone, 9-1-1 already queued up, ready for her to press Send.

"He–he won't hurt me," I tell her.

"Of course I wouldn't." Silas looks wounded. Disturbed. As if it's sinking in how far this has gone.

"You sure don't look like a guy who wouldn't," Lily says under her breath, putting herself between me and Silas, her eyes searching my face. "Are you sure?"

"Yes." Exhaustion seeps into me. "I–I'll come by tomorrow."

She hugs me. Second hug in a row where I'm saying goodbye to someone I wish I could hang out with. "If you need me, you know my number, right?"

"I do."

Glaring at Silas, she makes it clear she's not sure this is a good idea, but I leave with him anyway. Walking as fast as I can, I turn the corner away from the SUV.

I'm yanked back, crying out as my arm wrenches.

"Way to prove her right, Silas."

"I'm sorry." He sounds genuine. "I didn't think you'd keep walking."

"You could have said something."

"Words don't seem to work on you."

"But violence does?" I start to run away from him, the pain in my shoulder throbbing. It's useless. He catches up within seconds, but I keep running anyhow. If he touches me again, I really will scream.

Sometimes, moving the body beyond its limits is the only way to escape.

"I'm sorry," he pants as I run and he jogs like my sprint pace is nothing. "Truly."

You can't exist, I say to myself in an endless loop, the words taking on a beat. If Silas exists, then I have to acknowledge my heartbreak. If Silas exists, I have to look at him and remember how it felt to have his skin against mine, warm and loving, exotic and heated. If Silas exists, I am forced to remember the pleasure he gave me, the ecstasy of being with him, the rush of abandon that came as he made me feel more vibrant and sensual than I've ever felt in my life.

If Silas exists, then there is a separation. A schism. He will never touch me again in bed. He will never use his body and heart to comfort me.

If Silas exists and we're not together, then I'm *really* broken.

At the building, I go for the stairs, glutes screaming. The more my body suffers, the less I feel the pain in my heart, my mind, on my tongue. Pain crouches like a predator, waiting to strike. If I keep moving, it can't target me so easily. I would rather generate my own pain than be victim to someone else's. Torture is so much more endurable when self-administered.

On the second floor staircase, he says simply, "Jane. Please."

I'm cradling my hurt arm. I pause. I don't turn around.

"Let me help with your arm."

"No." My refusal echoes up the staircase, as if trying to break through the ceiling.

I push the hallway door hard with my good arm, storming onto our floor, marching straight for my apartment. I have to find my keys in the pocket on the side of my body with the hurt arm. Delayed by the injury, I lose precious seconds.

I feel Silas before he speaks.

"Leave me alone," I say, before he can try to tell me more words that do not matter. All the apologies in the world for grabbing my arm won't make up for what he's done to me in so many other ways.

The elevator dings. Footsteps.

And then the last sound I expected to hear.

"JAAAAAAAAANNNNNEEE!" squeals little Kelly, tackling my legs with a giant hug. She uses her whole body and full heart the way only a little kid can.

Silas steps in front of me and opens my door with *his* keys. His keys to my apartment.

That's it.

The tears start.

"Jane! Are you here to play Candyland with me again? Grandma says we are going to stay at her house for a while. We leave in a few days. Uncle Silas said Grandma's here until some man in a bathrobe decides we can go."

"Bathrobe?" I don't want to wipe my eyes and make it obvious I'm crying. Silas looks at me and sees it, though.

"Robe. A judge's robe," he clarifies.

"Ah." Behind the scenes, custody issues must be resolving. I wouldn't know, because I'm not part of Silas's inner world anymore.

Damn the tears.

My phone buzzes. I can't reach it without feeling the pain of something caught in my shoulder. Kelly touches the outside of my front pocket, frowning.

"Someone is texting you," she says. "A friend?"

"Maybe," I tell her, my panic rising as I see her grandmother come into view, her eyes lighting up as she sees me.

Ah. Silas hasn't shared his stupid belief that I had something to do with his sister's death. Hope rises again, its heartbeat in rhythm with the throbbing in my shoulder.

"Jane!" she says, giving Silas a funny look. He's standing back now, propping my front door open for me, stretched in a way that gives me the most space between us.

"Grandma, can Jane come over for Candyland?" Kelly begs.

"No," Silas says, just as Linda says, "Sure!"

Like every typical five-year-old, Kelly only hears the yes. "YAY! Jane's coming over!"

"Just for a short visit," Silas says gently. "So I can make sure her arm is okay."

"What happened to your arm?" Linda asks, immediately concerned.

"Someone grabbed it accidentally while I was walking. Some jerk who can't bother to see the world in front of him," I add in an acid tone. "You know the type."

"Oh, yes. The ones who think the world revolves around their perspective and no one else's?" she asks, matching my tone.

"Exactly," I say, the edge all too clear to Silas, who is seriously angry with me.

Good.

"Karma will get him," she assures me.

"Oh, it will," I agree.

"Come over when you've freshened up," Linda says. "We're only here for a short time." She lowers her voice. "Kelly's about to have a meeting with a social worker. We're a few steps away from being safe with custody, and then we can move her to Minnesota."

"Oh, wow. So soon?"

"I can't take much more time from work. And the legal bills..."

"Mom," Silas says sharply, ending conversation. Linda looks chastened, but recovers fast.

"Sorry. Given what Silas does for a living, I never know what I'm allowed to talk about," she says in a conspirator's voice.

I smile. It's the polite, expected response.

And then I go into my apartment, shut the door, and stand there, crying silently until my belly turns into a tight ball of pain my muscles reject.

It's worse right under my heart, as if the pain were clinging to each rib, being held back by some unseen force from storming the gates.

Silas was a Trojan horse. I thought he was one thing.

He turned out to be quite another.

Little Kelly leaves soon, so this is my only chance to see her once more.

I think through the moment in the flower shop as I walked away. Silas consciously reached for me, pulling me back into his world. The one where he makes all the decisions. The one where he tells me what to do. The one where he protects me.

The one where he hates me for committing crimes I didn't commit.

It's so easy to make someone believe a lie.

And so hard to convince them of the truth.

Backwards. It's all backwards. I feel like the kids in that series on Netflix.

Everything in my world is upside down.

And there's a monster out there no one else sees, coming for me.

I set my purse down and grab a tissue, wiping my face, blowing my nose, trying to find homeostasis. What now?

I check my phone. Hedding Stuva, texting me.

Tap tap tap.

I whirl around in surprise and open my door. No one's there.

"Hey!" I look down. Kelly.

With Linda and Silas right behind her.

"Sorry," Linda says apologetically. "The social worker moved the appointment up. We're leaving now, and Kelly insisted–"

"I wanna say hi. And I want you to have this," she says shyly, handing me a crayon-covered drawing.

I hold it up with my good arm as I crouch to her level. Silas notices, frowning.

"It's beautiful! I can see the princess in there. And are those candy canes?"

Kelly beams, hurling her little arms around my neck. "Yes!

Someday I wanna go to Disneyworld with you, Jane! Can we go and be princesses there?"

The lump in my throat threatens to crawl out and go hide under the covers of my blow-up bed, never to emerge. "Um," I say, stalling. I can't lie to her.

Silas rescues me. "Mom, why don't you take Kelly to the car. I'll be there shortly."

Linda nods, then pulls me in for a hug. "Take care of yourself, Jane. Hopefully we'll see you before we go back to Minnesota."

"*Mmm hmm,*" is all I can manage, smiling at her and Kelly as they go back to the elevator, Kelly pushing the button eagerly.

"You didn't tell your mom. You didn't tell her what Drew suspects about me," I say to him. It comes out like an accusation. I don't mean it that way.

"It's not just Drew who suspects," he says with a glower. "But no. I didn't."

"Why not?"

"I didn't want to add to her distress."

"You don't really believe that I had anything to do with your sister's death, do you?"

"I don't know what to believe. Trust me, Jane, that's a position I'm not used to. I don't like ambiguity. Not in combat, not in protecting clients, and certainly not when it comes to emotions."

"Life is filled with ambiguity. We have to learn to navigate it. It's what makes us human."

"I didn't say I couldn't handle ambiguity. I said I don't *like* it."

We're at a standoff.

And when you're at a standoff, you're basically playing a game of chicken.

I fold first, making my body turn away from him, consciously choosing to be the first to flinch. Without a word, I leave him hanging, walking away. There is no response good enough to meet whatever criteria he has in mind.

Because he might not like ambiguity, but right now, ambiguity makes me feel safer than the truth.

Whatever that is.

$\mathcal{I}$ find a tube of pain cream in the little first-aid kit in my bathroom and do my best to rub it into my shoulder. My phone buzzes repeatedly while I'm covered in pain lotion. Irony: whatever's in those texts will just cause even more pain.

I need to bathe in nothing but pain cream. Swim in an ocean of it.

Let it swallow me whole.

After washing my hands and taking a few deep breaths, I think about Alice. I stare at myself in the mirror. Red-rimmed eyes. Splotchy complexion. Slightly hunched-in shoulder. Wrinkled and rumpled, I'm nothing much to look at.

But in Alice's eyes, I was beauty. The light brought me in, made me more real than this world, made her paint me for all eternity.

I have worth.

I do.

Alice said so.

What I don't have is love.

I walk into the living room, flip on a show, and regroup. The pain in my shoulder is an endless reminder of Silas. I know he didn't hurt me on purpose. Remorse radiated off him, the apologies genuine. At least there's that between us: basic human decency.

And Kelly.

Soon, Linda and Kelly will leave. The little sweetie will have to learn to live all her future days without a mommy. Without *hers*. You can find substitutes. You can have friends. You can even, for a brief and shining moment, have an intimate partner who seems to genuinely care.

But not having a mother leaves a hole no one else can repair. You have to learn to navigate around it for the rest of your life.

If you fall in, the abyss is endless. And it calls you, like a mother whispering your name in the night.

Bzzzz.

My phone. Again. Grudgingly, I pick it up. Texts galore.

Lindsay: *Coffee at The Toast. Tomorrow. 1 pm.*

Harry: *I need you to come to The Grove. Now.*

Marshall: *You need to come to The Grove.*

"I need you all to go to hell. How about we have a meeting in hell? I'll bring the coffee," I mutter to myself.

Except for Lindsay. Lindsay's already been in hell. She doesn't need a return trip.

I text Harry and Marshall as a group: *I'm not leaving my place. If you want a meeting, come here.*

Instantly, Harry responds: *That would be a security risk.*

I reply: *For whom?*

Blocking his number is so tempting.

Nothing from Marshall. Silence from my father.

I pour myself a glass of wine and try to watch a political drama. Too close for comfort. Instead, I turn to a dystopian fantasy involving fascism. I make it through one episode.

I settle on old improv comedy shows.

One hour and two shows later:

Tap tap tap.

"Jane?" It's Duff. "Open up."

I do.

To find my father and Marshall in the doorway.

They walk in like they own the place.

"Good idea to hold the meeting here," Marshall says to me pleasantly. Harry looks around my apartment as if I live in a slum. Disgust is all over his face.

"I never said you could come *now*!"

"Best to get this over with," Harry says, looking me over. "You smell like sports injury cream. What happened?"

"None of your business."

He looks at Marshall. "Get the injury report from security."

"It wasn't—oh, forget it. You could have warned me you were coming over!"

"Security risk," Harry snaps.

"Your entire life is a security risk!" I lob back.

"Now you're starting to understand." Harry sits down on one of the chairs at my dining table. I only have two. Marshall gestures for me to sit, too.

"Why are you here?" I remain standing.

"We need to talk to you about what's really going on."

"You think I'm not experiencing reality? Have you looked at the news, lately? I'm real, all right."

Deep discomfort seeps out of Harry's pores. "That's bad enough, but we're here for other reasons."

"There's something worse than having my naked body exposed to the world and the tabloids covered with pictures of Silas and me kissing at The Grove?"

"Yes," Marshall says without irony. "We know your mother was innocent."

"You *what*?"

"And we know you are, too."

"Okayyyyy...."

"We also know that someone in the inner circle is sabotaging us. *And you*. It's someone very, very close."

My father looks at me. "We've narrowed it down to about eight people. You're not one of them."

"Gee, thanks for the vote of confidence."

"But Silas is," he adds as if he's ordering a side of bacon with his breakfast.

"Silas? You think *Silas* is behind all of this? You're crazy.

Legitimately, certifiably crazy." I start laughing. I'm not sure I'll ever be able to stop.

"Think about it," Harry says, eyes intense and full of determination. "He knows explosives. You're tracked by him. He's your main conduit of information. Drew's focused on you. I think he's blinded by loyalty and can't see Silas for what he might be."

"Which is?"

"A deep-state operative."

I can't stop laughing.

"What about Silas's sister?" I finally manage to choke out.

Harry's face tightens. "A junkie who overdosed? What about her?"

"Someone gave Drew an anonymous tip that *I* was behind her death."

"What?" Harry looks genuinely shocked. He gives Marshall a displeased look, as if Marshall isn't doing his job properly. Hope rises deep within me. I want to quash it. There is no way Silas will ever come back to me. None.

I can't let go, though. Hope springs eternal, right? But killing hope, even if it's unrealistic, is a kind of soul death I just can't handle.

"First I've heard of it," Marshall defends, giving Harry an earnest shrug.

"The heroin she took was laced with fentanyl. It killed her quickly. And now my entire life is being ruined–again–by someone telling *your* security team that I made her die."

"That's crazy," Harry exclaims.

"My entire life is crazy, Harry. Has been since before I was born." A yearning for my mother rises up in me.

"That's not true," he says softly. "We gave you a good life."

"We? *We?* We, who? You and my mother? You gave me twenty-four years of nothing but lies!"

"It was the best we could do."

"STOP SAYING THAT! It's just another lie! You could have divorced Monica and married my mother!"

"You're right. I could have. But Monica was pregnant, too. I wasn't about to leave my wife in that condition."

"But you'd do it to my mother? You sick, sick bastard."

"I'm not proud of how I handled everything. But I had a very difficult choice to make."

"And you chose Monica."

"Yes. I did."

"Because you love her more than you loved my mother."

"No. That isn't true."

"Then why?"

"That is personal."

"We're talking about *my* life here! You can't claim it's personal when your decision changed the course of my entire life!" I challenge.

"I can, and I am."

"What are you hiding? What makes you use people like this? Only someone with a disturbing secret would manipulate so desperately. What is it? What did you *do*?"

If Harry could flip the dining table, he would.

Instead, he stands, visibly shaken, running an angry hand through his hair. I can't look away, watching every move, trying to find myself in his gestures, his features, his emotional reactions.

"I'm only here to protect you. Drew told me you threatened to stop allowing the protection we provide. You can't do that," he tells me.

"Don't tell me what I can and can't do. I don't need you anymore. Alice's estate means I'm independent financially."

"That will take months, maybe a year, to trickle in to you."

"I don't care. I'm done taking 'help' from someone who doesn't believe me."

"I do believe you. I said so."

"If you believe I'm innocent, and you also believe someone in your inner circle is sabotaging you, you're missing the obvious." I want to say her name. I do. I'm about to, just as Harry's phone buzzes. He looks at it.

Abruptly, he leaves. Just like that. *Poof!* My front door shuts with an efficient click.

"Jane," Marshall says, his voice surprisingly casual and kind. "I know this is hard."

"For someone whose entire job is to spin, you are doing a bad job of it right now."

"How about I take off my spin suit and we'll just speak in blunt truths. Off the record."

"My entire life has been off the record, Marshall. Go for it."

"Your father loved Anya. Deeply. But he loved becoming president more."

"And he chose Monica because divorcing a pregnant wife for his pregnant lover would have ruined his political career?"

"Yes. But it's deeper than that."

"How?"

"Monica is... ambitious." He clears his throat, a pink flush mottling his neck. Marshall is fair in the way of Irish men, with skin flushes and thinning blond hair. He looks at me as if I'm supposed to decode his nonverbal signals to find some unspoken truth.

"Hard not to notice."

"And becoming president is all about building the right team. Making compromises to move up. Leveraging assets and relationships. Knowing when to be tough and when to back off. People have those skills–they're innate. You have them or you don't. And Anya didn't. She loved Harry for who he is. Wanted a quiet life with him. Was holding out for that. She didn't understand."

"You mean she wasn't a predatory, power-hungry bitch like Monica."

"Yes."

"You weren't kidding about the blunt part."

"I never kid when it comes to work," he says with a pointed smile.

"It really comes down to that? Monica was a better fit when it came to rising up the political ladder to become president? She was more of an asset as potential first lady?"

"That is a very watered-down version. I'd go much further. She has *made* Harry. He would be a state rep piddling away with quid pro quo contracts and private corporate payoffs if she hadn't worked tirelessly to get him into the U.S. Senate."

"Why?"

"She wants to be first lady."

"But why?"

"I don't know. I know very little about her. She's not the friendliest of people."

"Where is she from? What's her history?" It dawns on me that I've never asked this question before. I need to research her. Dig into her past. Understand more about her, because it turns out she's my enemy. Has been since I was conceived.

And I had no idea.

All these years.

"Why are you telling me this? Why now?"

"Because you know. *We* know."

"Did you know I was Harry's daughter before all this?"

"No. Rumors abounded. But the blood test confirmed it."

"Why did you make me go through that awful medical exam? You could have just asked for my blood."

"Orders from a different agency." He shrugs, as if that violation I faced were just another bureaucratic procedure.

"There are a lot of orders about me. Anonymous tips about me. But where is the evidence I've done anything wrong?"

"None exists. Trust me, we've looked."

"If Harry knew all along I was his biological daughter, why has he consistently tormented me like this? What kind of father orders a medical exam like that one?"

"It wasn't Harry who ordered it. Like I said, an agency. Acting on a tip."

"A tip."

We stare at each other, neither willing to break first.

"Marshall," I finally say, "there's a reason you're telling me so much about Monica, isn't there?"

"Yes."

"Oh." All the air in me runs away.

"Be careful, Jane. Be very, *very* careful." He slides a small box across the table. It's black molded plastic, the size of a laptop. As I touch it, the edge feels cold and unyielding.

I look at him, puzzled. He lifts one finger to his lips in a *shhhhh* gesture.

And with that, he stands up, plucks a pink peony from my vase, swallows the rest of his glass of water and gives me a somber nod good-bye.

"But I–"

My door snaps shut on my words. I jump up to click over the deadbolt. Duff is out there, so it's just a precaution, but one he's drilled into me.

I practically sprint back to the table and look at the black case. It has thick click-locks on it. I pop all three sides and open it.

It's a gun.

Tiny, with two boxes of ammunition. I've been to firing ranges before. Mom taught me how to shoot when I was a teenager. We always had a gun in a locked box, ammo stored separately, for home invasion protection.

But this? This is different.

Marshall has given me a *gun*.

The man acting on behalf of my father, Senator Harwell Bosworth, candidate for president of the United States, has given me a mysterious firearm after warning me about the future first lady.

Talk about *blunt*.

CHAPTER 25

My apartment is all an illusion of privacy. Every bit of it. Because within a minute of Marshall leaving, there's a knock on the door.

"Marshall?" I call out, my hand on the closed gun case, the heat from my palm making it feel like a hot poker.

"No. Silas."

"Damn!" I mutter, grabbing the case. It's heavier than I expect and I wrench my injured arm, dipping down but maintaining my grip.

"Hold on!" I call out, rushing into my bedroom and shoving it under the mussed covers of my blow-up cot. Racing to the door, I answer it to find a nearly nuclear man standing there, his face red, veins bulging.

Without asking permission, he comes in, closes the door behind him, locks it, and whips around.

"What the hell were Marshall and Harry doing here?"

"Playing Euchre. We need a fourth. Want to join us?"

"Damn it!" He slams his hand on the table. I jump, flinching enough to make him take deep breaths. "I'm not going to hurt you," he assures me.

"I know that."

"Don't look at me like that," he commands.

"But you did. You hurt me."

"I did. It was a mistake. I am sorry, Jane."

"I think coming here was a mistake, too, Silas," I say quietly, the words fighting with every part of me that wants to be in his arms again.

"No. I'm here because I need to be here."

"Why?"

"Too many unanswered questions. Too much conflicting evidence. Drew's convinced again that we can't trust you. But then the senator comes here for a confidential meeting with you. Why?"

I throw the same words he's said to me right back at him. "I can't share that information."

"Of course you can."

"Then let me clarify: I *won't*."

"Why not? Because it implicates you?"

"Nothing implicates me."

"Plenty of evidence sitting in Drew's office does, Jane."

"Rumors. Tips. Show me the evidence. Not someone's plan to turn into Iago."

"Throwing Shakespeare at me? We're not playacting *Othello* here. You think we're being manipulated?"

"Of course. I know you are. Why aren't you looking at Monica the way everyone else is looking at me?" I have to be careful. No one can know what Marshall told me.

Or *gave* me.

I expect Silas to tell me I'm crazy.

He doesn't.

"We are. But the proof is... sketchy."

"Of course it is–she's smart! Savvy. Covers her tracks."

"Drew thinks you're the same."

"What do *you* think?" The words are so much more than that simple question.

"If I knew what to think, I wouldn't be so angry."

"If you weren't so angry, what would you be feeling?"

His look is caustic, ragged, yearning, dangerous. In those eyes I see how wrong I've been.

Being apart hurts him, too. Not knowing who to believe is causing him so much agony.

The fact that he can't be sure about me hurts more.

"I want to know! Tell me you're honest! Tell me with every fiber of your being that you didn't do any of this! That you're not working with the deep state. You're not colluding and feeding The Grove's security codes to Harry's enemies. That you didn't use your contacts to kill my sister, or that you don't report to people who killed Paulson's and Foster's parents. Tell me I can flip the switch inside me that stays on guard, flip it off, sink into you and know to the core of me that you are true. Tell me, damn it."

He looms over me, staring down, as if I haven't been saying all of that since the day I was accused.

I give him the one true answer: "No."

"What do you mean, *no*? No, you're not honest? No, you're not innocent?"

"I am honest!" I shout, panting. "I am innocent! I've been screaming it from the rooftops, you jackass! *No* to your demand. *No* to your requirement. *No* to your rant. I've been saying everything you just asked for, Silas, and it's not my fault if you can't hear me!" I have to be closer to him, to make sure that this time the words make their way into whatever center of his brain processes anything I say.

I move, drawn into his space, not from allure but from the simple position of trying to reach him. Leaning in, I move my face within inches of his, standing on tiptoes to do it.

"This is not about me, Silas. Not one bit, and you know it. It's about you and loyalty."

"Loyalty? You expect me to be loyal to you, even when the evidence–"

"Rumors! Tips! And no. I don't expect it. But I do expect you to be self-aware enough to see that your loyalty to Drew is making you miss the truth. And it's not my fault you're missing it. So get your big head in the game again, Silas. There literally aren't enough words I could possibly say to you to make you trust me. Not one. That's on you. You have to do it. Quit putting the burden on me."

"Burden! The burden? Since when did the truth become a *burden?*"

"When you created an impossibly perfect version of the truth that no one–including me–can ever meet, which is so convenient for you, isn't it? If no one can meet your standards, then you never have to let anyone in!"

"I let *you* in!"

"And then you kicked me right back out because Drew told you something that made it easy. Made it safe for you again. You only feel safe when you suspect the woman you're with is going to betray you. And then you get out before she has the chance to love you."

He goes pale. "Love? I know we said it before but – is that really what this is for you, Jane? Are you sure you're not just adding the promise of love to your bag of tricks?"

I let his words hang there, like a cliff diver at the top of a waterfall.

And then he dives, kissing me hard, his lips brutal, his hands harsh and everywhere as I kiss him back, pounding on his chest with my fists, not wanting him to stop but also needing to hurt him. It makes no sense, but nothing in my life makes sense.

If life is chaos, might as well kiss Silas in an angry fit as part of it, his mouth demanding that I give him the truth, his hands extracting a promise I shouldn't have to give yet again.

"Stop it!" I push him away. If he needs me to declare my honesty until he believes it, he doesn't deserve my kiss.

I might, but he doesn't.

"You–you have to be telling me the truth!" he shouts, inches from my face, the taste of him on my tongue.

"I am! Why can't you believe me?"

"Because if you're lying, I'll have to kill you!"

For a few seconds, I stop breathing. Sound ends. All of the lines between my body and the world lose definition.

And then Silas walks out my front door, slamming it.

I drop to the floor, falling in the space between the kitchen and the living room, his last words ringing in my ears.

Because if you're lying, I'll have to kill you.

I stand and walk into my bedroom, pulling back the covers to find the gun case. It's a Beretta Nano, similar to the kind I used at gun ranges with Mom.

Someone has done their homework.

I load it, undo the safety, brace my stance and steady the sight. One trigger pull.

I'm just one away.

I redo the safety.

Marshall warned me about Monica. Harry thinks Silas is the culprit. Silas and Drew think it's me.

Muscle memory makes me imagine the sequence from trigger pull to discharge. It's like giving birth. Loading the weapon is like conception and pregnancy. Removing the safety is like water breaking.

And pulling the trigger? That's when we birth a new self.

Pow.

CHAPTER 26

J'm running in a big meadow around a lake, with mountains surrounding me, a circle of natural wonder that takes all the colors and uses them with mathematical precision to create the greatest beauty for the greatest good. The grass feels like silk against my bare legs, and I'm aroused. Naked and flushed, the wind turning my nipples to pearls, my inner thighs brushing against soft, warm water as I'm suddenly in a stream made of hot spring water.

It flows down from a mountain, a waterfall of rushing energy, infusing me through osmosis with an enveloping love. Like a shockwave, my body jolts, powered by pure joy. The source of this force eludes me. I don't care. My skin lights up, transported to a place where even the memory of pain is not allowed.

Banished by all that is good and whole, clear and unmarred by unfairness or treachery, pain has no home in this wonderland. Animals dart through the woods at the base of the mountains. I am unafraid. I am invincible.

I am invincible because I am loved here.

A computer screen appears, a grotesque monster the size of a human being, the screen its head, a human body making up the rest of him. An electronic mouse, the older kind with a cord, snakes out of his ass from behind. The screen changes to a video of me being attacked, naked and vulnerable, the horror movie in front of me. Averting my eyes is impossi-

ble. Evasive maneuvers don't work, the screen in front of me at all times, the monster blocking me from turning away.

It's always there.

It will never, ever not be there.

Suddenly, the signal dies, all the color distilling down to a single, solitary green dot. The monster falls, the screen cracking, spidering into a thousand tiny shards of glass that reanimate.

They come for me.

They come for a bloodletting.

Before the first one draws blood, I'm protected by a long, homespun skirt, layers weighing me down, my head covered by a thin cotton hat. I reek of body odor, an old, ripe scent that comes from weeks without showering, from clothes that retain the sweat and blood of past days like a physical memory. My arms are wrenched, the pain bearable if not for the betrayal.

For it is Silas who pulls me toward the pile of sticks with a tall wooden pole at the center. He's even stronger than usual.

"All witches must have a warlock, Jane," Silas says, his voice going deeper, his eyes drawing me in, until I don't know whether my soul is mine or the devil's.

"Caw! Caw!" calls out an onyx crow, the sound rhythmic, maddening, "Caw caw caw..." as it becomes too steady, an electronic sound of panic and terror.

I wake up to smoke, the dream all over my skin, my scent mixed with an aged woodsmoke odor that won't go away.

"JANE!" Someone's in my apartment, calling for me. I sit up, disoriented, wondering why I'm not burnt.

Duff's in my bedroom, with Silas right on his heels. I'm sleeping in a t-shirt and underwear, but I sit up, shocked by their appearance.

"Get out!" Silas says, shouting over the loud alarm. A second one, interwoven over the other, creates a horrid cacophony, making it hard to think.

Silas pulls a gun from his waistband and says to Duff, "This could be a set-up."

Abandoning all modesty, I climb out of bed and find my pj bottoms, shoving one leg in just as all the lights go off.

Alarms continue, but the power's been cut.

"Gentian!" Duff hisses. The glow of his phone screen lights the room. I finish putting on the pants, then feel on the ground for my shoes, finding only one.

"Get her out of here. Call for an SUV. This smells like a trap," Silas barks. Duff acts quickly, moving down the hall in darkness save for his phone's flashlight. I follow Duff, now smelling smoke, my injured shoulder banging a door jamb. I cry out but don't stop, my bare toes curling in reaction to the pain.

Silas says nothing behind me, his hand on the small of my back, gentle but guiding from the rear.

People pour into the hallway in steady groups, the muttering of the confused crowd like holding a conch up to your ear at the beach. Duff's in front of me, moving slowly, and Silas is on me, so close. Too close.

And then I realize what they're doing.

This isn't your standard fire alarm evacuation.

They are shielding me with their *bodies*.

We're downstairs, the bare grass tickling my feet as we move to a small black car at the end of a narrow sidewalk, my soles on concrete quickly. The lingering strands of my dream make the grass feel erotic. I stuff that emotion down, down, down as I realize it's happened again.

I've let them take charge.

Conditioned to obey, I just did what I was told.

I stop in my tracks so fast, Duff doesn't realize we have five, even eight feet between us for a few seconds.

"It's the small black car there," Silas says, as if I'm confused.

As if I don't know where to go.

"I know. But I'm staying here." A firefighter walks by, her pace slower than I'd expect, and as Silas starts to argue with me, I call out, "Do you know what started the fire?"

"Looks like a kitchen fire on the first floor. Small, contained," she calls back with a smile. "Just stay outside until we can clear the building and get you back in."

I give Silas a smug smile. "See? No internet trolls armed with fire-alarm-pulling skills. Just a boring domestic reason for the fire."

"For once, it wasn't someone trying to kill you," Silas says cynically.

"Don't sound so disappointed."

He just glares at me. For the first time, I take a look at him. Pajamas. Inside-out t-shirt. Gun in his pocket, weighing his pajamas down. Like me, I'll bet he woke from a dead sleep.

Did he dream my dream? Was he burning me at the stake in his subconscious? Is he the "warlock" in my cryptic message? Was my father's warning true?

Gaslighters and sociopaths take truths about themselves and turn them around, accusing you of the very negative attributes they hold. Is Silas a master manipulator?

Have I been played–body, mind, soul, and heart?

Duff walks over to us and interrupts, handing me a phone. "It's Senator Bosworth."

"Jane?" He sounds worried. "You need to do whatever Duff and Silas say. We haven't sourced the fire in your building." Notice how he doesn't ask how I am? I'm sure Duff briefed him. Why interact with me on an emotional level when your staff can do it for you?

"It was a kitchen fire."

"That's what they say, but until we do more research and–"

I hang up on him.

"ALL CLEAR, FOLKS! It was just smoke! Fire's out and you're fine to go back to sleep," calls out the same female fire-fighter I spoke to, clipboard in hand, her fingers cupped around her mouth to shout.

Like everyone else, I walk to the main doors and join the cattle call to go into my apartment. Duff cuts me off, moving in front of me, Silas behind.

"You're being unreasonable," Silas says in my ear, his breath heavy and intense as he leans forward, his voice coming through gritted teeth.

"I'm being careful. Has it ever occurred to you that maybe

I'm being told details about *you* that don't pass the sniff test?" I call back over my shoulder.

"By who?"

"Oh. Sorry. Can't tell you that," I say, smirking to myself. "Confidential."

"You're joking."

"Actually, no. Someone did warn me. Pretty credibly." I stop and turn around, looking him in the eye. "Thanks for ending it first. You saved me the trouble."

I don't mean a word I'm saying.

He can tell. I can tell, though, that my words also hit the bullseye.

"This isn't about what we are–*were*. It's professional. You're not safe."

"You're right about that." I take a step back from him. *Were*. Ouch.

"I don't mean you're not safe with me."

"I do."

"Do you really?"

Do I really? Some part of me screams for him, even now as he challenges me, our bodies in a nebulous place from our broken slumber, the twin stresses of fire and predators making us raw. I don't really, truly believe he's trying to hurt me, but the signals inside that my heart and my head send to the rest of me are crossed. Transposed. The mess of confusion inside unsettles me.

The confusion itself *is* the danger.

We reach the elevators but Duff takes me to the staircase, avoiding the crowd. He's also avoiding any chance we'll be trapped in a small space with no way out. Careful calibration of bodies in time and space is his and Silas's job.

I'm tired of being one of those bodies.

My phone rings. It's probably Harry. I ignore it. Duff's and Silas's phones both ring seconds after.

Now I'm *sure* it's Harry.

"Drew." Silas taps my shoulder. I ignore him.

"It's Drew on my phone. For you."

"I don't want to talk to him."

265

"He doesn't care what you want."

"And that's exactly why I don't want to talk to him, Silas."

A gentle but insistent hand on my arm stops me. "You have to talk to him."

"No. I don't. What are you going to do? Pin your phone against my ear and make me listen?"

I hear Drew shout from the phone, "Is Lindsay giving her lessons? Good grief, Jane. Just come to The Toast today. 7 a.m." His voice ends abruptly.

"Message delivered," Silas says tightly.

"That doesn't mean I'll obey." I put my hands up like a dog, begging. I stick out my tongue and pant. "Good girl," I say. "Go fetch the stick. Go to the meeting. Submit to the exam."

Fall in love with a guy who can't trust you.

We reach our floor. I walk into my apartment. I close the door. I know Silas is out there, deliberating. I have to pretend. Pretend he's not there.

This isn't a game of Candyland, though. I'm not a princess, and we aren't surrounded by sweetly spun sugar in a fairytale that feeds my imagination. Emotional needs aren't fantasy. They're very real. Humans are wired for connection, and I'm down to Lindsay and Lily. That's it. My only friends are a flower shop girl I click with and the woman the media thinks I betrayed.

The clocks in my apartment all blink out of sync. My phone says it's 5:33 a.m. Sunlight shines through the dining area. There's no way I can fall back asleep.

I set up the coffee pot. Turn it on. Take a shower. A semblance of normalcy is better than the alternative. If I have to pretend Silas isn't there, I might as well prop up as many parts of the facade that help me to fit in as possible.

Two cups of coffee later, I decide to torture myself with my phone. Hundreds of ignored notifications, texts, and emails, already filtered by Drew's team, do not instill confidence in society's capacity for compassion.

Or decency.

We really haven't evolved past our baser impulses. Not one iota. Social media makes that abundantly clear.

Shake it off, I tell myself, searching for Lindsay's text. I brighten as I think about seeing her again.

One notification from an online bookstore makes my heart race. I click to the book, a long line of reviews under it. Sorting by "most recent," I find Lindsay's very, very coded message.

The book is about the abuses of patriarchy.

I laugh, the sound dying in my throat as I read the book review. Five stars, as usual.

The phallic symbolism discussions alone are illuminating, but understanding how women need to be armed with their own version of phalluses is its greatest contribution to the literature.

That was Lindsay's entire review.

Huh? She wants me to... grow a penis?

And then I get it. A chill runs through me.

Phallus.

Gun.

I go to the locked box under my bed and pull it out. Opening it feels like unlocking a gate to hell. I do it anyway.

I pull the gun and the clip out. There's another layer beneath it. I pull up the insert to find a small holster. It's designed for something smaller than a shoulder.

It's for the thigh.

All the pieces fall into place. When you don't know who to trust, you arm yourself. Physically, psychologically, emotionally–it doesn't matter. You do whatever it takes to feel safe.

I find a loose, long maxidress. It's similar to the one I was wearing when my car was firebombed. The thin straps of the thigh holster feel exotic. Almost sexual. The gun rests along my inner thigh, just above the knee. I have a phallus between my legs.

But this is one I point at the world. Not one that invades me.

For a long, long time I stand at the window and stare into space until finally my vision goes white. The landscape of the busy city fades to nothing. I am nothing. My life is nothing. All that is left is self-preservation.

But what self am I preserving?

Who am I? What's left of me?

I shake myself out of it as someone taps on my door. It's inevitable. Duff will take me to see Drew.

I acquiesce.

The car ride to The Toast is uncharacteristically quiet. No Silas, Duff's being somber, and the radio isn't on. The gun under my skirt feels so obvious. So blatant. Like the world can see it and thinks I'm an idiot for imagining otherwise. This feeling is familiar. I've always felt as if everyone can see my thoughts and feelings, no matter how carefully I hide them. It's as if the rest of the world has some secret trick for how to be obscure, and I missed that lesson.

Duff pulls into the lower level of the parking garage next to The Toast. He takes a sharp turn and goes into an area marked "Restricted."

Silas is standing right there.

He looks bigger. *Angrier.* The suit he's wearing shows off more muscle and breadth than I remembered. Is that how this is going to work? Every second of pleasure we shared will be seared in my memory, but my understanding of his body will fade over time?

I have no perspective. No way to compare this experience to any other. He is my first. My one and only.

And this is killing me.

Maybe he's spent the last few days bulking up. When I'm stressed, I drink coffee and go for walks. Maybe when Silas is stressed, he lifts weights. I don't know.

What I do know is that the way he looks at me is so different from that night at Alice's, when she painted and we, well...

We were *we*.

Now we're Silas and Jane.

And in his eyes, I'm not even Jane.

I am the enemy.

"Go away," I tell him, seriously starting to wonder if Harry's warning is true. My skin turns prickly with panic. What if Silas really is my biggest threat? Why would he be here now, in a dark, sheltered space? Have I been lured to my death by Duff and Silas?

It's silly. Stupid. Paranoid and bizarre, but the doubt is there. So strong I can taste it, metallic and cloying.

I press my knees together, the reassuring solidity of the gun ready for me to access at any time if I'm quick enough.

Duff leads me to an elevator, exchanging a look with Silas that spikes my heart rate. Duff turns around and goes back to the car. I linger, brain racing to find a way out. I need to escape. Screw the 7 a.m. meeting at The Toast.

I need to *flee*

The air feels sinister. Deadly. I can't explain it. I can only feel it. The elevator appears and Silas motions for me to get in. I bend at the knee, buying time.

Not enough time.

All witches have a warlock.

What does it all mean?

The doors start to close. As Silas steps forward to stop them, inspiration strikes. I lunge up and pull a fire alarm lever on the wall next to me, the ear-splitting sound so close, the speaker right there. The elevator doors freeze in place, just narrow enough to make Silas pause. He's too big, so *big* today. The frozen doors are just enough.

I run.

I run as fast as I can, the gun rubbing against my thigh, lumbering up a set of stairs and out into the sunshine. No thought, no mind, no strategy. I realize Duff will be after me, Silas at his heels. I need cover.

Another parking garage appears. I turn hard and run down the stairs, around and around and around in a spiral that feels like circling the drain until the stairs end and I burst out into a gas-scented level of hell.

Heart pounding, I find a giant pickup truck with space between it and the wall. I hide.

I wait.

Footsteps, loud and clacking, precise and searching. I can't feel my hands and legs anymore. I'm detaching, nothing but blood that runs through an imaginary body. My head feels like it's going to float away. I'm dead already, aren't I?

That's how this feels.

I slide my skirt up, the slip of fabric against my gooseflesh-covered calves a reminder I'm alive. The gun is loaded, safety on.

Slowly, slowly, I lift the safety.

Shoot to kill, my range instructors taught me.

Aim for the heart.

It's not so different from love, is it?

The footsteps sound softer, fading out as the person leaves. The tinny echo of movement in the stairwell lessens. My thighs scream in pain, hamstrings tight, overworked, overwhelmed.

I stand. The coast is clear. Carefully, I move away from the wall, closer to the ramp up to ground level. I hold the gun in both hands, one palm gripping the base of my other hand and wrist, braced to fire at will.

A twitch. A scratch. A sound I would never hear under normal circumstances, but this is definitely abnormal. Instinct takes over and I twist, gun at eye level, right index finger on the trigger, sight instantly level.

As my vision shifts to take in the target while tracking the sight, I come face to face with my pursuer.

It's Drew.

And he's pointing his gun right at my head.

CHAPTER 27

"*P*ut the gun down now, Jane."

"*You* put the gun down, Drew."

"You don't even know how to shoot."

"Try me." I squint and even the sight. He's so close I could shoot right into his eye and leave a nice, clean hole. I may have been shaking the first night Silas and I made love.

But I'm steady as a rock right now.

My father was wrong. Silas isn't the inside saboteur.

It's *Drew*.

"Jesus!" Silas shouts from behind me, his breath heavy, footsteps hard as he finds us.

"You, too? I knew it. *Knew* it!" Drew bellows.

"Knew what?" Silas chokes out. I'm so focused on Drew, on my breath, on not moving, on being ready to move, on ignoring the blood that courses through me at a million miles a second, at not fainting. You can live every single second of your life in one breath.

I know that now.

"Knew you two were working together," Drew barks at him. "I suspected it all along. Lindsay said no, I was crazy. She defended you, you piece of shit!" I don't know if he's talking about me or Silas.

Or both.

"Of course we're working together! You assigned him to protect me!" I scream at Drew, trying to break the tension, hoping he'll stand down, but knowing my fate is sealed.

"I don't mean that. I mean Gentian turned traitor. Harry told me. Warned me," Drew spits out. "Your father tried to warn me, Jane. Warn me about you and Gentian."

"What?" I'm shrieking. We're making a scene, and any second now, someone will call the cops. Right? Please, for once, let someone call the cops. My hand starts to shake. My vision goes into a spin. I can't faint. I can't! If I faint, I'll never wake up.

Because Drew is about to kill me.

Silas glares at him. "Cut the crap. You've been increasingly paranoid, Drew. I would never, ever betray you. You know that."

"It's not paranoia if you're *right*," Drew bellows.

"Then you need mental health help, because you're wrong. I'm your best friend," Silas says in a puzzled voice, full of emotion and clearly trying to de-escalate. "Put the gun down." Every word is a clear threat.

"No." Drew's gun is pointed right at my face. We're at a true standoff. Every second edges one of us closer to death. My sight on the gun blurs. I can't keep my hand even. What does a bullet through the chest, the forehead, feel like?

I'm about to find out.

"Then you leave me no choice." Silas reaches up swiftly, his gun in his hand. He starts to close the distance with Drew, but pulls back. I keep my attention on Drew, but realize this is a new threat.

Two men with guns. Only one *me*.

As he moves, Drew screams, "DON'T DO IT, GENTIAN! DON'T DO IT!"

Silas ignores him, the gun in his hand now pointing at --
Drew.

Silas' reflexes are so swift, I can barely see his arm, the blur becoming deafening as Drew's eyes narrow, his body pivots, the gun off me as he pulls the trigger.

And shoots Silas in the heart.

~*~

SILAS AND JANE'S story continues in *A Shameless Little Bet*. Find out what happens next in the stunning conclusion of Silas and Jane's pulse-pounding story!

ABOUT THE AUTHOR

USA Today bestselling author Meli Raine writes romantic suspense with hot bikers, intense undercover DEA agents, bad boys turned good, and Special Ops heroes -- and the women who love them.

Meli rode her first motorcycle when she was five years old, but she played in the ocean long before that. She lives in New England with her family.

Visit her on Facebook at http://www.facebook.com/meliraine

Join her New Releases and Sales newsletter at: http://eepurl.com/beV0gf

She also writes romantic comedy as Julia Kent, and is half of the co-authoring team for the Diana Seere paranormal shifter romance books.

www.meliraine.com

Printed in Great Britain
by Amazon